HE'S A KEEPER

SPECIAL EDITION

STACY TRAVIS

PROLOGUE

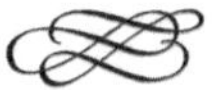

$\mathcal{H}$olden

Two Years Ago

I'm front and center in a large TV studio audience when my girlfriend starts singing a love song about another man.

For a moment, I still feel the rush from hearing her soft, raspy voice, believing she only sees my face in a crowd of thousands, knowing I'm the guy who gets to take her home. My brain is slow to process the full meaning, even though my heart has plummeted to my gut and left searing, choking pain in its wake.

The lights make it impossible for her to see my face, but she knows where I'm sitting. She'll give me a sign it's not what I think.

"Your brown eyes are my homecoming in a desolate world," she sings, her voice pitch-perfect and mournful.

My eyes are gray.

The camera pans to me and I don't have to look to know my face is on the jumbo screens that flank the stage where Shyla Winters sits on a lone stool under the spotlight, her throaty voice a dead ringer for that of Stevie Nicks. I try to compose my face, giving a stiff, closed-lipped smile because I can't react badly on camera to her love song, even if it isn't about me.

The audience shrieks and howls, evidence they love it after just the first few lines. Why wouldn't they? She's singing about infatuation so strong it levels everything in its path. Who doesn't dream of that?

I did.

Fuck.

My chest feels like it's being sliced in two by a steel blade. No one can absorb that kind of emotional blow, not even a soccer player at the top of his game. A thousand hours of sprint training on the field, yet now my lungs don't work quite right. I want to bolt from the room first, ask questions later. Get out of my dress shirt. It's suffocating.

This can't be what it seems. Right?

I look to Shyla for some confirmation, but the lights blind her view. Eyes drifting closed, she smiles like she's dreaming of a faraway time and place.

"On a mountain top hike at sunset, I wanted to kiss you, but you kissed me first."

We've never been on a fucking hike.

I'm not a paranoid guy. After eleven years of professional soccer—yes, I know it's football in most of the world, but since I live in the US, I need to avoid people confusing me with linebackers—I don't let negative thoughts or doubt enter my field of vision. It doesn't help me, and it doesn't help my game.

Jesus, I have a game tomorrow. I should be home, resting up, stretching, and icing my muscles, but instead I'm here to support the most important woman in my life. No other option when you're in love.

Normally, hearing Shyla sing about some other dude's eyes wouldn't make me flinch. It could be someone from her past or even an imaginary kiss on a hill. But she's been weird lately, acting fake-happy, like she's overcompensating. The pieces start careening into place.

Then there's the fact that I stopped by the studio with takeout one night when she said she'd be there writing, yet no one had seen her there for days. I knew she was lying, and I suspected something wasn't right, but I never expected to hear about it from her lips to a television audience of millions.

She does like drama.

A lone light beam seems to enclose her in a protected cone of stardust on the otherwise dark stage. She looks beautiful, her wavy blonde hair shimmering gold in the light, her face ethereal and turned toward the cameras at the perfect angle. She's a pro at using her eyes to enthrall people she's never met for the sake of selling records. It never bothered me before tonight.

Now, I'm wondering why she invited me to sit in the audience of this episode of *In Key*, the mega-hit reality TV singing competition that made her a megastar in the past year. Sitting in the judge's seat sent her already-huge career into the stratosphere, and she's been warning me for months that her upcoming touring schedule combined with my San Francisco Strikers' game schedule will likely mean we won't see each other much.

Like a loyal love-struck boyfriend, I told her I'd jump on redeye flights to meet her for two nights in Paris or Houston, the romance of it all fueling my willingness to be dead tired at a soccer match the next weekend.

I'd sacrifice sleep for her but in no way would it impact my game, never the game. It couldn't.

Shyla told me she cared too much about my soccer season to let me make that kind of sacrifice. I feel my quads flex under the denim of my jeans just thinking about playing. I'd rather be on the pitch or just about anywhere else right now.

No, get me to the pitch, where I can pummel a soccer ball with my foot until I've flattened the damn thing.

Her plaintive voice rings out over the strumming of an acoustic guitar and some quiet piano notes. I can't deny that she sounds good. Looks great.

"On winter nights, your kisses melted the snowflakes. They melted me," she sings.

We've never been anywhere in the goddamn snow together.

But thanks to a recent spread in *People* magazine, I know who just bought himself a log cabin in Lake Tahoe and has spent every weekend there writing music—Peej Tinselman, one of Shyla's co-stars on the show, a hip-hop artist who's sitting in his judge's chair beaming at her.

Don't even get me started on his name. Just. Don't.

And now that I'm aware, it's clear as cheap crystal that she's singing right to him. The small smile playing on her lips is for the memory of his mouth on her, not mine.

For the past three weekends, Shyla has left town to "hole up and write." I didn't question her process when the studio has been jonesing for a new album. What the hell do I know about songwriting?

So, I sat in our San Francisco penthouse looking at the view of the Bay Bridge alone, while she was riding the dick of a guy with a blue fauxhawk and neck tats.

All at once, I'm grappling with fierce emotions that want nothing to do with each other. There's the pain of knowing she's not singing about me. There's the sickening longing I have to rush to her side and ask her all the questions that will lead her to an explanation. There's the positively ill feeling I have knowing that I still love her even though she's long gone.

I sit there like I'm carved from wood, immobile except for a tick in my jaw. Hopefully the cameras don't catch that part, but honestly, I don't really give a shit now.

"He was cruel, loved the game more than me. I wanted to be

everything, but to him I was nothing. And it drove me to you, my love," she sings, her voice drawing out the notes, milking them for every bit of angst and sympathy, flat-out blaming me for her choices. I'm no poet, but her lyrics aren't exactly veiled in metaphor.

By now, people are catching on. Shyla finishes her song, and the audience goes wild, applauding what will surely be another hit, and instead of looking to where she knows I'm sitting, her eyes go to Peej, who is giving her a standing ovation.

She walks to the edge of the stage, and he extends a hand, helping her down to her judge's chair. Then the ballsy jerk leans over and kisses her cheek.

What the actual fuck is going on?

I know Shyla has a plan. She's brilliant at crafting viral moments and this bombshell will push her new single to the top of the charts by the end of the night.

But I don't need to be part of her goddamn moment. I push out of my chair, aware that nearly every pair of eyes in the room has shifted toward me. I've got nothing to say. Just need to get the hell out of here before my skin catches fire.

As soon as I've slipped out the side door, an entertainment news reporter has a mic in my face. How he managed to get wind that Shyla planned to end our relationship on national television is anybody's guess, though I have a feeling Shyla tipped him off. I feel like a nonplayer character in someone else's video game.

I hem and haw and try to get past him without saying something I'll regret. I feel a strange sense of obligation to my girlfriend. Maybe I got it wrong. Maybe I misunderstood. It's just a song. People sing about all kinds of things that have nothing to do with reality.

Before I can bring my blood pressure down low enough to ensure I won't rupture a vessel, paparazzi are buzzing around me like a new set of flesh-eating vermin. "Shyla gave a statement earlier saying your relationship has been over for months. Do you have a comment?"

"What?"

In that same moment, the door opens and there's Shyla with Peej standing right behind her. She meets my eyes with a mixture of apology and firm resolve that tells me she's not on Team Sanders. Not anymore.

That pushes me over the edge. I lash out at her in front of all the cameras, doing every stupid thing I've been media-trained not to do in public. I yell, I get up in people's faces, I act exactly like the uncommitted asshole she's led them to believe I am.

"You're right. You are nothing to me." I know I sound like a spurned teenage boy. Like I give a shit.

Except that every goddamn cell phone is aimed at my face.

I could go out and smash something up, get into a bar fight or two, crash my car. I could get stinking drunk and act like all manner of asshole after being publicly humiliated by a woman.

But I don't do any of those things. Well, I do get stinking drunk, and I stay that way for upwards of a week. Or longer.

It's a wakeup call.

Bad news, my girlfriend cheated on me—and wrote about it in a song that'll probably hit the fucking Top Ten on the Billboard charts and told the world it's because I only love soccer. The good news is that I'm this close to getting an offer to play for Tottenham Hotspur in the English Premier League. If I had any hesitation because of how much I loved Shyla, it's gone now. I can blow out of town and forget about her and Peej. I'm cured of wanting any distractions in my life.

From now on, I'm done with women, done with relationships. I don't need the distraction or the grief.

I'm a soccer player. End of.

CHAPTER 1

Molly

PRESENT DAY

After three years of doing the exact same thing every day, I have my afternoons down to a science. By the time the dismissal bell rings at the all-girls high school where I'm head librarian, I've already packed my laptop away and slung the saddlebag over my shoulder.

A wave of chatter erupts before the shrill bell stops, as teen girls in navy blue skirts and white button-downs emerge to crowd the narrow hallways of a century-old building with high arched ceilings and thin carpet on the floors.

I weave between bodies and backpacks, shoving at blond tendrils that come loose from my ponytail as students jostle me. Out of habit, I push my brown rectangular glasses to the bridge of my nose with one finger, even though they're in no danger of falling off.

"Bye, Molly." Olivia, an outgoing senior with a sparkly nose piercing and purple streaks in her hair this week, waves as she elbows past me to catch up with her friends. It's a school policy to have students call faculty by their first names to foster an egalitarian environment. She's gone before I can respond.

I don't have a second to spare. If I want to make it to my other job on time, I need to beat the student drivers to the parking lot and race away before the glut of cars blocks my exit while students linger, check their socials, say endless goodbyes, and make plans to see each other in five minutes.

The key to reaching the local library across town lies in efficiency. That means making every green light, paying attention to traffic advisories, and eating a protein bar in the car—the chocolate-coated type that doesn't leave crumbs and has enough nutritional value to provide an excuse to eat chocolate. Sort of.

I also need to stop for a latte, which I know may sound foolish when I'm crunched for time, but it's life or death when I've been up since six and I still have five hours of work ahead.

Priorities.

If all goes according to plan, I sail into the children's section with one or two minutes of breathing room, every hair tucked neatly into place, pink lipstick freshly applied. No flush on my cheeks from hurrying out of the parking lot. No sign of struggle under the heavy bag of books thumping against the flesh of my thigh.

If my plans go awry, I roll in the door late, apologetic, sweating, frazzled, but still smiling because a smile offsets many transgressions.

In three years, I've never experienced Scenario A.

Bonus points for my eternal optimism?

Today, I'm only ten minutes late to the Opera Plaza branch of the San Francisco Public Library, which puts me ahead of my performance the past two days but doesn't save me from my boss's angry glare as she pointedly checks the clock overhead.

As I quickly pad through the carpeted checkout area, I dab at the sheen of sweat on my forehead and ignore the boob sweat that I can do nothing about. Loose strands of hair partially obscure my vision, my lipstick has gone MIA, and I left my reusable water bottle on my desk at work, so the protein bar is half-lodged in my throat.

Nevertheless, I persist, waving at my boss, Judy, as though no time can be wasted with idle chitchat. As usual, she places her reed-thin body in my path, and I nearly fall over from halting in my tracks so I don't knock her over.

"Hi, Judy." I give her my brightest smile, hoping to blind her to my tardiness with sheer enthusiasm for all the bookish good I plan to do for the kids who come this afternoon.

The woman can't weigh more than ninety pounds including the long, cabled cardigan sweater she probably knit herself. For as long as I've worked here, Judy spends most of her time glaring at her employees from her desk where she knits various things, all of them black.

Her tidy short, silver hair gives her a severe expression, as do the bright blue eyes that always seem to fix on me like lasers boring into my soul. "Everything okay, Molly?"

She asks me this every time I come to work, and every day I answer the same way, with a smile. "Yes, traffic. So much worse than usual."

Normally, she scowls and mutters something about my work ethic. It's a silly daily dance—her the austere leading partner and me the curtsying, obedient one with two left feet—but it gives me a level of comfort that nothing changes. Until today.

Today she has a brand-new knife to insert with her bony little hands and twist. "I'm not sure we can keep you as an employee."

"Because of afternoon traffic?"

"No, because of the mayor." She draws out her vowels so that each word contains one very long syllable.

Maybe she's bluffing.

I look around as though the mayor of San Francisco is hiding amid the stacks. Instead, I see a homeless man sleeping at one of the desks and a few high school students with headphones working in the study area. Otherwise, the library could pass for long-forgotten book warehouse under a domed ceiling with yellow pendant lights.

"The new budget mandates a higher ratio of patrons to employees."

I smile. "So we need more people to come to the library, that's what you're saying?"

Nodding, she adds for clarity. "You're the parttime hire, so yours is the salary I need to justify." Official-sounding words to say that if more people don't show up, I'm out of a job.

"Great!" My grin could conquer Everest out of sheer will.

Her eyes go wide at my enthusiasm. Or apparent lack of understanding. "I have all kinds of ideas for how to bring more people in, lots of great ideas." Without further explanation of what those ideas may be—since I don't yet have a clue—I sweep past her as though I don't have a moment to lose.

The smile stays plastered across my face as I rush to the children's book area in a corner of the library with painted murals of winged Dr. Seuss and Curious George books flying across the walls. In the center, a rainbow rug divided into colored squares makes for easy seating for the kids – one per square.

I find it mostly empty, save a pair of twin preschoolers and their mother who looks more frazzled than me.

I've seen her here for the past few weeks, and her ragged expression turns into an idea. "Hi. I'm Molly. I've seen you here with your kids."

"Yeah, I'm the one trying to keep my twins from killing each other for two hours before the dinner and bath routine," she says.

"Ha. Twins, I don't know how you do it." I watch as the tow-headed kids face off, each with a large book about trucks in hand, wielding them like swords. Those books will end up on the floor in a matter of minutes.

"Back when I was pregnant and running a start-up, I thought I'd won the efficiency lottery—one pregnancy, two babies. Then I discovered that two kids the same age are somehow four times the effort of one. My oldest has a playdate. And I'm pretending to work." She holds up her phone. "My office in the palm of my hand."

She couldn't know it, but she's given me the perfect setup for what I'm about to propose. "So, would it help you—and maybe other working parents you know—to be able to have the kids engaged here in a reading hour where they could listen to stories, and you'd be free to sit in a quiet spot here and work?"

Her eyes grow large and for a moment, I think she might weep. She nods. "Yes. Yes, please. I'd love that. And I'm sure it would be a big draw. Will you do it?"

Extending a hand, I touch her shoulder. "I think I might." As my idea unspools, I envision guest speakers and famous authors and kid whisperers, oh my!

I can already think of one perfect person for the job.

"Esther, I have a great idea for you!" I wave my jazz hands at the seventy-four-year-old volunteer who spends every Wednesday helping me.

She pats her cheeks as though primping for a photo shoot and ambles toward me. As I explain my idea for a daily reading circle to Esther, I wipe beads of nervous sweat from my brow with the back of my hand while shelving the rainbow mountain of books the twins have pulled from the shelves to use as shields and weapons.

With her hair drawn up in a tidy salt-and-pepper bun, pink lip gloss, and a belted, pale blue linen dress with nary a wrinkle, she looks the complete opposite of how I feel. She rides a bike here from her house in Noe Valley, and how she stays so put together remains a mystery.

"You're going to read to the kids?" Her skeptical expression tells me I haven't done a good job of explaining.

"No, special guests are! Like you. You'll be great at it. I'll pick out books, maybe around a different theme each week, and you can make it fun for them because you're such a great reader." My voice comes out in a pleading whine. "Please, Esther? I need you to do this for me. I need it to work."

What I need is security at my part-time job now that Judy is threatening to downsize me. I can't let that happen because the pay here is good, the hours work with my school schedule, and I really need the extra income.

Plus, this library is the real reason I spent two years in grad school—I wanted to create new programs and make libraries lively community spots. Didn't necessarily want to have my job on the line in order to do it, but an opportunity is an opportunity.

It's more than I'll get at the high school, where I'm mostly an annoying shush-er who stands between the girls and the raucous party they want to have in the library every day.

I get it. I went to high school. Probably annoyed a few study hall proctors with my giggling and gossiping, but the librarians were always my friends. They were the gateway to the books I loved almost more than life itself.

"You need a man." Esther's voice pulls me out of my reverie.

"My dating life isn't the problem."

Well, it's not the problem at hand.

"Not that. You need to find a bigger draw. A handsome man. And some seat belts." I follow her gaze to where the twins are playing tag among the bookshelves, and I have to admit the chances they'll be willing to sit for a half hour seem slim.

But she's wrong about the other part. "The love for books and reading is the draw. Kids love books and reading." My gesture at the empty children's section kind of sinks my point.

Esther shakes her head and pulls a pair of cat-eye reading glasses from her pocket. As she begins swiping across the screen of her phone, I marvel at how much cooler she is than me in my purple Chucks, dark blue skinny jeans, and an oversized gray sweater that feels like a cocoon. I'm lucky that my school's egalitarian policy extends to letting faculty dress how we want, and I want to be comfortable. Even my glasses, which I only need for distance, have plain, dark rectangular frames because anything else makes my round face look even more round. And makeup? Only whatever remains from this morning.

"Here. Read this," she says, showing me her phone. I quickly peruse the article about how a renowned pastry chef opened a bookstore in Arizona and serves cake to everyone who comes into the shop.

Feeling another wave of sweat gloss my forehead, I hand back the phone. "That's completely different. She owns the store, and that doesn't say anything about a man."

"Speaking of which, you dating this week?"

"Esther, focus."

"Thirty-one, you should have a man in your life." Esther tsks, part of her weekly mission to needle me about my lack of boyfriend. I've considered lying just to appease her, but it doesn't sit right with me when she's the closest thing to a grandma figure I have. Besides, Esther is a human lie detector. She'll know.

"I have men in my life, they're just not around more than a night or two," I admit, hoping I can scandalize Esther into silence. But she doesn't bat an eye at my love 'em and leave 'em ways. And if I'm honest, it's been a while since I even liked anyone enough for a hookup. A long while.

"That's all well and good when you're twenty-three. Or my age. But you should find a nice man to keep you company on a steady basis. I'm not saying you have to fall in love, but you can give a man a chance to make you happy."

"Eh, relationships aren't for me. I've got the perfect situation. It works." She doesn't have to know that the perfect relationship currently exists between me, a pile of romance novels, and my vibrator.

Her quirked eyebrow tells me she does.

I shrug and spin off to shelve some books. Esther follows, eyeing me suspiciously. Hands on her hips, she tsk-tsks me. "That feels like an excuse."

"It's not."

"Fine. I'll mind my own business. Today. But on the other thing, trust me. You don't need to own the library to come up with something to draw people in. Invite a series of lecturers or something. *Male* lecturers."

"You think a bunch of old dudes lecturing is going to pull in the under-ten crowd?" I give up on organizing the pile of books when the twins race past us and knock the stack I've been making to the ground.

"Boys! Settle down," Esther calls to them. They slow their run slightly. "I don't know why you let them get away with acting like hooligans."

"Because at least they're here. Sooner or later they'll notice there are books around."

"Exactly. First you have to get them here, and who brings them? A parent, generally a mom or a babysitter. Usually a female, is what I'm saying. Who said anything about old dudes? I'm talking about young, hot men who like books, guys who will draw in the bored moms *and* their kids. The kids don't have a way of getting here without the chaperones."

Esther carries a stack of books toward the Fiction section, grumbling, "Those boys took out every Agatha Christie and used them as airplanes."

I look toward the kids' section as I weigh her opinion. Still empty, dashing my hope that it's filled up in the five minutes we've been chatting.

When I turn to follow her, I run into a hard blue wall. The library doesn't have blue walls, and I realize it's a wall of human —tall, muscular, and…angry. I immediately apologize.

He merely grunts and crosses his arms over his chest. "Be careful." His tone is more annoyed than cautionary.

"I am careful. Normally."

"Maybe do it all the time."

Wow, he's crabby. Handsome—at least what I can see of his face under a baseball hat shading his eyes—with a strong stubble-covered jaw, full lips, dark hair curling around the sides of his hat. And…I'm ogling a grouchy stranger. Esther is right. I need to get me a date before my libido starts making bad decisions for me.

"Um, okay. Can I help you find something?" I kill him with my sweetest smile, honed to melt the frostiest shell.

Just not his. He doesn't smile back, doesn't crack the irritable façade. "DVDs."

The demand jolts me, not because of its gruff delivery, but because it's probably been a year since anyone's shown interest in the dusty collection of old movies. In fact, there's been talk of eliminating the entire section to make room for a romance section, and I am all for it.

I point to the back corner and I'm pretty sure I hear a muttered "thanks" as the man's back recedes in the distance.

Rude.

Whatever.

"Now there you go." Esther sweeps over and catches the last glimpse of the man as he bends behind a rack of DVDs. "That's what I'm talking about. A *man*. Or multiple men. That'll bring the ladies and their kids."

She may have a point of drawing in women, but it can't just be any man. Someone like that guy is a human repellant, even if he is nice to look at.

"Multiple men? What, are you suggesting I bring in the local fire department and do a calendar shoot in the kids' section?" I laugh at my own joke, but Esther's eyes light up like I've just found a youth elixir that tastes like cake with no calories.

She pokes her finger in the air, revealing a purple cocktail ring. "Now *that*, my dear, is an idea."

olden

THE STRIKERS' stadium is alive with cheers and chants from the crowd in the final minutes of our match against the Sounders. Standing in the center of the goal, arms outstretched, light on my feet, I let the electricity of the crowd fuel me.

Moments like this are what I live for.

Our team has dominated possession for most of the game, but the score is tied, nil-nil. For a goalkeeper, that counts as a win—I didn't let anything get past me.

I'm ready, watching every player from my perfect vantage point, a pass from Weston, our center mid, a long cross from our striker, Donovan Taylor. No goal.

The Sounders' keeper hurls the ball back into play, and I watch each quick pass, a change of possession, the amped-up energy of every player in the final few minutes of the match. Everyone is itching to take a shot.

And when they come my way, I'll be ready. I've worked my ass off to be at the top of my game.

It took…a while.

Months.

Almost a year.

Not gonna lie, Shyla's affair with that douchey rapper fucked with me. I'm a pro, but it was near impossible to keep her from getting in my head, not when pictures of the happy couple appeared on every damn tabloid and they were all anyone talked about for months. Not when they became social media darlings and posted pictures of cozy weekends, domestic bliss, and open-mouthed kisses. Not when they went on a tour of late shows to talk about their magical love.

Fuck me.

I made some bad decisions—a lot of bad decisions—got into a few bar fights, showed up late to practice, earned a reputation as a hothead with a foul mouth. Unfortunately, the Strikers paid the price with a few brutal losses that were my fault.

My brother finally shoved some sense into my thick skull, and I remembered my priorities, cleaned up my fucking act.

The "foul mouth" part isn't going anywhere. Neither is my total commitment to the sport I love. I fought my way to this spot, and I'm not going anywhere.

The Sounders are moving the ball up the field, and in seconds I anticipate someone taking a shot. My eyes are everywhere, body coiled like a puma, ready to jump or dive.

Clint Chisholm's foot connects with the ball. It's a hard, clean strike and the ball sails to his left, my right, just where I'm currently in the air on my way to the corner in front of the goal. Stretching my arms as long as they'll go without dislocating my shoulder, I reach for the ball which flies toward the corner of the net.

Tapping it away with the tips of my gloves, I send the ball back into play, which isn't the best idea. Better if I'd been able to dive on top of it or grip it in my gloves, but I still denied Chisholm a goal.

Now my teammates rush in and scramble with the Sounders' players, feet gnashing against feet, legs tangling. At what feels like the speed of light, another bullet flies off someone's foot and I dive, which takes me far enough out of the goal that I'm going down in a scrum of players, feet flying everywhere, one of them connecting hard with my head.

Too hard.

Hard enough that I see black and a jolt of air rushes from my lungs.

What happens next is a blur of bodies and turf and shouting voices. "Coach!" "He's not moving!" "Sanders…Sanders! Hey, you okay?"

I can hear him, but it takes me a minute to blink myself back to full consciousness. At first, dull shapes come into focus, then outlines of heads and rough details of faces staring down at me.

"Yeah," I mumble, my throat dry. I blink slowly and try to pull the faces around me into focus. I'm seeing two or three of everyone and my head feels like it's being squeezed in a vise. I confirm, "I'm good."

Am I good? I have no idea.

I have no idea about anything, except that I need to know whether I succeeded in defending the goal. "D'they score?" Why does my voice sound like I'm talking through a mouthful of marbles?

"Nah." It's the only answer that matters to me.

Fighting against blackness that threatens to descend again, I blink harder, needing something to come into focus. Nothing is clear except the searing pain in my skull.

I've had concussions before, none of them taking me out for more than a few weeks. This is probably more of the same. Fortunately, we're right at the beginning of the season, so missing a few games at most won't hurt us.

"What day is it? Where are you?" I hear the concussion protocol begin before I'm even standing up.

I mutter my replies to the various questions on autopilot.

I know what follows now—tests and monitoring, a CT scan, a series of mental and physical hoops I'll have to jump through before I can get back on the field. I'll do whatever it takes.

It's fine. I didn't let the Sounders score, and we got the win. That's all that matters.

~

Two weeks later, I haven't been released from concussion jail and I'm getting a little testy.

Sitting in the training center at the practice facility, I feel like I can hear the muffled grunts and shouts of my teammates practicing outside, but it's probably my imagination. I want to be out there so badly, I'm hearing phantom balls kicked at my head.

"Come on, Mickey, I feel fine," I tell the team doctor, knowing he probably doesn't believe me.

I don't feel a hundred percent fine. I still have headaches, and I've been working with a physical therapist and a medic daily, but mostly the prescription is rest.

In other words, I'm going batshit crazy because I can't attend normal team training sessions.

Going from running six miles daily and having hours of keeper-specific training to basically sitting on my ass has me ready to pounce on the first person who looks fit enough to wrestle.

My temper is hot, my patience is at a new low, and the only thing that's keeping me halfway sane is the sliver of possibility that I could still play in the Premier League. There have been new rumblings of interest from a Premier League team, and at my age, it's my last shot.

I hope my time off the field doesn't make anyone reconsider.

I knew I deserved it when the Tottenham Hotspur offer never materialized in the aftermath of the Shyla debacle. That's when I really woke up and realized I'd let the fallout from a relationship ruin the career I'd worked my whole damn life to achieve.

No woman is worth the sacrifice, and even if I'm known now for my bad attitude and relentless scowl, it's fine.

And now this. Out for four more weeks, give or take. My own personal hell.

"You're better, but you're not fine," Mickey growls.

His name isn't really Mickey, but he reminds me so much of Burgess Meredith's character in the Rocky movies that it's become an unofficial nickname used by most of the team.

"So, another week?" My optimism is borne of desperation. I need to get back on the pitch, and I need to get medical clearance before I can do that. A before B, B before C. Even my concussed brain understands this.

Mickey is Point A, and he still won't even let me look at my cell phone screen, or any screen for that matter.

I shift on the bench and try not to grimace when I feel the ache behind my eyes that tells me I'm not close to ready for a contact sport. I can't be rash about returning to play. A second concussion on top of a first could take me out of the sport for good and likely result in brain damage. I know I need to listen to the doctors. It's just really damn hard.

The whole reason I started playing soccer in the first place was that my parents saw my whirling dervish tendencies, and need to kick things, and signed me up for a rec league at age five. Three different times they took me in for testing on the suspicion that I had attention deficit hyperactivity disorder. This came at the suggestion of teachers over the course of grade school and middle school when I irritated them sufficiently with my inability to sit in a chair for more than ten minutes.

But my attention and focus weren't the problem. I just had an absurd amount of energy. Even with soccer as an outlet, I needed a couple hours each day to run laps around the park, endlessly juggle a ball, and climb any tree I could find.

"What about walking?" I grunt. Walking bores me, but I'll do it.

He shakes his head. "Sure, if you were a normal person who intended to walk a mile or something, but I know if I give you permission, you'll get on a treadmill, crank the incline to fifteen, and walk all day."

Sometimes it's a problem to work with people who know you so well. I can't get away with shit. Closing my eyes, I sigh, not caring if he sees my childish agony. He's seen worse. "I'm going crazy. Feels like I'm gonna jump out of my skin."

His bony hand thumps my thigh. "Take the opportunity to expand your horizons. Find something else to focus on."

"No shit. But what? You won't let me watch game tape."

"That's not something else. That's still this."

"So, what? You want me to take up knitting?"

He runs his fingers through the thinning shock of white atop his head. "Wouldn't be the worst idea, but it might give you a headache. How about volunteering?"

"Hard pass." I'm determined to be disagreeable and spread my misery to Mickey

"Wouldn't kill you to do something for the community—get photographed holding

puppies at an animal rescue, volunteer at a soup kitchen, something. A little positive PR will help you clean up your bad boy image a bit. Good optics, especially if you still want a shot at the Premier League."

"I hate when you sound fucking reasonable."

"Whatever. You figure it out. Something low-tech and non-jarring. Take your kid for ice cream, sit and watch the seals at Pier 39."

"You know I don't have a kid. And there's something sketchy

about those seals. They just lay around all day. It's not normal. Freaks me out watching them."

"Just make sure it doesn't involve a screen or a level of physical activity beyond a twenty-minute walk."

"You're such a ballbuster, Mick. Fine. Enjoy training my ass when it's full of lard after sitting around for another two months."

"It will be my pleasure." He bows like he's seeing royalty out of the room.

I have no idea how he puts up with us. I may be the surliest on our team, but a lot of the guys run a close second.

Meanwhile, I can't think of a single hobby that doesn't involve a ball or a lot of running. That leaves me open to other people's dumb ideas—which is how I end up agreeing to babysit my brother's kid, who wants me to take her to the goddamn library.

CHAPTER 3

$\mathcal{M}$olly

"AND THE SAVAGES DESCEND," a deep voice intones when I walk in the library, two weeks after instituting my Good Cookie Reading Circle. It's not an official title, but it's how I think of my new program which now has me baking into the night and sending kids home with treats.

Okay, bribes.

But if it gets them in the door, I'm not above buying them off. Unfortunately, the sugar fix isn't proving to be the library gold I'd hoped for. There are marginally more kids here today than a week ago, but I feel my job teetering on a ledge no wider than Judy's knitting needles.

"Please, Seth?" I beg my friend who runs the information desk at the library. He fiddles with his green bow-tie-of-the-day which features tiny rubber ducks. It's paired with a white short-sleeved button-down and a black vest with jeans.

"Like I said yesterday, and like I'll say tomorrow when you ask

—no. Not reading. Those six-year-olds have the vocal power of sixty normal people." Seth smooths his blond goatee, which doesn't need smoothing.

"You'd love it. The kids are adorable." Maybe he's the male energy Esther had in mind. "Have you tried reading to kids?"

"Have *you*?"

"Yes. Obviously. I just like to offer the opportunity to others, spread the love." And so far, I've found enough "special guests" that I haven't had to do it myself.

"Okay, I'm not touching that pile of bullshit with a hazmat suit on. We'll discuss whatever phobia this is later on."

"It's not a phobia." Maybe it's a phobia. Kids freak me out a little bit. I realize that's a bit of a problem for a children's librarian, but let's be honest—I'm not really a children's librarian.

I'm a library scientist.

Seth chuckles under his breath. "You're ridiculous."

"Why am I ridiculous? Because I don't want to read to kids? I don't have a degree in that. I'm not a parent."

Now his amusement grows into a full laugh. "We don't have time right now, but later, please explain the entrance exam and advanced degrees people get before becoming parents. Meanwhile, you're Mary Poppins come to life. If anyone can charm a roomful of kids, it's you."

I mock-scowl at his description of me. It's not the first time I've heard someone compare me to the perfect nanny, but I don't happen to agree. Just because I'm cheerful doesn't mean I have a magic touch with children.

The main reason kids freak me out is that I'm pretty certain they hate me. Generally, I get the feeling they think I'm strange. I'm one part scary adult, one part owlish book lady. I may have a slight Mary Poppins vibe, but kids make me insecure—I'm worried I'll break them.

So instead of working on that part of myself, I take the easy route and outsource the spoonful of sugar bit to the professionals, aka Esther and anyone else I can find.

Someday, I plan to be an awesome parent and love my kids beyond measure, but that's the difference—they'll be my kids. I'm not always sure I'm equipped to say the right things to other people's kids, even when I have a book in my lap as a crutch. There's nothing more intimidating than a child's wide eyes willing me to outright enchant them when all I've got is my shaky book reading voice.

I head back to the kids' section and pick up the tiny metal windchime from its perch on top of the shelf of picture books for early readers. Holding it up, I jingle it around until a melodic tinkling sound gets people's attention. Two of the kids sprint toward the reading area, which has several small beanbag chairs alternating with the rainbow-colored seats. The beanbags are a favorite and the first two kids dive onto them and get settled.

A couple more kids sit down, two boys on their parents' laps on the rug, one blond girl in a chair. Her dad is standing over her with his arms crossed while she tries to tie her shoes. He looks like the rude guy from couple weeks ago, the insanely hot man with the bad attitude.

The blond girl's large eyes implore him to help, but he shakes his head. "Use your fine motor skills, Small Fry." His voice is gruff.

Yup, same jerk.

She's frustrated, pigtails swatting her cheeks as she shakes her head at the impossibility of the task, but when she looks at her dad, it's with pure adoration. Dads and daughters are my favorite, especially when the little girls gaze into their dads' eyes like they've hung the moon and stars.

And when the dads gaze at their girls like they don't ever want to see them grow up, I feel such a pinch in my chest at the few memories I have of my own dad that my brain spins off into fantasyland—the childhood trips to the park I could have had if my dad hadn't left, the teen years where he'd see me off to the prom with tears in his eyes, the someday wedding where he'd give me away.

The inevitable record scratch brings all those fairy tales to a halt, and I project all my hopes and dreams onto the little girl in front of me, hoping she'll have everything I wished for. Hoping her dad is worth the adoring gaze.

"Fine. Last time," her dad grumbles, bending to tie her shoe. Gleeful at winning the battle, she picks up a stuffed turtle from her lap and kicks her legs back and forth, oblivious that she's making tying her laces extra challenging.

I can only see the man from the back. He's hunched over, wearing jeans and a long-sleeved black Henley. He's the only dad there—if he is her dad. I shouldn't make assumptions.

I catch a couple of the women in the reading area checking him out. They're not subtle.

They have a better view than I do of his face, so when he settles the girl down in her chair, tosses his baseball cap on the floor, and sits in a chair, I take a good look.

And yeah, those women weren't wrong to ogle him. Wow. He's pretty spectacular, even with his arms crossed defensively and a scowl causing a muscle in his cheek to pop. The crossed arms accentuate his biceps, and the twitching muscle highlights the handsome contours of his jaw.

His dark hair is a little mussed, which is totally my catnip. I love it when a hot guy isn't too perfect, when he's a little rumpled like he just rolled out of bed looking tired but spectacular. And this one is spectacular. He also doesn't seem to be aware of his effect on the ladies around him—or it's abject disinterest. He probably has an ego the size of Kansas.

Sigh.

He has a jawline sharp enough cut ice. High cheekbones. A few days' worth of dark stubble makes me think he works in tech or some creative field where he doesn't need to shave or show up in a suit. Probably owns a start-up or something and sets his own hours, hence his appearance here at five on a weekday.

Shuffling through the books in the pile I made yesterday, I decide I'll read the one about Flat Stanley first. Even if kids already know the story or the series, they all love the origin story where Stanley gets flattened. I have a limited-edition version with color illustrations, and I'm hoping that excites at least a couple kids.

"Okay, everyone. I'm Molly. Are we ready to get started?" My voice already sounds choked and uncomfortable. I half-expect the kids to stage a coup and tell me they don't want to sit still for an hour. Then they'll challenge me to a game of dodgeball, only with books instead of balls.

It's one of my recurring nightmares, though where young kids are concerned, I'm far more comfortable having books hurled at my head than being their source of entertainment. Kids always have questions. Always. Then I get into trouble because my stream-of-consciousness thoughts fly right out of my mouth before I can edit them, which either bores the kids or scares them.

I know this. I've watched it happen and had no way of stopping the crazy train. If I alienate the few kids who've shown up today, my job here is toast.

And while I'm lost in that worry, the little blond girl's dad walks right past me, headed for the exit.

He barely glances my way, and I can't see much of his face under the baseball cap, but I do notice that he walks with a swagger that says he knows his jeans fit perfectly. And because I'm human, I also allow myself to notice how nicely his shirt hugs the muscled contours of his shoulders and back as he...leaves the library.

"Wait!" I call after him a bit too late for him to hear me. Kids aren't allowed to be unchaperoned during story hour. It's one of my rules. Even if their parents want to browse or work somewhere else in the library, they need to stay inside.

Book in hand, I hurry over to Seth. "Hey, can you entertain the kids for a sec?"

He looks skeptical. "Is this your way of tricking me into reading them a story while you mysteriously disappear for the entirety of the hour?" He taps a pen against his lip.

I practically throw the book in his lap and dash to the front door. "No. I'm not pulling a fast one. I've got a runner."

CHAPTER 4

$\mathcal{M}$olly

WHEN I REACH the glass doors, I expect to see the irritable man outside scrolling on his phone. Or, if he really doesn't understand the rules, he'll be walking to his car.

But he's nowhere.

Glancing back, I see Seth dutifully sulking toward the story area, his shoulders hunched like I've sent him to the gallows. Still, he's going.

That gives me a couple minutes to track this man down. I should've asked his daughter for his name so I can yell it.

The library is a one-story building on a corner. A small square of grass sits on each side of the front walkway, leading to the sidewalk where the city hasn't trimmed the overgrown trees in years. The result is patchy brown areas where the grass doesn't get enough sun and trees that nearly block out the sky.

I head around the side of the building to where the tiny parking lot only has room for a handful of cars. My fugitive stands with a pair of preteen boys each holding a skateboard under one arm. All three stare up at one of the trees.

From my vantage point, I can't see much except a whisp of what looks like orange fur on a high branch. The boys are doing their best to mask their nerves with a façade of bravado.

"Dude, you do it. I have a basketball tourney this weekend and my dad'll kill me if I get injured," one of the boys says, dropping his skateboard and stepping on one end so it flips back into his hand.

The other boy, who has a shock of blond hair, tosses his board onto the grass and cranes his neck toward the ball of fur in the tree. "Nah, he's really high up. Dude, if he falls and dies, it's totally your fault for letting him out."

"I didn't let him out. He ran out before I saw him."

"Whatever. You were the one who opened the door."

"You're the one with a cat who's too dumb to stay in the house."

"Not. Helping," the man scolds, turning his baseball cap around so the brim hangs over the back of his hair. Now I can see his eyes, though with the way he's squinting at the tree, I can't discern their color, just that they burn under aggravated brows.

It's also crystal clear that my initial take on him was spot on—he's so good-looking that he uses it as a hall pass to be a jerk. Even his stance, with his arms folded so his biceps pop and his shoulders pull at the fabric of his shirt, shows anyone within viewing distance that he knows what to do with hundred-pound barbells. And he does it.

"I don't want him to die." The blond boy wipes his sweaty palms on his jeans and takes a few steps closer to the tree, surveying the climb.

"He's not going to die. Cats are ninety-five percent tiger. They have eighteen toes, so they're built for climbing," the man says. "Plus, they have double the neurons in their cerebral cortex as dogs. They're smart. Your cat's only climbing as high as it's safe."

It's like dinner theater seeing this brawny dude with the bad attitude rhapsodize about cats. I can't tear myself away.

Suddenly, he jumps up and grabs the lowest tree branch, executing the most manly pullup I've ever seen. His biceps ripple as he hurls himself vertically, ending up in a squat on top of the fat horizontal branch. The legs of his jeans stretch taut over his thighs, and he balances like some kind of ninja. From there, he reaches for another branch overhead and does the same.

It's like Tarzan with a zoology degree.

I inch a little closer to get a better view. The boys are fixated on him and don't notice me until I whisper a question. "Do you know that man?"

"Nah, he's just some dude who walked out here," says the blond boy. "I hope he's got extra toes too."

"You know an awful lot about cats," I call up to him.

From the way he flinches when he turns toward me, he had no idea I was there. Holding on to a tree branch, he stuffs his other hand into his pocket and looks back at the cat, who's used the momentary distraction to scramble higher on the branch. "I almost fucking had it."

"Hey. Children are present." I put my hands over my ears to demonstrate, stuck in my library lady persona because, as I said, I'm bad with kids.

"Are you one of them, Mary?" He smirks. It's not a bad look on him because it almost looks like a smile. Except that the upturned corner of his mouth makes me want to punch it. And why's he calling me Mary when I introduced myself to the group right before he left?

"Hardly." I square my shoulders as though I need to prove to him that I'm not a child, which seems childish and makes me want to punch him again. "Anyhow, you can't be out here."

"I have no idea what that means," he growls, stepping further along the branch, which looks flimsy under his weight.

He's nearly twenty feet in the air and pretty close to the

orange and white cat, which is no bigger than a grapefruit. It sits perched on a high branch meowing like it's singing opera. Cute little thing.

I don't have pets. It kind of goes along with my fear-of-kids thing. I worry the responsibility of caring for a pet might be more than I can handle. What if I forget to feed it for a week? What if I let it escape and it ends up in a tree?

But this cat has fate on its side because Tarzan scoops up the small thing and tucks it into his chest. From the way his head is bent toward the cat, I can tell he's talking to it.

Using his free hand, he deftly slips down to a lower branch and balances on it while he surveys the best path down. Lowering into a squat, he calls out to the boys. "You said you play basketball, yeah?"

"Sure," one of the boys says.

"You're going to catch this kitten like it's a buzzer beater from downtown. You miss, you lose. Ready?"

The boys prepare themselves, hands open, squatting like the ballers he's daring them to be. "Ready. I'm open!" the blond boy yells, instantly in game mode.

The man drops the furry, striped body to where the boy grasps it surely in his hands. He scruffs it under the collar and tucks it under one arm while he and his buddy grab their skateboards.

"Thanks, man. You saved my bacon," the blond one says.

As he swings from the lowest branch and lands in front of the boys, the man is already brushing off their appreciation. "You never have to worry about cats. They're climbers. He'd have come down on his own, so if he does it again, wait him out. Don't break a bone. Speaking of that, cats have more bones than people —they're just small." He spouts all this information sounding irritable and inconvenienced, though it's not like anyone asked for an encyclopedia entry on cats.

"Cool, good to know." The boys mount their skateboards and

thank him again as he flicks some stray pieces of bark from the sleeves of his shirt.

Then his gaze locks on mine, and I notice the hardness in his steel-gray eyes which have dark rims like they were drawn with charcoal pencil. Pretty, but unyielding.

He stares at me like I'm the one who isn't where I'm supposed to be.

"I need you to come back inside," I say again. His eyes roam over me from head to toe and back again. He makes no attempt to hide his slow perusal of my form, and I feel a flutter in my belly that irritates me because I don't want to react to him. I fold my arms over my C-cup chest.

"I'm sorry?" He cocks his head to the side like a dog who only hears words but doesn't know what they mean.

"You need to stay in the library."

"I don't think there's a law about leaving the library. Aren't you the one who's supposed to be inside? Who's reading to the kids, Mare?"

The kids—as though he isn't the biggest child among them.

"My name's not Mary."

He shrugs.

What he doesn't know is that I wrangle headstrong, hormonal teenage girls for a living, and if I can get them to work quietly, I can handle one unpleasant man-child. He doesn't intimidate me. He does, however, beg me to spend a little more time staring at his strong jaw, even though he glares like he's weighing the odds of murdering me and getting away with it.

I exhale a long breath, prepared to explain the rules, but my mind drifts to a subject that's more intriguing. The drift isn't a problem when I'm alone, but when I'm having a conversation with someone, it can lead people to think I have focus issues.

Maybe I have focus issues.

Drifting back, I point at the man accusingly. "How do you know so much about cats? Are you a vet?"

He huffs a disbelieving breath, stuffing his hands deep into his pockets. "I have a cat." His icy stare makes it seem like he's unhappy about it.

"You have a cat?"

"I just said I did."

I shake my head as if to knock the errant words from my ears because I can't have heard him correctly. In no world does this tightly-wound grump take care of animals, unless he's skinning them for their pelts. Which makes me worry for the safety of his cat. "You have a cat. As a pet?"

He squints his eyes, which causes the corners of them to crinkle. Strange, until I realize they're laugh lines that accompany another smirk. He observes me with his hands on his hips. "As opposed to...?"

"I don't know, like maybe you're planning to feed it to some larger animal. Do you also raise coyotes and watch them devour cats for sport?"

He mirrors my stance, and I can't help but notice the bulge of his biceps when he crosses his arms. He looks slightly menacing, and I worry for a second that I'm poking a beast that's best left alone. He shakes his head.

"I don't know what kind of weird shit you're snacking on behind the reference desk, but no, I'm not into torturing animals. Any other questions about my cat?"

"What's its name?"

"Greta."

"Huh." Is it wrong that I expected him to have a male cat? I picture him with a surly tomcat who hunts for mice with him in the dark. "Greta," I confirm.

"Garbo. She's a European Shorthair. Swedish. I like old movies."

A Tetris block drops into place. "The DVDs. You were renting oldies?" It happens that our branch has a big collection of classic films on DVD, and some people come from across the city for them.

His brow furrows. "What?"

"A couple weeks ago. I ran into you?" Obviously, he doesn't remember. Why point it out? "Never mind. But if you're a Garbo fan, I feel compelled to admit I always liked *Romance* better than *Camille*. I know it's controversial."

I glance to the side, thinking about the two movies. When my attention drifts back, he's studying me like I'm an oddity. I'm used to that look. Yes, I'm the library lady who likes books—and even movies—more than people.

It's why I get a perverse thrill at hiding details about my life and letting people assume what they want. If I admitted to a one-night stand here or there, there'd be questions. Assumptions. Maybe even invitations to hang out after work with some of the male faculty at school. Easier to let people assume I'm a sunshiny little hermit on my way to becoming a spinster.

What people think is irrelevant, which is why it surprises me when this guy picks up my conversational tangent like it's normal. "*Camille* might be a tad overrated. I agree there. But *Romance* isn't my favorite."

"Which is your favorite?" I'm suddenly willing to abandon my job responsibilities to stand out here and talk about old movies with him. I kind of love it.

"*The Kiss*." His gray eyes bore into mine until I can't take the weight of his stare any longer and look away. I feel the heat rise in my cheeks and prickles of warmth crawl up the back of my neck.

Must be hot out here.

When I recover my composure and look at him, he's smirking like he knows the effect he has on me. "Anyhow, I gotta go." He starts walking toward the parking lot, forcing me to move quickly to keep pace with his long stride.

"Oh. No. No, no, no. We have to go back. You need to stay inside the library."

"Why?"

"Because it's a rule. Parents stay."

We reach the parking lot and he stops by the door of a sleek-looking Porsche. I half expect him to speed away without finishing the conversation, but he doesn't pop the locks. "I'm not a parent. I'm here with my niece. We're *bonding*." His grimace and the irritated tone of his voice makes bonding sound as much fun as being stapled naked to a tree.

"It doesn't matter. You're her guardian. Parents, guardians, nannies, babysitters, uncles—all of those people need to stay if they bring a kid to the library. It's not daycare."

"Not my rule."

Pressing his lips together, he glares at me like I'm a gnat he'd like to flick away. It draws my attention to those lips, which look like they could do heavenly things to a woman's body, and I'm immediately annoyed with myself for noticing.

I offer him my most meaningful stare, which is challenging as my body cranks up the heat again when he looks at me – to say nothing about my pounding heart.

Stop it. He's just a man. A normal human man.

Okay, he's not normal. He's spectacular, gorgeous, stunning—all the adjectives. But still, just a man. The wind chooses this moment to kick up behind me, pushing a bunch of flyaway strands out of my ponytail and into my face like runaway tumbleweeds. For a moment, I can't see if he's decided to make a break for the fancy, fast car.

"Be a better guy than that," I mutter, taming the strands behind my ears.

Something in his eyes shifts, softens, if only slightly. "Fine," he says, turning back toward the library. "Not like I have any place to be." I catch the sarcasm in his tone and the view of his broad shoulders as he swaggers away.

"It's one hour. I'm sure you'll manage. It'll give you more bonding time, and if you really can't stand it, the place is full of books. Maybe you'll find a new favorite author." I can't help the brightness of my tone. I love books.

"I said it was fine," he says over his shoulder, but his fierce, sweeping stride makes it clear he dislikes my terms. He walks ahead of me, so I'm forced to keep pace if I want to see his face, which is marked by a resigned lack of enthusiasm.

"What's your name?" I ask.

"Holden."

I extend my hand, which he grips firmly before dropping it. I swallow hard when I feel a small zing of pleasure erupt over my skin at his touch. It only because I haven't been touched by a man in a while. Nothing special about this one.

"Nice to meet you. I'm Molly." It's not particularly nice, but I'm not about to alienate one of the few people who showed up today. I need about twenty more of him.

"Molly, huh? Given your whole spoonful of sugar vibe, I could've sworn it was Mary."

"Nope, Molly." I ignore the Mary Poppins reference. He thinks he's so original.

He stares me down. "Okay, Mare. I mean, Molly." He says my name slowly like it sticks in his throat. Charmer.

I decide to kill him with kindness. "Appreciate you being so easygoing about this. You have any other friends with nieces who might want to come to the library?"

"I'd only subject enemies with nieces to this."

Wow, he's seriously grumpy. It doesn't really bother me. I work with teenagers all day long—I've dealt with so much worse —but I can't figure out what his problem is. If he really wants to bond with his niece, he should spend time with her, not zoom off in his Porsche and do whatever flawless men do.

When we're back inside, he sits behind his niece, who bounces on her knees with so much enthusiasm that her scruffy pigtails look like cheerleading pompoms. I relieve Seth and take my seat in front of the group.

Oddly, there are at least a dozen more people in chairs and on the rug than there were when I chased Holden down fifteen minutes ago. And most of them seem oddly focused on him, shooting surreptitious looks his way. I even notice a couple women taking selfies that just happen to catch him in the background.

Weird. Well, maybe he's some tech billionaire or something. Or an actor. Even so, I don't recognize him, and I'm up on my Marvel movies and all things Netflix. Based on the attention he's getting, you'd think he was some rare, exotic species never observed in the wild.

And he's ignoring it all.

"Any requests for what book we read?" I ask the group, having lost my Flat Stanley mojo. One of the boys raises his hand and I point to him and read his name tag. "Jet, what sounds good?"

"Something about diggers and machines."

"Okay." I pretend to think hard, even though I have a stack of construction books tucked away by my feet. Always a safe go-to. "Oh, I know a good one! Anybody else?"

The boy sitting next to him on the rug holds up a book, waving it around. I reach for it, looking at the title *Why Do Cats Have Twelve Toes?*

Interesting.

According to a certain man who swings from branches, cats have a lot more toes than that. Not to mention, he has a wealth of other factual tidbits about cats at the ready, facts I'm certain the kids would find fascinating.

A sudden traffic jam of ideas crowds my brain, horns honking and people yelling obscenities, but I manage to discern a few. Getting this man engaged might make him enjoy being here a little more, which will make his niece enjoy it more. Getting him to show up to a few more reading sessions might be good for building a crowd, based on the apparent interest in him among female library-goers.

I'm desperate enough to keep my job to make a deal, if not with the devil, then at least with someone who shares his personality.

My eyes dart to Holden, and I point to the book title and smile. I can see the shadow of doom descend as he realizes what I'm about to suggest.

I wave my hands at the kids because I'm suddenly excited, instructing, "Let's take a five-minute bathroom break, then meet right back here to talk about why this book isn't telling the truth." I see wide eyes among the faces, scandalized at the idea that a book got it wrong.

Then I make a beeline to Holden before he can run from the room again.

olden

"HELL, NO," I tell the annoyingly perky woman, while warning myself to look away from her sassy, sweet grin before it does things to me that will make it harder to hold my ground.

The only idea I like less than being forced to do "low-tech, minimal-jarring" activities is helping her read books.

Even if she is adorable.

Fuck. Five minutes into taking my niece to the kiddie section of the library, and I need a cold shower. This is what I get for agreeing to take Kathryn to the library—the kind of distraction I've avoided for two years.

Well, it won't hurt to look at her. My concussed brain deserves some fucking distraction.

"Lovely language in front of the kids." She crosses her arms in front of her and taps one foot in a spitting imitation of a cartoon schoolmarm. It does nothing to dispel the adorable factor. To the contrary, it has new fantasies blooming in my brain about a stern librarian slapping me on the wrist. Along with a few other places. And I wouldn't hesitate to slap back.

I make a big gesture of looking around the alcove where she has me buttonholed by the overflowing returns cart. "I don't see any kids. They're safe from my lovely language."

I'm used to people asking me to do things—it goes with the territory of a high-profile job. Somehow, I thought a library in a random corner of San Francisco would be the exception.

She bites her bottom lip and scowls. Even scowling, she looks about as threatening as a baby otter. And biting her lip only serves to emphasize its pink, full shape. I have a sudden, raw urge to drag her lip between my teeth and discover what it tastes like.

The instant surge of lust shocks the hell out of me because it's so foreign. I reason that it's perfectly safe because nothing's going to happen here. This woman is hardly the average jersey chaser, and she's plainly disinterested in me.

With her stern devotion to books, she's the polar opposite of most female fans who approach me after games or when I'm in a bar with my teammates. They're athlete-fuckers, not necessarily fans of the sport. Some of them have mainlined makeup tutorials from YouTube and show up in revealing outfits barely safe for public view. I'm generalizing, but there's a type. They want a hot, fun fuck from a player, and they flaunt their assets to make it crystal clear.

Not saying I don't look. I appreciate beauty, and there were many years when I happily accepted the fruits of my labor on the field.

Not anymore.

I'm not even tempted, or at least I wasn't until I gazed upon the uncomplicated beauty of the petite librarian. She's somehow convinced me I'd rather watch her read to rowdy kindergarteners than go anyplace else.

With her large brown doe eyes, rosebud lips, and take-no-prisoners attitude, she has me about ready to agree to anything, just so I can look at her some more. And once more for the people in the noise-canceling headphones, I'm only looking.

My rules are my rules, and they've served my game well.

The fiery look she gave me a moment ago has dissolved into something that looks like determination. She's going into battle. "I really need this," she grinds out between clenched teeth, almost like she's telling herself, not me.

Her shoulders drop and her long lashes hide her eyes, which focus on the floor. She seems exasperated by me—I'm not editing my surly tendencies, and it's not her fault I'm frustrated as fuck about all the time off the pitch.

"Look, I know I'm a jerk. I just don't do the whole circle-time-with-kids thing."

"And yet you're here with your niece."

"I like my niece. I don't like other people's kids."

A flicker of something flits across her face then disappears. She's probably judging me for that statement, but I don't give a shit. "Right," she says.

"I'm just being honest. I'd rather be an honest son of a bitch than a lying nice-seeming person."

Her laugh rolls out so abruptly it seems to surprise her. "Yeah, well, I wasn't likely to be confused." She cocks her head, her wide eyes fixing on me as if seeing me anew. "You don't normally bring your niece to the library. I've seen her here before with a woman."

"Yeah, that's my sister-in law. Me bringing her is a new thing. A temporary thing." I can't allow myself to believe I'll be off the pitch for much more time, even if talking to this woman is the least annoyed I've felt since I got my head bashed in.

"Still, it's sweet of you."

I huff a laugh. "Yeah, that's how most people describe me. I'm super fucking sweet." That gets me an eye roll, and damn if her mounting irritation doesn't make me want to taunt her a little bit more. She's hot when she's aggravated.

"You don't need to be Mr. Rogers. I'll read the book. All you have to do is rattle off a few of those cat facts like you did back there, and it'll keep them entertained. They'll love it. It'll be so great. And next week you can tell them facts about something else." She claps her hands and for the life of me, I can't understand how a person could be this excited about having me spout useless information about cat toes.

"Wait. Next week? When did this become an ongoing gig?"

Pressing her lips together, she answers by fixing those big pleading eyes on mine and clasping her hands in prayer.

I don't have a good reason *not* to do it. Nothing she's asking goes against Mickey's rules of disengagement, and it might help in the image makeover department.

Not to mention, I'll probably score a million favorite-uncle points, which will keep my brother out of my hair for a while.

"Just try it. For ten minutes. Talk to them about your vast knowledge of cat claws and see how it goes." She seems a little desperate and I'm dying to know why. When she goes back to chewing her swollen bottom lip, I take a step forward, getting in her space a little bit. I'm not trying to intimidate her; I just don't want her to have an easy exit.

"This seems important to you. Why is that?" I get the pro athlete cachet, but her desperation seems like something different.

Leaning my forearm against the wall, I study her. She's easily a foot shorter than me, with blond hair in a tight bun and strands of it spraying out in all directions, like she spent an hour at the hairdresser having someone style the perfect messy bun. Only I know that's not the case because I watched the wind whip half of it out of the hairband earlier. Then, she shoved part of it behind her ear like she doesn't care how it looks.

It looks amazing, and it startles me how intently I'm clocking these tiny details.

She wears a loose-fitting pair of jeans rolled up at the bottom with orange Chucks and a black sweater that looks three sizes too big. Maybe she borrowed the whole getup from her boyfriend after she slept over last night. I feel a surprising stab of rage at the thought of a boyfriend, but I push the thought away.

The dark frames of her glasses could be military-issue for librarians, but she rocks them in an I-have-lacy-lingerie-under-my-drab-clothes kind of way.

Yet she seems slightly uneasy in her skin. Or maybe in the library. Her lips twitch like she's about to speak, then she reconsiders and frowns. "Forget it. It was just an idea."

She moves to leave, but I've successfully hemmed her in between the wall and the rack of books. Undeterred, she starts rolling the rack out of her way.

I reach for her arm, and she turns. "Hang on. I'm not saying no. I just wanna know why you want me to do it. If you tell me your reasons, maybe you'll convince me."

"Or you're just toying with me because you get off on tormenting people."

"I thought we established that I only torment cats."

That earns me a reluctant smile, and it looks good on her. I feel relieved. I'm not a complete asshole, and I'm not trying to make her life more difficult. Then again, I didn't make pro soccer at twenty-one by giving up when I want something.

And I want to know. "Why do you want me to help you?"

Her shoulders rise toward her ears, and she looks at the ceiling. Then she lets them fall and exhales. "Fine. I'm not the best with kids. I'm bad at entertaining them. I was just hoping for a little help and people seem to be interested in having a guy here."

Huh. To her, I'm just "a guy." Not a soccer player, not a league all-star, not Major League Soccer's most eligible bachelor—none of the goddamn titles that I carry on my shoulders on and off the field. And especially not the guy who got his heart handed to him on national television two years ago and now takes special pleasure in being a certified asshole whenever possible.

It doesn't even offend me that she doesn't recognize my stupid concussed face. If anything, it's a relief that she's asking me to help purely based on a few facts I know about animals. Granted, most of the other people in her little reading circle couldn't post their selfies fast enough when I sat down with Kathryn, but to her, I'm just a guy.

I kind of like it.

And the part about a children's librarian being bad with kids…I *definitely* want to know more about that.

"You don't like reading to kids? But you're a librarian. Isn't that part of your job?"

"Why do people keep saying that? No, reading to children has nothing to do with library science. One is the study of book cataloguing systems and globally-accepted practices, and the other is basically babysitting with mild entertainment."

"I see you've put some thought into it."

She shrugs. "Some." Her fingers trail down the binding of a book on the cart and she smiles. The sight causes a visceral response in me, a chill over my skin that feels surprisingly good. It knocks out two years of shutting myself down and building resistance to the human touch.

Watching her hands makes me want to know how that book spine feels. My brain starts silently quoting Romeo Montague's line about a glove against Juliet's cheek. It's so foreign, I almost can't accept that I'm capable of feeling these things, and yet I do.

In the past fifteen minutes she's distracted me so thoroughly from my incessant misery that I feel willing to do whatever she asks. That's something.

Actually, it's a lot. But I can hardly let her believe I'm agreeing in order to help myself.

"Fine. I have a little bit of time on my hands for the next couple weeks, and I promised my niece I'd bring her here anyway. If you're going to force me to stay for the entirety of 'story time,' I might as well make myself useful."

"Why did you do this?" she asks, mimicking my air quotes. "Are you making fun of story time? It actually *is* a time for stories. What would you call it?" Standing there with her hands on her hips biting her lip again, she looks like every fantasy I never had of a hot librarian, but I'm sure as hell having them now. And the way she's glaring at me only makes the fantasy better.

As I debate how to rile her up even more, we're interrupted by a stern-looking woman who shushes us first, then glares at Molly. "Are we aborting story time? Have you given up on your grand plans so quickly?" she asks, daggers practically shooting from her eyes. If Molly's glare was hot, this woman's is the opposite—just plain, cold-as-death frightening.

"No, not at all. I'm just consulting with our...guest speaker." Her eyes turn toward me, and I see her ball her fists.

A part of me wants to wait and see if she's going to haul off and punch this other woman, which would be entertaining, but I get the impression there's an equal chance of her punching me. I also don't want to get her fired, so I grudgingly nod and tell her through gritted teeth, "I'd be delighted to talk about cats. Happy?"

She gives me a stiff smile, nods enthusiastically, and guides me back toward the reading area, turning her back on the other woman who likely skulks back to a viper den somewhere near the Death Cults section.

"Who is that basket of pain in the form of a human?"

"Judy. My boss. She threatened to fire me but I..." she says, still smiling through clenched teeth. She may look demure and put on a bright-eyed façade in front of the kids, but I can already see there's something stormier beneath the surface. And despite myself, I want to tug at her and learn more.

Why? You've got two weeks tops in library purgatory, then back to soccer twenty-four-seven.

I don't have time to answer my own question before I'm ushered to a chair in the reading area. Molly stands beside me as the kids all race back to assume their positions. My niece, Kathryn, has the biggest damn grin plastered across her face, positively delighted by the embarrassment I'm about to endure.

The brim on my baseball cap partially blocks my view of the faces staring up at me, which is just fine.

Molly pulls over a chair, seats herself next to me, and I try to ignore the sudden heat that warms my bones.

She begins reading, and her lilting voice sounds stronger and more sure of herself than she implied a few minutes ago when she admitted she was crap with kids. On the contrary, she's great at this.

Every child in the room stares at her like she invented the very concept of reading aloud. Her large, brown eyes dance as she meets the gaze of each kid on the rug and draws them into the story with her obvious joy.

When she gets to the part of the book about why cats have so many toes, she breaks with the text and grins mischievously. "Here's where we have to take the things we read in context. Does anyone know what that means?"

Not a single hand goes up. A few of the kids look around the room, wondering if anyone has the answer.

Of course they don't. They're six.

It doesn't matter—she owns the room. They'll follow her down a tunnel of Socratic methods if she asks. Molly plows on, undeterred, willing them to join her. "It means that just because you read something in a book—or see it on TV or in a YouTube video or wherever someone is giving you information—it doesn't mean it's an inconvertible truth."

Again, the kids aren't so much with inconvertible truths. Most seem baffled but equally fascinated by the secret portal she's opened to them.

I stare at Molly, more and more curious about this woman the further she gets from kindergarten curriculum. I'm about to grumble a joke about Greek salad at a Socratic seminar when one of the kids raises her hand. Molly nods at the small, dark-haired girl who's been sitting solemnly taking in everything Molly has said with matching wide-eyed delight.

"So, are you saying some things aren't true? Even what we read in books?"

Lighting up even more, if that were possible, Molly pushes a finger into the air. I half expect her to tell the little girl she's "grrreat" like Tony the Tiger. "Exactly, Caitlin. Like this book, for example. It talks about cats having twelve toes. If you read this and go off thinking all cats have twelve toes, you only know one fact about cats that might deserve to be questioned."

She leans in, her voice a stony whisper, and drops the money shot, "Cats have more toes than twelve and the reason they have them is fascinating." She leans back in her chair, leaving them slack-jawed and primed for more, but she presses her lips together and waits.

A chorus of "Why?" "Tell us!" "Please, Molly!" erupts from the kids on the carpet. My niece's voice rings loudest.

Molly nods slowly. She *has* them. And in some deep place I'd left for dead a long time ago, she has me. I'm hanging on her every word just like the kids.

She's the last thing I need, but admiring her from afar seems harmless enough.

"I have a special surprise for you." She presents me like I'm reading circle royalty and I'm stunned at how much I like it. "Let's call him the Cat Whisperer because he can coax them down from tall trees and tell you all kinds of cool stuff."

Like a professional shell game swindler, she's effectively finished reading after about ten pages and shifted all responsibility to me.

I'm so dazzled by her sleight of hand that it takes me a second to realize the kids are now waiting expectantly. But her quick pass is the closest to soccer I've gotten in a while, so I take it and run.

"That's right, you guys. Not only do most cats have eighteen toes, but one lucky cat set the record at twenty-eight." I wait and let my factoid sink in. It's something I read about after I learned that Greta has a few extra toes. My pint-sized audience looks riveted, so I pull some more useless facts out of my hat. "Next time you see a cat, pay special attention to how it walks, and you'll notice something interesting. Cats walk with both right feet, then both left feet. The only other animals to do that are camels and giraffes."

I can't imagine how the kids can possibly find this better than listening to Molly read. I sure wouldn't. But as I inwardly roll my eyes and prattle on, I see Molly glowing with something like pride and relief, which makes me want to do whatever it takes to keep her looking like that.

The intruding feeling sends up a warning flare.

Her happiness should be irrelevant to me. The last thing I need is any sort of complication in my life courtesy of a woman, and this one, with her perky smile and bouncy ponytail, could have me shelving every book in the place if she smiles at me once more.

Turning my attention back to scrounging useless trivia about cats, I mostly succeed at ignoring her for the remainder of the hour. Every so often, I hear a contented sigh slip from her lips when the kids laugh at one of my stories about Greta and her boundless excitement about yarn. Each time, the sound jars me out of my train of thought. It takes all of my mental fortitude to keep from thinking about other, less G-rated ways to make her sigh.

And now I'm thinking about what an asshole I am, sitting in front of a dozen kindergarteners and fantasizing about fingering the librarian.

After I finish up, she thanks me, extending her hand like we're old business partners. "Holden, thank you. Sincerely. You really made this great." She wastes no time locking me in for next week before I can tell her I don't want to come back, sit next to her, and fight the urge to stare at her.

The words wrestle around on my tongue, but she levels another blow before I can untangle them.

"We make a decent team. The kids loved it. Really, really loved it." Then she smiles, and I'm a goner.

In two years, I've stuck by my self-imposed ban on women. Not a single date, not one no-strings fling with a jersey chaser. It wasn't even hard to resist them. Or any woman.

Until now. Until her.

One smile and I'm considering rewriting all my rules. They're good rules, put in place for the sake of my sanity and the importance of my game. Why would I risk changing something that's working? The game is everything, now more than ever since I can feel how it sucks to watch from the sidelines.

I should step away and tell her this was a one-time thing. I should. Instead, because of that smile, those doe eyes, that boundless joy over feline fiction, I turn my back on common sense.

"Fine, Mare," I growl. "See you next week."

CHAPTER 6

olden

"Two weeks in a row, I'm impressed, Uncle Holden. I thought you'd tap out after one trip to the frozen yogurt shop, but I hear you're going back to the library next week," my brother Edward says from the ground below the tree where I'm currently sitting on a high branch.

I seem to be finding myself in trees quite a bit lately.

The orange tree is probably as old as my thirty-two years, its life improbable for so many reasons. Citrus trees do famously poorly in the Bay Area climate, at least in the area where Edward lives. It's generally too cold and foggy to give these trees the kind of sunshine they require, but this one has managed to survive.

A developer bought the tract of land in Portola Valley that eventually became a group of houses and leveled everything on it except this particular tree. The developer originally slated Edward's house as his own, but then he took a job in Los Angeles and sold the place. Edward was the beneficiary.

"Yeah, what is it with the yogurt place giving your kid a vat the size of a Home Depot bucket and calling it a serving? She must've loaded thirty kinds of toppings in there—gummy worms, cookie dough, some kind of weird orange fruit things that burst in your mouth…"

"Boba. It's boba."

"I dunno, man. She gave me one to try and it kind of creeped me out. But she's cuter than shit, so I'd do it again."

Jane, Edward's wife, took one look at the chocolate ring around Kathryn's mouth and gave me the kind of glare that turns lesser mortals to stone. "Ice cream before dinner, Holden? Really?" she said.

"It's yogurt, Mommy. Don't worry, it's healthy."

At Jane's eye roll, I tried to get on her better side. "If it makes you feel any better, I ate most of it," I lie. I'm lucky to look enough like Edward that she spares me the really deadly laser stares because I have no doubt they'd kill me. She swatted my arm and pointed to the backyard.

"Go. If you're going to make trouble, do it outside, please." Then she shuttled Kathryn over to the sink to wash her hands and mouth before serving her a plate of spaghetti. I did as told and promptly ended up here in the tree.

Half the oranges on Edward's tree have gone unpicked because they're too high for the fruit picker contraption he uses to grab them.

Uncle Holden to the rescue.

"It's pretty damn peaceful up here. I may never come down," I say, finding a spot at the crook of two branches that's a comfortable resting spot. As I lob oranges down to Edward, aiming at the gray bucket in his hand, I think about bringing a few to Molly next week when I go to the library.

Then I wonder why she'd have any interest in a bunch of oranges. Then I ask myself who wouldn't want a bunch of oranges? We all need vitamin C.

Yeah, I'm thinking about her. Better than thinking about our game this past weekend, where I sat on the sidelines and watched our team get slaughtered. The only thing worse than feeling responsible for letting in a goal is feeling like a helpless pansy who can't do a damn thing about it.

That's right, I said it. I'd rather have an entire stadium blame me for missing a save than have to watch our number two let something in that I know I'd have caught. It was the worst kind of misery, and I have at least a few more weeks of it. The docs won't let me fly to away games—the changes in cabin pressure aren't good for my swollen brain—but I'll screen every minute of those on the big flatscreen in my house and clock any mistakes in high def. No-screentime-rules be damned.

Edward rubs a hand over his face and retreats to his patio a few yards away. "I'm pretty sure tree climbing isn't part of concussion protocol." He plops into a rattan chair with a big white cushion. If he's not picking up the oranges I'm throwing down, I'm done picking them.

"Yeah, well, fuck 'em." I drop down one branch and lower myself to the ground. Then I raid the bar fridge behind his barbecue for a bottle of water.

"When are they clearing you to play?"

Shrugging, I blink hard, ignoring the tiny ache behind my eyes when I do. I know it's not a good sign. "I'm not going to be stupid—other than the trees. I've still got double vision and my sleep is all messed up."

"Really? Can't sleep?"

"The contrary. All I want to do is sleep. I can normally get by on six hours, and right now my body wants nine. I don't have time for it."

He nods. "You're still recovering. It's normal." Edward is a dentist and he's married to an orthodontist, so I'm not sure what he knows about recovering from a concussion, but I'll latch onto any shred of positive news I can get. "You still have the brain fog?"

"Yeah, a bit. Getting better." I have brain fog to blame for most of what went down at the library the other day. My thoughts felt like an egg scramble when I was sitting with Kathryn, which was why I ended up rambling about cats with the kids outside. I was half wacky when Molly started scolding me about leaving, though I'll admit that some of the fog cleared when I looked at her.

I sip the water, enjoying the chill of the afternoon fog settling in. It's one of the things I immediately loved when I moved to San Francisco to play for the Strikers. Edward already lived in the city, and I'd visited him a few times, but it wasn't until I moved that I realized how moody and relaxing the fog could be. For a guy who's always amped up trying to train and think about the game and win the game, having a weather pattern take hold of my energy felt profound.

Whenever the team is training or playing at home, I let the foggy afternoon vibe wash over me and take the edge off of whatever game stress I'm carrying.

Today, the sheet of white creeps in slowly, and I can still see blue sky through the veil of descending fog. A few hours from now, it will be so thick that I won't be able to make out my neighbor's house across the street. I like it.

The past hour that I've spent with my brother has relieved me of the need to think about why I want to go back to the library.

But now I'm thinking.

"Anyhow, your willingness to keep taking Kath to the library wouldn't have anything to do with a hot librarian named Molly, would it?" He feigns an innocent expression which quickly dissolves into a smug grin.

"Who says she's hot?"

Edward shrugs. "Kath mentioned the librarian convinced you to help her tell stories and you're not exactly Hemingway."

"I resent that. I did major in English, you know."

"Yeah, the language you grew up speaking. Big reach."

"You're an idiot. I didn't spend college learning the English language. I spent it reading. Lotta Shakespeare. You might want to try it sometime. It's good to know things."

According to our mother, my brother and I came out of the womb disagreeing and giving each other shit. As my fraternal twin and only sibling, no one on earth knows how to get under my skin more than Edward. And I pay it back in spades.

But other than a general resemblance and equal reliance on sarcasm, we couldn't be more different. He won every mathlete and science award at our high school, while I captained the soccer team and played for an elite academy that put me in front of major league coaches before I got a full ride to play soccer at UCLA.

When I was ditching my English classes to fit in extra keeper training, Edward double majored in chemistry and history before leaving college a semester early to travel the world before heading to dental school. Our paths crossed in Spain, where I was a bench player for Real Madrid before getting my current starting spot on the Strikers.

Leaving the higher-level European leagues was a tough decision—I scarified prestige and a higher level of play—but with no guarantee I'd play a single minute of a game in Spain, coming back to the US felt right.

The Strikers offered me a sweet contract and really seemed to want me. I took it and ran.

My mind often drifts back to that decision, wondering, as I often do, if I made the right choice. Edward's fist connecting with my shoulder pulls me out of my reverie.

"So? What's up with Molly? I heard you agreed to be her assistant. Is that some kind of role play during sex?"

"Your kid has a big mouth. And no."

He smirks and wanders over to the bar fridge, which he opens with the flourish of a game show host.

"My kid is awesome."

"Your kid *is* awesome, and I think I've committed myself to helping the hot librarian with her kid reading hour or some nonsense. I dunno. Guess I'm a sucker for a pretty girl who asks nicely."

Continuing the Vanna White routine, he gestures at the bottles on the bottom shelf. "Microbrew or IPA? And don't tell me you're good with water. You're not training tomorrow, and a beer might help you sleep."

I shrug, no idea what I want. He hands me a dark bottle of something with a colorful label and flops his out-of-shape body on a lounge chair next to a square of grass barely big enough for a two-year-old to keep busy with a soccer ball. But the house is perfect, and I won't be surprised if Kathryn gets a sibling one of these days.

Rather than argue, I reach for the opener that hangs from a string near the barbecue and crack open my bottle, then his. The cold beer goes down easily, and I realize it's been a while since I've allowed myself to do this—hang outside with another person and unwind for five damn minutes.

"Thanks, man. I didn't realize I needed this."

He looks at me quizzically. "Who doesn't need a beer?"

"I mean, I needed to remember that my life didn't end when I got carted off the field on a stretcher."

Patting the blue cushion on the lounge chair next to his, Edward insists, "Get out of my sun. Sit." I obey, and I'm pleasantly surprised at how comfortable it is. "Now, tell me why you're so gloomy. I know you're having endorphin withdrawal, but is that the only thing? Did the librarian turn you down?"

"What? No. I haven't asked her out."

"But you're going to."

"I don't need that in my life."

"Why not?"

"You know why."

He shrugs. "I know what your excuse is. Shyla handed you a good one and you've milked it for two years, but now it's getting ridiculous."

"So says the guy who married his college sweetheart. Trust me, it's safer to look and not touch."

He crosses his legs at the ankles and tilts his lounge chair back, letting the afternoon rays warm his face. If anyone ever asks me what job allows for the best income with the least amount of stress, I'll say dentist every time. Just looking at my brother proves it. He's as relaxed as I am wound up. "You're right. Turning away all the women who want you for nothing but filthy sex sounds like torture. No wonder you're pissed off all the time."

I roll my eyes. "There's no point."

"No point in what?"

"Talking to you, for one thing. Risking my game for a jersey chaser is another."

He shrugs. "Your game's on hold right now anyway, so there's nothing to risk. Just have a little fun. Not every woman is evil. Make yourself happy for once."

"I am fucking happy," I bite out.

His barking seal laugh startles me. "Sort your shit, man. You're happy enough on the pitch—*maybe*—when you're winning. But what about the rest of your life?"

"The pitch is my life."

"What happens after you play your last game?"

"Ugh. Go away." Throwing an arm over my eyes, I pretend I'm alone. Much better than sitting here having my twin tell me I'll be old enough for retirement in a few years.

I just want to drink my beer and distract myself from those depressing thoughts. Which is maybe why I keep letting images of Molly wander into my brain. She's sweet, she's goddamn gorgeous, and I'm fairly certain she's hiding something more complicated and interesting behind the perky façade. If thinking about her provides a tiny distraction from the depressing thoughts roiling my brain, what's the harm in that?

"I don't want to think about my last game right now. I'll deal with it when it happens."

"Fine. Ask the librarian out. You've got a good month before your game's at any risk. Most relationships barely make it a month anyway."

"Fine."

"Yeah?"

"If you'll shut up about it and not blab to your kid, I'll ask her out." I'll say anything to make him shut up.

"Great." He smiles like he's just solved all my problems. I shoot him a death glance and drink my beer.

If there's one thing I'm not doing, it's complicating the shit-show that is my life by asking Molly out. Even if I can't stop thinking about her.

CHAPTER 7

Molly

THE CROWD in front of the library tells me something's different.

But the smile on Judy's face is the real indication that pigs must be orbiting the planet on wings made of bacon. I'm late, as usual, and she beelines for me as soon as I walk through the front door.

Her blue eyes are aflame, but she doesn't look angry, and I'm pretty certain she's done something different with her hair, though I can't say what. It looks fluffier.

"Nice to see you, Judy," I say, hurrying through the entry area.

"You've risen to the occasion." Her tone is accusatory even though the words sound complementary. She points at the kids' area which is partly obscured by a row of book racks which aren't normally there.

"I'll clear those away, don't worry."

She starts walking with me toward the children's section, so I brace myself for another reprimand. "No, no. I had Seth put those there. For crowd control."

Now I'm certain she's off her rocker because this is a library, not a Kendrick Lamar concert. But then I see a large group milling around the kids' book area, mostly women with kids in tow.

There are easily fifty people and every one of the beanbags and small chairs is full. So is the carpeted area. And still, a couple dozen people stand around the periphery. Then I realize...

"The fliers! Oh, I went around over the weekend and posted fliers near all the elementary schools in the area, urging people to come hear the guest speakers. People must be super excited about the idea." I'm suddenly nervous, however, because this is far more people than showed up yesterday. Holden said he'd help out, but I don't see him, and I don't know how he feels about crowds.

If he's a no-show, I have to command most of this circus myself. We still have fifteen minutes before I plan to start, so I don't panic. Yet.

Nearly every square on the rainbow carpet has a kid sitting on it, and adults either sit behind them or they stand in the back. Having all these adults in the room calms me. I know how to discuss literature with adults and teens. No problem. I'll just focus my attention on them as I read. Tune out the littles.

For the next few minutes, I busy myself adding more books to the large pile I have in front of my chair. Then I shelve a few books on the cart because, let's face it, I'm stalling for time.

But at a few minutes past five, I sense the kids getting restless and Judy glares from her desk. I need to start with or without Holden, and after one more glance toward the front of the library, I conclude that I'm on my own.

I can't decide how I feel about it. On one hand, his gruff attitude and scowl might alienate some people. He's nice to look at, so that might balance out his personality.

But it hurts a little that he's going back on our deal. It's a combination of feeling like I've been rejected by a man and the annoyingly persistent feeling that I failed to convince him to help me.

Then, there's a third thought tugging at me. Despite his irritating personality, I was kind of looking forward to seeing him again. I'm just a few days away from the anniversary of the death of someone in my past, and Holden's pretty face would be a welcome distraction.

Oh well. Buck up, Mary Poppins. It's show time.

Taking my seat at the front of the rug, I pull a book from the stack I've curated with the help of some children's book bloggers. I want to start off strong, and with today's crowd, I'm glad I prepared.

In one hand, I hold up a factual book about African tigers, and in the other, I show the kids a fiction book about a group of warrior cats on a knight's quest. "Hi, everyone. I'm Molly. Who's ready to read?"

There's a stir in the crowd and a rumble of assent. I start with the Warrior Cats book, but one boy pipes up, "Where's Holden Sanders?"

I open my mouth to come up with an excuse when a chair slides across the floor next to me and Holden drops into it. "Yeah, I'm late," he says, a scowl on his face. "Fucking traffic."

I've never been more delighted to have traffic as an excuse. I'm sure the wattage of my giddy smile makes the overhead lighting unnecessary.

"Ah, bane of my existence," I whisper, a feeling of calm washing over me now that my kid crutch is here.

He scoots his chair a little closer and looks over at the book I've chosen, nodding his approval. When I begin reading, I'm suddenly hyperaware of his body near mine. I thought I'd imagined the heat drawing me to him last week when he had me cornered near the returns cart. Now, I know the man possesses some kind of force field.

I'm also aware of people snapping pictures of Holden with their phones. I feel certain they're not just responding to a male presence.

Holden Sanders. The name isn't familiar, but I feel like I should know who he is.

I don't hear the words as I read from the book. My attention is pulled to Holden, and my brain shuffles through my late-night TV binges—admittedly mostly romances—and since he's clearly not a British amateur baker, I know I haven't seen him on *Bakeoff.*

As I turn the page, I sneak a look in his direction and find him watching me, his ice-gray eyes drawing me in to stare way longer than I should. They're a little hypnotic.

And…I've lost my place in the book.

I stammer to continue, feeling a blush creep across my cheeks. I know he sees it, and that embarrassing thought is enough to keep me from looking his way again.

But it doesn't keep me from thinking about him and his Henry Cavill jaw.

After a few minutes, I stop reading and let Holden tell the kids more arcane facts about cats. He explains that not all of them hate water and some know how to swim.

When I pick up the book again, I hear an audible groan in the room.

"Can we read a different type of book?" a freckled boy whines from the front row. My eyes close in defeat when I realize I'm slowly torturing a roomful of America's future, making them believe that reading is just a process of acquiring cat knowledge.

So I cave to the tide of reason. "Sure. What kind of book would you like?"

"Soccer!" he yells, and immediately the area erupts into gleeful agreement. They all want the same thing, at least, so I hop over to the sports section and select a few books with characters who play soccer.

As I flip open the first book, the boy with the constellation of freckles raises his hand, waving it so fervently that I'm certain he needs the restroom. "Can Holden Sanders read it? That would be so cool!" He stares wide-eyed at Holden, who shrugs.

The rickety apparatus in my brain finally kicks in. Oh. He's a soccer player. Explains all the selfies. And maybe the crowd.

Also explains why you need to get out of the library on occasion.

"Wanna read?" I ask him. His face is half suffering, half smile, which forms a dimple in one cheek. I think I actually flutter my eyelashes at him.

His expression turns pained, and I worry my lashes have offended him until he admits, "I can't read."

Momentarily taken aback by this blunt admission, I stammer. "Oh, okay. It's fine. A lot of people don't know how to read. I didn't mean to assume—"

A noise interrupts me, and it's so uncharacteristic of him that I don't recognize it at first. Holden is laughing quietly, his eyes crinkling at the corners and mouth tipping into the most gorgeous smile. I almost fall out of my chair. "Sorry. I know *how* to read. I just can't for now." He points to his head. "Concussion."

"Oh. Wow, okay. I'm sorry to hear that."

"It's fine. I'll just make up a story. Is that okay?"

"Sure. Great." I'm still partially stunned at the smile playing on his lips. It's so beautiful that it blinds me to everything else in the room, and at first I don't notice the complete hush that falls over the crowd when Holden starts his story. Then I realize he has everyone captivated.

His voice, suddenly deeper when he takes on the characters' dialogue, continues to heat all different parts my body, and for a minute, I forget that I'm sitting in front of a roomful of kids and their attentive female chaperones. I visualize myself sitting alone with Holden while he reads poetry in the same deep, sultry voice he's using right now. "...Then I'm out of the box, slide tackling him and hurling the ball away."

He could slide tackle me. To say nothing of what he could do to my box.

Until...

"And then I say, *hell no*, not in my house. And I dive right, get a hand on the ball, and smack it away for a fucking epic save."

I swallow hard and shoot him a look. He has the good sense to realize what he just said without me having to make a bigger deal of it in front of the kids. "Excuse the colorful language," he tells them, but no one cares. Every kid in the room—and every parent, for that matter—is riveted to him, waiting for whatever comes next in the story.

"So, you did it? You made the save?" The boy with the freckled face has scooted up so close, he's able to grasp Holden's shoes in his small hands, white-knuckling them at the story.

"I did. And you know what? That save kept us from dropping three spots on the table, so it's a good lesson. Never think that you can't make a big change with a small action. Even if you don't know it at the time. Always try your hardest."

And with that, he's delivered parenting gold. The wide-eyed kids nod like zombies, and he's redirected the rebellious ones with his words. A few of the phones probably recorded it for social media posterity.

The hour flies by as he and I tag team our way through a little bit of reading, a lot of stories about soccer, and my growing gratitude for making my interactions with children bearable.

By the time the kids and parents file out of the library, it's nearly six o'clock and Kathryn is dramatically staggering like she hasn't eaten all day. I've been bringing my home-baked treats on Mondays and Fridays, but I tell myself I need to step up my game and bring them every day.

"Ooh. I have something you might like." I dig into my purse for a chocolate-covered chewy granola bar and present it to her.

"Can I, Uncle Holden?" He nods and she accepts the small offering, tearing open the wrapper. I walk them toward the exit, lest Judy catch Kathryn eating in the library and blow a gasket.

"Wow, you killed it. That was great," I tell Holden.

"It wasn't torture," he grumbles. "So…I assume you need me again next week?" From his eye roll, he's dreading it. I do need him, though, so I nod enthusiastically.

"Yes, please, if you don't mind. Thank you."

Holden holds the door open for me and Kathryn. I adjust my glasses as I walk through, which means I don't see his foot in my path until I trip on it. Falling against him, I brace my hand on his hard chest to stay upright. His eyes darken and he holds my gaze. I swear I hear a growl of what sounds like torture rumble from his chest.

I step away before he sees how much his gruff smolder affects me. And oh, it affects me—in a snaking ribbon of pleasure that ends between my thighs. Holy hell, this man is a danger to any female who needs to concentrate on something other than him.

"Anyway, yes. I'd be grateful if you came back next week."

He taps a finger against his lips, which are turned up into a smirk. "I'll admit I don't know a lot of children's librarians, but are all of you terrified of actual children?"

I frown, caught. "Oh. You figured that out, huh?"

"Pretty obvious."

Inhaling the cool air outside, I glance around, half hoping a stranded cat might distract him from his line of questioning. I see only a small traffic jam of cars leaving the parking lot and commuters passing by on the sidewalk. "Well, first off, I'm not really a children's librarian. I work at a high school. This is just a part-time thing, and they need me in the kids' section, so…"

"You didn't choose it. Makes more sense."

"And second, I'm not terrified of them." I'm lying and from the way he taps a finger against his lips and waits, he knows it. "I just have a low-lying fear that I'm ruining them without knowing it."

He points to Kathryn who's strayed a few yards away from us. She sits on a bench, legs swinging, taking small, measured bites from the granola bar. "She likes you."

"Yeah, bribing them with chocolate is always helpful." Drawing my hands up, I massage my temples.

"You okay?"

"Just a headache. Long day. Nothing new." I don't want to bore him with my boring life.

"Trust me, I know about headaches."

"Yeah?"

He points to his temple. "This concussion's given me a headache going on three weeks now. Guess we're in the same boat."

"Yeah, well, your traffic problem didn't help my stress level. Maybe you should call the library if you're running late next week."

The smirk is back. "Were you worried I was going to leave you defenseless against the angry masses of six-year-olds armed only with cat books and granola bars?"

I feel my cheeks flush—again—at the memory of how I felt when he sat down next to me. "I'd have been just fine."

"Liar." He points to the front pocket of my jeans where my phone sticks out. "Here. Take my number. If I'm late again, you can rip me a new one via text. I find that to be a great stress release."

I note that he's not asking for my number. There's no reason for him to have it. We're not planning a future date or something. That's not what this is.

So why do I feel slightly disappointed?

He hands the phone back. "There you go. In case of emergency, text away."

I put it back in my pocket, thank him again, and say goodbye to Kathryn who fist bumps me like a pro. Holden hoists her onto his shoulders, and as they walk away, I can't help but marvel at how good he is with her, despite his obvious dislike for most people. Everyone should have a doting uncle like him.

Then I go back inside the library, certain of one thing—I won't be texting Holden Sanders. Ever. Even in an emergency.

CHAPTER 8

olly

"*Pride and Prejudice* is the gateway drug," Preeta says in her clipped British accent, as she pops the top on a can of Diet Coke. Taking a healthy slug of her drink, she twists a strand of her long, dark hair. I hear tiny slurping sounds and marvel at how quickly she can drink a carbonated beverage without stopping for air.

Her large, brown eyes peer at me from under dark lashes. I hold my tongue and smile, which drives her crazy.

"Come on, say you disagree with me." Her thick lashes move like butterfly wings. Preeta Bodapati teaches calculus and advanced statistics, and even though we're the same age, our brains could not be more different. While I could get lost for hours analyzing one passage of literature, she could spend hours solving one math problem. But on Jane Austen's classic novel, we agree.

"I'd love to get into a debate about it, but I happen to think you're right. For many lovers of romance novels, their first toe dip into the genre came when they fell in love with Darcy."

"Well, bollocks. I was hoping for some lively debate, but now you're going all bookish and serious on me."

"It also works in reverse. Some of the girls at school here will read romance novels all night long but they don't realize that Jane Austen was the OG romance writer. Once I turn their thinking, they start devouring the classics."

"Now I know why the English department tips you well over the holidays," she jokes and finishes the can, which she tosses into my recycling bin after banking it off the wall.

"Nice shot." It leaves a small stain of dripping brown liquid, and I take a paper towel off the roll on my desk to wipe it down.

"Thanks. I'm sporty, you know."

"Yes, I do know." If I had a dollar for every time Preeta mentions her epic basketball career—which ended with a torn rotator cuff in grade eleven at her London prep school—I wouldn't need my second job at the public library. "What I don't know is how you can drink that sludge at nine in the morning." I gesture to the discarded can.

"It's caffeine. Don't judge, coffee addict. I don't drink that rubbish, so I have a few colas throughout the morning." She shrugs. The thought of that much sickly-sweet fake sugar makes me shiver, but she's right. I have no problem slugging down three cups of black coffee before noon.

Preeta has office hours in the study hall area of the library, but no students have sought her out this period, so she's lurking around the reference desk.

"So you convinced this bloke to come and sit there like eye candy so women will bring their littles into the library? Elizabeth Bennet might have a thing or two to say about that."

Biting down on my lip, I'm forced to agree. "When you say it like that, it's pretty cringey. Though she'd probably like looking at him. He's very nice to look at."

"Wait, this sounds good." She grabs one of the rolling chairs from an empty study carrel and pulls it over, spinning it around, throwing one of her long legs over the seat, and leaning her lean forearms on the headrest. "Tell me more."

I debate not telling her he's the San Francisco Strikers' starting keeper. Yes, I went straight home and googled him. Who wouldn't? Most of the recent news detailed his concussion and speculation about his return to the game. There were photos of him being carried off the field after his injury and lots of action shots of him sweating, smoldering, and growling. I mostly just looked at the pictures.

He looked good sweating, smoldering, and growling.

"He's Holden Sanders," I blurt.

For a second, she's quiet. Then her eyes grow wide, and she shrieks. "Wait. Bloody hell, wait. Your library volunteer is the famous footballer?" She starts tapping on the screen of her phone and shows a picture of Holden to me. More smoldering.

"He's a soccer player."

"We call it football where I come from. And this guy? You know he's a legend, right?" Of course, my closest work friend has to be a sports nut.

I nod, pressing my lips together as though it will prevent more rogue words from escaping.

"How? Why? Tell me everything."

I give her the barebones of our arrangement and she somehow infers from it that we'll be "shagging" by the end of a month.

"I feel like you didn't hear a word I said. He's just helping for a couple weeks while he's benched. I'll keep my job and he'll get himself some positive PR. Nothing more.

She looks at me skeptically. "But he's gorgeous. You have to at least try to shag him. Though is it true what everyone says? He's completely closed off and angry?"

"I wouldn't say angry. Just grouchy."

"Not that I blame him. That was a shit move Shyla Winters pulled, but still, he's had ample time to get over her." When I look at her blankly, she unfurls a tale of his horrifying public breakup with his mega-star girlfriend and the messy aftermath where some bad boy behavior and a worse attitude derailed his shot at playing for the Premier League.

It surprises me that I feel a small twinge of jealousy at the mention of him dating Shyla Winters. She's gorgeous and famous, only proving that whatever small fantasy I might have had about chemistry between us was all in my head. He doesn't date librarians.

Still… "Is he dating anyone now?" I ask, since Preeta seems to know everything about his social life.

She shakes her head. "He's all about football. Sort of famously doesn't date. But I assume he still needs to meet a need. You must give me details every Thursday morning about whether your library time leads to a shag," she says, slapping a hand on my desk with last four words. "Now let's go get some food. Today they have breakfast burritos. Pleeease…" She's whining like the students do when they want to take over the library for social club meetings.

I point to the canvas tote I use as a lunch bag. "Not spending money on burritos. I brought stuff from home. I need more money coming in than the amount going out. As a math teacher, I'm sure you're familiar."

Pinning her dark eyes on me, she pulls a tube of pink lipstick from the pocket of her dress and refreshes her lips. Rubbing them together, she uses me as a human mirror. "Passable?" She shows me her teeth. Not a lipstick smudge on them.

"You're good."

"Great. Now explain your voodoo finances to me. You make a decent living here—granted, you should be paid more. We all should. But you're the only one I know who works a second job to live in a studio near the freeway. Are you supporting a family someplace that I don't know about?" She chuckles at the thought.

"Oh, you're funny. You know, I buy things impulsively online, get tempted by the salad bar at Whole Foods and a cold brew coffee, and I'm down half a paycheck. Regular single-woman bad habits. I'm just not good with budgeting."

I'm very good with budgeting.

And I can't remember the last time I bought something impulsively online.

Even though Preeta is about the closest friend I have, I don't want to share everything with her. Maybe it's *because* she's such a close friend. I don't want her to know all of my crazy. Some things are best kept private.

Instead, I let her think I'm just bad with numbers.

She gives me a slow, skeptical nod. "One of these days, I'll get to the bottom of this." I give her a closed-mouthed smile that I hope tells her I won't be bullied. "Anyhow, mainly I came here to make sure you're okay. I remember tomorrow is your big wallow. Want some company or anything? We could go to lunch after."

"Feels like you're always trying to feed me."

"I'm trying to distract you."

"I'm good. No distracting needed. It will be the usual wallowing."

"Promise me you'll be easy on yourself?"

It's easier to lie than to explain why I can't make that promise. "It's only one day. Don't worry."

The bell rings sooner than either of us expected and she sighs. "Back to the bowels of Wheeler Hall for me. Hope you get another quiet hour so you can read..." She picks up the book from my desk and looks at the cover, rolling her eyes.

"I should've known." She tosses my dogeared copy of *Pride and Prejudice* back on the desk and gives me a sympathetic look. But I'm merely revisiting an old favorite. It has nothing to do with the fact that Holden reminds me of the grumpy Mr. Darcy.

Nothing at all.

CHAPTER 9

olly

EVERY YEAR, I think it will be different. Easier.

And every year, I'm surprised all over again when unfamiliar emotions overwhelm me. Preeta was right—I don't know how to go easy on myself.

Adam died four years ago today. Adam was my boyfriend, or at least he was on the way to becoming my boyfriend. We'd only dated for two months—ten dates—but ten dates feel substantial when they're all you'll ever have. Then he died. I still blame myself, even though people say I shouldn't.

Long story.

Bad story.

So bad, I try not to think about it most of the time. Three hundred sixty-four days out of the year, to be exact. I'm happy in the present. I'm a naturally happy person. But once a year, on the anniversary of his death, I let all the sadness in and wallow.

I grieve for Adam's loss of life because it was tragic. And a

75

grieve a little bit for myself because I'll never let myself get close to someone I could lose. Then, I move on.

Some people pay emotional penance for a perceived misdeed. Others donate to a charitable foundation and pay it forward. I do both because I don't know what else to do.

Every year, I go to the cemetery and sit by Adam's graveside. I talk about the news like I'm giving someone an update after a vacation without Wi-Fi.

"Life is strange, you know? I look around and see crap humans living until old age, and then someone good and honest like you isn't here anymore. It doesn't make sense. Or maybe it's just random and I should stop trying to look for logic where there is none," I tell the flowers and grass at my feet.

I don't think I'm actually talking to Adam, but it's a ritual, going there and spilling out a year's worth of thoughts, goals, hopes, secrets, and fears.

It grounds me to come here and remember him, even if I have no certainty that we'd even know each other anymore if he'd lived. His death froze our relationship in time and made it my origin story. I doubt he'd want it that way, but he's not here to argue.

Adam's headstone lays flat on a wide expanse of grass that also contains markers for his great grandparents and his grandfather. The sky is unmarred by clouds, all the morning fog having burned off by noon.

After an hour, I drive to Richmond and visit Adam's parents. His mom, June, greets me at the door like she always does with at least one oven mitt on her hands. She cooks on Saturdays for Sunday nights when Adam's brothers and their wives visit. Today, from the smell, it seems like she's roasting chicken.

"Come out to the yard," she says, offering me a glass of iced tea and calling to Joseph, Adam's dad, who's building some sort of contraption. Like he always is. Last time, it was a wooden bench. Today, it's a bird feeder shaped like a two-story, pitched-roof house.

"You were at the cemetery?" Joseph asks, knowing the answer because he knows my ritual. He has his own, which includes a visit later in the day with June.

I nod and tell them I can't stay long. I don't want to say long. I hand them an envelope containing a check, enough to pay a tuition scholarship for one student at the private school where Adam went, just like he planned to do when he finished law school.

Even though his parents tell me, as they do every year, that it's overly generous and not necessary, they take the money and add it to a scholarship fund set up in Adam's name.

I've never seen the school, but I assume it's similar to the one where I work. It feels like a good thing to do, even if it means I need the extra job to fund it.

For most of the rest of the year, I'm able to live my life outside of the dark cloud that hung over me along with shock that someone so young could die so suddenly. It took some therapy. Probably not enough therapy, but my insurance only covered a certain number of sessions, so I'm as healed as I can be.

So I embrace the life I'm lucky enough to have. I try not to squander it. Life is for the living. Adam believed that, or at least I feel like it's something he'd believe. So if I try a little harder than some people to look at the brighter side of things, it's intentional.

"You seeing anyone?" June asks, hopeful as she always is while she waits for my answer.

"No, not right now," I tell her.

Joseph shoots her a don't-meddle look while he holds two walls of the birdhouse together so the wood glue can dry. Turning her back, Joan pointedly ignores him. "You need to get over him, sweetheart. I want to see you happy," June tells me, like she does every year.

"I am happy. Don't worry." I give her my most convincing smile and sip my tea until she seems satisfied.

It's sweet that she worries, but she doesn't understand that I'm not grieving a guy who I may or may not still be with if he were alive. I'm grieving the fact that I will never open myself up to a relationship again.

As a kid, shiny-faced and hopeful, I trusted that my dad would stay with my mom forever—stay with me forever. But he left her when I was a kid and didn't take much of an interest in either of us once he had a new family. Then I watched him leave that family too.

I grew up with an inherent distrust of men. I was my mom's cheerleader and best friend—we hated men together. She taught me that it's better to be independent and keep fierce control over your heart than to open yourself up to getting hurt by a man.

When she got remarried, she took her words back, but they had already cemented themselves in my consciousness.

Adam pursued me for almost a year. A year of trying to wear down my defenses before I relented and went out with him. Two months later, I felt ready to shout from the rooftops that I'd embraced the optimistic side of life and love. A week after that, I stood at his funeral.

Lesson learned. You don't have to be a shitty husband or father to break someone's heart.

"You let us know if you need anything." June pats my hand and walks me to the door, ending the annual ritual.

"You too."

"We're fine. We've made our peace with God's plans for us in this life. You should too." I nod and wonder what it would feel like to believe so fervently in a god that it allows a mother to make peace with losing her son.

As I leave Adam's parents' house, I feel a weight lift off my shoulders. Another year behind me, a little more money in the scholarship coffers. A tiny easing of the memories.

Heading south on the freeway, I make my way back toward the Bay Bridge, back to my tiny, crappy studio, which I love for its simplicity and its proximity to public transportation.

I call my neighborhood SoMa-adjacent because it's close enough to the hip South of Market neighborhood to be accurate without revealing that I live in a hellhole.

The sun starts to drop as I lace up my running shoes and jog uphill through the Presidio. Even the painful ache of my lungs straining to pull enough air feels good right now. Because I'm alive. I don't have survivor's guilt; I have survivor's appreciation. I can't let any opportunity slip past me. Can't forego looking at the sunset when I have the chance. Can't forget to smell every rose. It's exhausting sometimes, but I can't complain because I'm alive.

Each time my feet hit the pavement, I feel an awareness of the world around me, my heart beating, my hair flying behind me in its ponytail.

By the time I reach my block in SoMa-adjacent, I'm running so fast that my lungs are taking in air in a jagged, desperate quest for survival. My feet pound, my throat feels so dry it might crack, and the taste in the back of my mouth might be blood.

Then I round the bend, slowly regaining my composure, transitioning from where I'm sucking in air to where I'm not thinking anymore about breathing. It only takes a minute for my chest to stop heaving and my thundering heartbeat to drop back to normal levels. I've been running the hills of San Francisco for years, so my body accepts it.

The front door to my building croaks like the voice of a lifetime smoker when I stab in the code on the front panel. It's become a comforting groan that signifies to me that I'm home. Then the smells. My downstairs neighbor is always cooking something that seems to involve cabbage or brussels sprouts. Then there's a meat component, just not a meat I can identify. I suspect it might be in the bird family.

When I get inside, I change out of my wet running clothes, hop in the shower, and slip into pajama pants and a T-shirt, no bra. Not going to see anyone, so what does it matter?

Then I attach a small speaker to my phone and scroll through my playlists until I find the one called "Good Vibes." I add to it occasionally, any time I hear a song that gives me perspective and lifts me out of a mood. There's some Taylor Swift on there, Alanis Morissette, and some covers of classics by Merry Clayton whose gorgeous voice gets me right in the feels.

Her rendition of "Gimme Shelter" starts to play and I feel my shoulders relax. Whatever the run didn't accomplish, her voice finishes off.

Then I go to my fridge for sour mix I made a few days ago from lemons and sugar water. I rub a little salt on the edge of a juice glass, drop in a few ice cubes, and temper the sour mix with a healthy pour of tequila. I'm thirsty after my run, but instead of drinking water, I slam down an entire margarita in under a minute.

Rookie mistake. I make a fresh one and vow to sip it more slowly.

My small two-room studio only has space for a desk or a table in the kitchen room area. I wanted a desk, but I saw a gorgeous, reclaimed plank table at a yard sale and couldn't resist.

It feels strangely formal to drink margaritas at the table, so I hop up on my countertop and test the soil of the gardenia plant that sits by my sink. Dry.

I sprinkle some water into the pot and lean against the cupboards to sip my strong drink. The sweet and sour flavors mix with the harsh burn of cheap alcohol and glide down my throat.

Stashing my festive drink near the coffee maker, I hop down and spin in the kitchen, arms in the air, belting out lyrics to a song by Pink that makes me feel empowered.

A little more margarita. A little more dancing. I really should eat something, but I don't. Instead, I'm overtaken by Bruno Mars, moving my hips, dancing with an invisible partner.

Due to the lack of space, I don't have a ton of furniture, just a lot of plants, which I work hard to keep green and healthy, and a bookshelf along the one wall without a door or window. No surprise, it's stuffed with books, the spines arranged together in waves of color—a group of reds next to a group of blues, then another group of reds next to pinks.

If I had infinite shelf space and infinite funds, I'd have an awesome library, but since I spend every weekday surrounded by books, I'm okay with a smaller personal collection.

It makes me more selective about the ones I buy in paperback or hardcover.

The pitcher of margaritas is nearly empty, and my dancing starts looking a little more like wobbling. The alcohol has gone straight to my head, and the pleasant numbness comes in a wave of relief.

Lots of people live alone. I have a good life. I have everything I need.

For some reason my thoughts turn to Holden Sanders. I wonder what he's doing right now. He probably has a lineup of women on speed dial. Of course he does. One of them is probably relieving the pain in his head right now with a neck massage. Or a blow job.

At that slightly disturbing image, I scroll through my phone to his number in my contacts, not that I have any intention of texting him. I just stare at the digits on the screen.

The rumble in my stomach reminds me again that I've been pouring all the tequila in the world into my body on an empty stomach. And what I really want is a bag of spicy nacho cheese Doritos and a pint of mocha chip ice cream. I know better than to bother looking in my pantry, but I do it anyway. All I see is a variety pack of oatmeal, a box of chewy granola bars, and my emergency supply of bottled water.

There's also no point of checking the freezer either. The only time I buy ice cream is when I'm making a dessert to bring to a dinner party, and that happens about once a year. But the mocha chip craving is real.

I can't drive to the store in my drunken state, but biking there seems slightly less dangerous. That is, until I get downstairs to where I locked up my bike in the back alley, only to find the front tire missing. Not the wheel, just the tire. Who steals a tire? "Are you kidding me?" I whine to no one.

Suddenly, I feel exhausted. Too exhausted to walk to the store.

I'm also frustrated over my bike and drunk enough to think that throwing my keys at the wall is a great idea. It feels good to hurl them and hear the metal clank against the beige stucco. I've never taken a good look at the wall behind the building, at least not good enough to notice the storm grate at the base of the wall that keeps the basement from flooding in the rain. But there it is, taunting me like a gap-toothed metal smile which just swallowed up my keys.

"Nooo!" Crouching down, I shine my phone flashlight down into the sewer, hoping they're right there, easily retrieved with a bent hanger. But they've fallen down into the bowels of whatever lies beneath the city. I shudder at the thought and slug the wall with my fist for good measure.

"Text in an emergency."

He didn't really mean that.

But he said it, and "an emergency" kind of includes right now —now that I have a bruised fist, no way inside my apartment, and no bike. Something about the gruff star athlete who takes care of his niece and owns a cat feels like the kind of comfort I need right now.

Plus, he's sinfully hot.

The bajillion margaritas fuel my lust, and I might as well entertain myself. It's better than crying.

I'm a drunk mess in pajamas, so I'm not really going to text him. I'm simply going to amuse myself with texts I'll never send until my apartment manager calls me back.

I type out a message, addressing it to Holden's biceps since I haven't been able to stop thinking about how good his tight shirt looks when he crosses his arms and scowls. And who am I kidding? The scowl is hot too, so I include that in my text.

Because I'm amused, I keep going, sending an open-ended invitation to his pecs as well to come pay me a visit. It's the first time I've smiled a little bit all day.

I swear, I intend to delete the text.

The arrow next to the string of words looks funny to me. Is there always an arrow? I aim my finger for the backspace key, but I'm a little wobbly.

And all of a sudden, the message appears in a blue bubble. My heart drops to my feet.

Holy shit.

CHAPTER 10

*H*olden

TONIGHT FEELS like some kind of a victory, even if it's not the kind I'm used to and definitely not the kind I'm craving. Sports has taught me to see small achievements as foretelling larger ones, so I don't let anything escape notice.

I should be sulking like the rest of our team because of our three-game losing streak, but for the first time in weeks, I feel okay about our crummy record. The team has a new owner with big ideas and big money to spend executing them, and the poor play will soon be in our rearview. I can feel it.

And finally, the doctors have cleared me to start walking longer distances on the treadmill. Normally, the idea of walking indoors gives me hives. I can't imagine anything more boring, especially when I've been instructed to limit my pace to three miles an hour.

"Last thing you need is to be launched off the back of the

treadmill because you're trying to walk an eight-minute mile and you trip," the doctor told me earlier today. I can't decide if I'm annoyed or heartened that he knows me so well. Mostly annoyed.

Doesn't matter. I'm working that treadmill like it's the most joyful downhill ski run on a spring morning. I don't care if I need to hoof it on that thing for ninety minutes in order to break a sweat. Whatever it takes, I'll do it. The jones to do anything resembling exercise is that great.

The team fitness area is empty, partly because it's the day before a game so the guys are resting up, but also because it's dark out on a Saturday and my teammates have wives and girl-friends—in other words, they have lives.

I'm an hour in, pretty warm from walking on an incline, but not in a full sweat. Music blares through my Bluetooth head-phones, and I feel the blood pumping in my veins. The windows of the facility face the practice pitch, and the sun has long since dipped behind the bleachers. That's when my phone pings with a text.

It's a number I don't recognize, and I'm about to ignore it when Molly's name catches my eye.

Molly: Hey Holden's biceps. It's me, Molly. Hope you're not lonely. If you want some company, come on over. Bring the scowling hot guy you belong to and some spicy Doritos.

Wait, what?

I look around as though someone's messing with me. But I'm alone, so I read the rest of the text.

Molly: And Holden's pecs, I don't want you to feel left out. Come join the party and bring that tight black shirt you were wearing at the library the other day. It was hot.

By the time I finish reading, I'm pretty sure she's drunk. Or crazy. Or both.

I'm also a little turned on. I shut down the treadmill and wait to see if there's more of what seems like stream of consciousness texting. It's not offensive. Just confusing. And a little bit charming.

I respond and ask if she's okay.

Dots bounce on my screen. Then disappear.

Is she okay?

It worries me that she can't seem to answer my question, at least not without a fair amount of consideration. Finally, the dots reappear but no message shows up.

She's…trying to figure out if she's okay? She fell asleep? I have no idea.

I also don't know if I should be worried. Is she drunk texting or is this a cry for help? Maybe she does this with anyone who's dumb enough to enter their number into her phone. But somehow, I don't think so.

The dots come back, and her response appears a moment later.

Molly: Oh shit.

Not the response I expected, which just makes me double down on my impression that something's wrong. I debate what I'm about to write, partly because I barely know her and I'm not even sure she knows it's me she texted.

Me: You don't seem okay.

Molly: I'm probably not.

Me: This doesn't seem good, Mare. Should I come by?

Not sure why I wrote that, and I immediately wish for a "delete" option in the virtual world. I don't know where she lives, and the last thing I should do is come by.

But the words have been sent, and I cringe at what sounds like I've offered a booty call. Hell, I can always make it even worse by sending another text, so I do.

Me: I mean, do you need anything? Groceries?

Groceries? Hell, I've gone from Magic Mike to Postmates.

My itchy trigger finger has already sent that one too before my brain has a chance to catch up. Before I can text some other stupid offer, she responds.

Molly: Need a bike tire and a jumbo bag of spicy Doritos. Do you have either of those?

Okay, maybe I can ignore the suggestive texts and help with her bike. Or give her a ride. I can handle that without seeming like a creeper or a delivery service.

Instead of continuing the text chain, I dial her number. She doesn't sound great—far less perky than the woman at the library—but she drops a pin with her location and agrees to sit tight until I get there.

In the name of expediency, I ignore her request for Doritos. She's in a dodgy part of town, and I don't want to leave her hanging there for too long.

~

FIFTEEN MINUTES LATER, I've traversed half of San Francisco in record time. I didn't bother to shower after my tortoise-like walk on the treadmill since I didn't even break a sweat.

Slowly, I drive down the street where Molly seems to be. What is she doing riding through this shit neighborhood that looks eerily vacant save for a homeless woman pushing a shopping cart? Even if I barely know her, I'm not above giving her a safety lecture.

I find her in front of an old gray Victorian a few doors down from a body shop in the Mission. She sits on the front steps, listing to one side with her cheek on her fist. Pulling in front of the neighboring driveway, I roll down my window. "Molly, hey." When she doesn't answer, I speak a little louder, "Where's the bike with the bum tire?"

At the sound of my voice, she picks her head up, blinking slowly and offering me a partial smile.

Gone is the bright ray of sun I met at the library. She looks sad, tired, defeated, I don't know what—I just know I don't like it.

I leave my truck where it is and hop out, but she doesn't make any move to get up and show me the bike. So I walk over to get a closer look at her. "Hey. You okay?"

She shrugs, and the movement has the effect of making her lurch even more to the side. Putting her hand out to steady herself, she looks up at me through thick lashes. "Yup. Just fine."

"Liar." I crouch down in front of her to look her in the eye, but she won't meet my gaze. The beige pajama pants she's wearing are pushed up above her knees, and the vintage U2 concert T-shirt is so big it swallows her.

Tipping her chin up with my finger, I get her to look at me.

Despite her watery eyes and messy ponytail, she radiates an inner light under a slightly disheveled exterior. Her flushed cheeks and plump lips make her look that much more vulnerable, and I feel an urgent need to help her, even though I have a feeling the bike tire is the least of her problems.

I can smell the tequila on her breath. She's plastered.

"Who fucking did this to you?"

She looks confused. "What? No one. I just…made margaritas."

As much as her inebriated state concerns me, I'm a little relieved that it's all I'm dealing with here. Countless times over the years, one teammate or another has ended up drunk and incapacitated. I know what to do.

"Okay, first things first. Where's your bike?"

She gestures to some point behind her, but all I can see is peeling paint on the apartment building whose steps are doing most of the work in holding her up.

"Can you be more specific?"

She lets out a deep sigh and tries to stand, but however much alcohol she's consumed makes her unsteady, and she falls into me. My hands react with a goalkeeper's swiftness, intercepting her and keeping her on her feet.

Catching her feels like the best reason to have put in a million hours honing my hand-eye coordination.

She feels pliant in my arms and an untapped part of my brain wants to keep her here and wrap her in whatever comfort I can provide. As she folds into my body, her gentle curves feel better than they should against my chest.

But I also need information, and the side of me that's been weaned on discipline for my entire athletic career knows there's an order to things.

When I feel like she's steady enough on her feet that I can release my grip. I back up enough to look at her again, still holding on with both hands to steady her. At the same time, I'm trying to coordinate a plan that makes some fucking sense since it's seeming less and less likely that she's capable of doing it herself.

"Okay, here's what we're going to do. You're going to show me where your bike is, and we're going to put it in the back of my truck. I'll drive you wherever you need to get it fixed, assuming we can find a bike shop open at this hour. But first I'm going to feed you something and get you sobered up. Then I'll take you home. Deal?"

She starts to protest, but I refuse to let her out of what seems like the most sensible option. Pressing two fingers against her lips, I shake my head. "You're not staying here. Just...let me help you."

She nods and I remove my fingers. "Was just gonna say, can we get some spicy Doritos?"

Her determination over this particular snack amuses me. "Yes. Whatever you feel like, though you might want to eat something a little healthier, or at least something that can soak up the damn tequila."

"Margaritas," she mumbles. Her half-lidded eyes make her appear charmingly sleepy and innocent. I'm suspicious about who else was involved in plying her with enough margaritas to get her in this state, but I'll deal with that later. First, I'll get a gallon of water into her, and, as requested, some spicy Doritos.

"Let's get your bike." She allows me to walk her to my truck, where I hand her a bottle of water from my cup holder and get her seat belted in. Then she directs me around to the backside of the building to an alley that looks even more decrepit than the front where she was sitting.

I know this probably isn't the best time for a safety lecture, but I can't help it. "Dammit, Mare, you can't leave your bike back here. It's really dark."

"S'fine." She dismisses my concern with a wave of a hand.

The bike lock sits unlocked, and as indicated, it needs a replacement tire. A phone, flashlight still on, sits on the ground next to the bike. I turn off the flashlight and hold it up so she can see it. "Is this your phone?" Pushing the door open to inspect, she has to blink her eyes slowly in order to focus.

"Yes. Thass mine." Her words are more slurred than they were a few minutes ago, which means the alcohol is still making its way through her system. It's probably too dark for her to see my mounting concern, but she explains anyway. "I threw my keys at the wall. I wasss mad about the bike."

"Okay. Where are your keys now? Do you have them?" I'm not sure what the keys have to do with the phone, but I trust that she's going somewhere with her story.

"N-no. They fell in there." She points to the grate at the bottom of the wall.

"These were bike keys? Or house keys?" I hope for the best, fear the worst.

"Both. And the landlord isss not answering."

I close my eyes against the reality of what I need to do. She has no way of getting into wherever she lives and I'm not even sure the answers she's giving me are accurate. "Okay, I'm taking you to my house. Then we'll sort everything out and figure out what to do next. Yeah?"

I tell myself it will be fine, that spending more time with her —even in her drunken state—won't produce any feelings and make it harder to stick to my rules about getting involved with women. And I need to stick to them like a gnat on flypaper.

She doesn't seem inclined to argue, but she does require clarification. "So, you want me to go to your house, even though I'm…" She gestures to herself, pointing to her clothes and face. I crack a smile.

"You're fine. My house isn't a fancy place."

"But you're super famousss. I googled you." She's slurring but kind of adorable despite her sorry state. And as much as I'm a little sad that now she no longer thinks of me as just "a guy," at least I don't have to hide my life from her.

The more pressing issue is what could have happened to her in a dark alley with no functional bike and no house keys. Before I can sort through all the lectures I feel the need to give, she pushes herself out of my truck and wobbles when her feet hit the ground. "I don't feel so great."

Her face has gone pale, and I know what's coming next. I'm grateful that she got out of my truck at least. I'm sure this alley has seen its share of puke and who knows what else? Putting a hand on her back, I guide her to an area of dirt and weeds.

I barely have time to gather the strands of hair that have flown loose from her pony before she heaves into the plants. Hands on her knees, she goes a couple more rounds. It's all margarita. Probably still cold. She has no food in her system.

When she stands up and looks at me, the color's returned to her face and her eyes are glassy. "Oh my God. I'm sorry."

"It happens. Don't apologize. Do you feel any better?"

She nods, and I grab a container of wet wipes for her. While she freshens up, I carry her bike around and stash it in my trunk. When I slam the hatch shut, I catch her watching me. "I thought you drove a fancy Porsche." Now that some of the alcohol is out of her system, she's stopped slurring. Not that I have any idea what she's talking about.

"What?"

"At the library, when I came out that first day, you were standing by a Porsche." My brain is getting whiplash following her train of thought.

"I don't have a Porsche. I have this." I gesture to my three-year-old Toyota SUV, the large model that's more truck than car. It's perfect for carting around sports equipment or heading up to Lake Tahoe for a weekend, where one of my teammates has a place. "I'm not into the whole fancy car thing."

"I like that. I'm not into fancy either." She gestures at where her bike was a minute ago. At least, I think that's what she means. "Anyhow…thanks for coming to get me."

For the first time since I arrived, she relaxes her lips into a smile. It feels hard-earned, and for some reason her gratitude evokes a twinge in my chest that makes me feel like the lucky one.

"Great. Let's get out of here," I tell her, even though I don't have a plan yet. I doubt any bike shops are open at this hour, so the tire will have to wait. The alley weirds me out and even though I feel confident I could win a fist fight with the average guy, I'm not taking any chances.

Tucking her into my front seat again, I move to the driver's side and speed us out of there. Molly's quiet, so at the next red light, I look over to make sure she's doing okay. Her eyes are closed, lashes fanned out against her cheeks, her expression peaceful.

Beautiful. Even at her worst.

At least, I'm presuming this is her worst.

If it's not, well, I'll deal with that when I get there.

CHAPTER 11

Molly

I WAKE UP WITH A HEADACHE. A really, really bad headache. Like an icepick is jabbing at my skull behind my eyes. Relentless, furious stabbing.

Make. It. Stop.

For a second, I feel disoriented. Is it morning? Do I need to hop in the shower and get ready for work?

No, I won't be hopping anywhere. More like staggering or crawling with my eyes glued shut to keep out the light.

Ugh, the light. Someone, please turn off the sun.

I don't hear my alarm, so that's not what woke me. Then I turn my head from side to side, feeling another round of throbbing, and manage to pry open my eyes. I don't recognize my surroundings, but I feel comfortable, splayed out on a giant bed covered in a pristine white comforter that feels like a cloud.

I like my bed, but I love this bed.

This is the kind of bed that begets fantasy dreams of reading all day with piles of puppies and drinking hot chocolate from a never depleting mug. The incessant pain in my head starkly contrasts with the feathery softness beneath it, where two soft pillows support me like a life raft.

Where the hell am I?

If I've been abducted and forced to live in these surroundings, it actually qualifies as a life upgrade, so I'm not too worried about the Stockholm syndrome that has seemingly already set in. When I tilt my head to the side and see a damp washcloth on the side table and a trash can beside the bed, unwanted memories start nudging their way back into my consciousness.

Shit.

Or rather, shitfaced.

What did I do?

I vaguely recall my missing bike tire and the frustration I felt at not being able to ride to the store for snacks. That still annoys me. Still doesn't explain why I'm not at home, and last I recall, I was alone. Pretty sure I wouldn't drunk-stumble my way into a five-star hotel.

I feel something in my hand, and when I lift it enough to look, I see that I'm holding a brand-new toothbrush, which I desperately need. A kindness from whoever put it there. I assume there's toothpaste somewhere nearby, but my head feels encased in cement, so I can't move it to find out.

Wracking my brain puts a strain on it and only makes my head hurt more. In an effort to check out the rest of this well-appointed bedroom, I roll to my side, careful not to move too quickly because of the insistent, relentless nausea.

The cloudlike duvet absorbs my movements so it's no surprise I don't disturb the person sitting in a chair several paces away from me. The face of my abductor surprises me, maybe because he isn't wearing a ski mask or holding some sort of torture device. Is that…?

No!

Reclined in an oversized chair that's practically the size of a loveseat, Holden Sanders sits wearing headphones and leaning his head on one hand, partially obscuring his face. Nevertheless, it's him. No question…it's him.

Shit. Shit. Shit.

That's when the rest of the memories spill forth like the last offending drops into an overfilled margarita glass—a second earlier, everything was contained under a bubble swelling over the rim, but there's no stopping it now. The seal has been broken and unwanted recollections of drinking my eleventeenth drink, texting my hottie soccer star library assistant's biceps—why, oh why, did I do that?—and puking in bushes while he held back my hair.

So. Beyond. Pathetic.

If I was in college, possibly acceptable, but certainly this is not behavior befitting an educated librarian who has her life together at age thirty-one. Um yeah, because maybe I don't.

My hand goes to the messy pieces that always fall out of whatever bun or ponytail I wrap my hair into, but instead of wayward strands, I find my hair held back with a wide fabric headband.

He did that? Along with mopping down my face with a washcloth?

Blood surges through my heart at the thought. It's sweet and mortifying in equal measure.

I press my addled brain to recall anything else I may have done or said that will elevate me from mere embarrassment to the permanent hall of shame. If I tried to seduce him or some other nonsense, I'm going to need to slink out of here, grab the first Uber I can find, and promptly join the witness protection program.

While I'm gaming out how to do all that, he shifts in his chair and looks in my direction, his face opening into a partial smile when his gaze lands on me. He removes the headphones. "You're awake and alive."

"Awake. Not sure I'm alive."

His smirk tells me he experienced way more of my near-death state than I'd prefer. His expression turns to empathetic concern, which looks surprisingly charming on his grumpy face. "How're you feeling?"

Good question. I take a deep breath and assess the damage. Other than a headache and nausea, I mostly feel disoriented and a little groggy.

Pushing myself to sitting doesn't make my head fall off, so I have to conclude I'll survive. "Oh, you know. Never better."

I have no idea what time it is. The room has the shades drawn and they're the blackout kind I've only seen a couple times in hotels. They're very effective. What I thought was sunlight is the bright bulb on a floor lamp next to Holden's big chair. The rest of the room is sparsely decorated, save for a round low table where Holden has his feet propped.

Shutting my eyes to block out further mortification, I don't notice he's come over to sit on the bed until the mattress sinks beside me. My eyes pop open,

"So. You live here?" I indicate our surroundings with outstretched hands. A part of me is disappointed it's not a hotel. A hotel, I could revisit. But after whatever shenanigans I pulled in my drunken state, I know I'll never see this place again. Frankly, I'm surprised he let me in the door.

He lets out a low chuckle. "Yeah. Works out well since you threw up on my doormat."

I drape an arm over my eyes. "Ugh. I did not. Please tell me that's your weird sense of humor." I hope it's his weird sense of humor.

"I'd offer to prove it, but the doormat is already in the garbage can out back."

"Nooo." Leaning back with my arm still over my eyes, I feel

the mortification color my cheeks. If the hue matches my level of shame, I'm the shade of a cranberry. "I'm so sorry. I-I don't normally do that. Ever. It's-it's just been, you know, a *day*. Is it even still the same day? How long did I sleep?"

Holden fishes his phone from the front pocket of his jeans and swipes across the screen a few times. The blackout shades start to rise, revealing a sweeping nighttime view of the San Francisco Bay, city lights twinkling just beyond the Golden Gate Bridge. From our vantage point and the billion-dollar view, I gather we're somewhere in coastal Marin County, possibly Belvedere Island off of Tiburon.

Nice neighborhood. Incredible neighborhood.

"Only about two hours. And since you don't seem to remember much, I'll save you the trouble of worrying—you only puked here the one time on the mat. After that, you pretty much passed out."

Great. I'm not sure what's worse, acting like a stinking drunk in front of him or hearing about it now. Not to mention that my head feels like someone's tap-dancing to a showtune on my skull with each beat of my heart. I'm not even sure this qualifies as hungover yet because I'm pretty sure I'm still half drunk.

I consider waiting him out. If I lie here long enough, he'll have to go somewhere, right? A sports dude party? His knitting group? An urgent gym workout?

Or maybe his concussion will heal and he'll go play soccer or something. Then I can skulk away without ever having to look him in the eye again.

He seems to have other ideas, gingerly lifting my arm from over my eyes, which I then squeeze protectively shut. "Mare. Open your damn eyes."

I shake my head slowly, which hurts nonetheless. "I can't look at you. I feel so bad about all this."

"Don't," he says, and I feel the back of his hand brush across my forehead. "Really. I've seen much worse, trust me."

Popping one eye open, I search for signs he's telling the truth. His somber expression says he's not messing with me, so I open the other eye.

"I don't know if I should be sorry to hear that for your sake or a little relieved because I'm not the bottom of the pile."

"You should drink a shit ton of water is what you should do. And take some Advil. Are you hungry at all?"

I stare at him and say nothing.

"What?" he asks.

"You're acting like it's normal for me to be at your house in the middle of the night after puking on your porch. Why are you not throwing me in a cab and telling me to get my sorry ass out of here?" Apparently my day of self-loathing still has a hold on me. And yet, I'm intrigued enough by his motivations to wait around for some answers.

"Well, first off, it's only eight o'clock. And second, apparently you chucked your keys into a sewer. Third, I'm not a total asshole, despite what you might believe."

"I don't think you're an asshole. I never thought that."

"Good to know." His gruff tone does nothing to disprove the idea that I've overstayed my welcome, though, so I stand up and find that I'm less wobbly than I feared. Toothbrush clutched in my fist, I scoop a tube of Crest off the bed and start moving toward the bathroom. Mercifully, he doesn't follow, so I brush my teeth, gargle, rinse my face, and pee.

I can't help but notice the hand-painted tile in the enormous bathroom with its sunken tub that elicits an unconscious sigh from me. Could I make things much worse if I locked the bathroom door and took a luxury bubble bath?

Yes. Oh, yes. You. Could.

When I feel a modicum more human, it's time to make a run for it. I head for the closed door of the bedroom, looking around for my shoes.

Before I reach the door, he puts a hand on my arm. "You're not racing out of here."

Turning to face him, I need to tip my chin up in order to meet his eyes. His face is achingly beautiful and that makes my head hurt more, purely from how painful it's going to be when I look away.

It surprises me that I didn't notice how tall he was the couple times I saw him at the library. He's…very tall. Elegantly tall and chiseled from granite.

The ogling makes me feel slightly less nauseous since his nice face and body provides me with something to focus on other than the queasiness in my stomach.

His eyes suddenly widen. "Are you sure you're okay?"

"I think so. Do I not—oh, whoa…" Then it hits me, a wave of dizziness bigger than my ability to control it. Before I can figure out what to do, Holden has scooped me up with ninja speed and kept me from fainting to the floor.

I hang limp in his arms while he lays me back on the bed. "Why don't you take it a little slower?"

I'm so helpless, and it's just so mortifying. After a minute, the wave of dizziness passes and I sit up. "I'm gonna get out of your hair," I tell him, looking at the floor.

I really need to go.

"No." The single word surprises me in its decisiveness and its authority. The shock must register on my face because he softens his tone. "I mean, you don't have to go. Stay, have some dinner, if you feel like eating, then when you're ready, I'll drive you home."

To an outsider, it might sound like a sensible plan. Except that we barely know each other and I'm still beyond mortified. Then again, if my landlord hasn't called me back, I don't have a way into my apartment unless I call a locksmith, and the after-hours fee is money I'd rather not spend.

"Okay, thank you. That's really nice." Still looking at the floor, I start shuffling toward the door before I feel his hand on my shoulder, turning me around. "That's the door to the closet. Come. This way."

His hand slides down to the small of my back and he guides me to the correct door. He walks us past the bathroom and opens the door to the hall, revealing a small brown cat.

He points. "Greta."

I nod.

He bends and scoops her up in his other arm without losing his hold on me and ushers us both down a carpeted hallway to where a long staircase leads down. At the bottom, he puts the cat on the floor, where it pads along right next to his ankle.

Holden shows me through his entryway to the open kitchen. It's so stunning that I gape awkwardly.

"Wow, are you a master chef?" My body begs me to find the nearest place to sit, but my brain is buzzing as it takes in stainless steel, marble, and wood. My entire apartment could fit in this kitchen.

He runs a hand over the dark scruff on his chin and shakes his head. "Not me. But during the season, I hire someone to cook. Keeps me honest about my diet." I'm about to ask about that when he starts unloading two brown grocery bags sitting on the kitchen island. One bag after another of Doritos—cool ranch, nacho cheese, and spicy nacho. Next comes bottled water, along with a container of Advil, which he hands to me. "You need this."

But I'm not thinking about that. "You bought me Doritos?"

He shrugs. "You did mention wanting them about a half dozen times. It seemed important."

Despite everything else he's already done for me, this strikes me as the kindest thing a person could possibly do.

It's also one more thing about the past few hours that I don't fully remember. "Ugh, I did? I'm so sorry. Again."

"Stop apologizing." He's saying the words, but how could he possibly mean them? I'd feel more comfortable with the grumpy flight risk I met that first day outside the library than this nicer guy who seems to have rescue tendencies. I'm wary of someone like that.

Holden guides me to one of the metal bistro chairs near a round, marble-topped table in one corner of the kitchen. The moment I land in the chair, I slump onto the table with my head in my hands. "This is not how I usually am. I feel like it's important that you know that."

He pulls out the chair next to mine and drops into it. I hear the twist of a cap on a bottle of water, which he pushes toward me. Then he gently takes one of my hands from my face and places it on the bottle. "First of all, drink this. You're dehydrated."

I obey because he's right, but I still can't look him in the eye. I'm not sure where to look, so I settle for glancing over my shoulder at where his cat sits perched on the back of a very long gray sectional couch. "So, this is Greta Garbo."

"The one and only."

"Does she like strangers?"

"Not sure. I don't usually have strangers in my house."

I call to Greta who eyes me silently from her perch. Her tail begins sweeping along the back of the couch, but she doesn't move. Seems like a decent sign. At least I haven't scared her away. I won't see her again after tonight, but I still want her to like me.

"Here, Greta," he says, making a clicking noise with his tongue. She gives him the same appraising look she gave me. A second later, she leaps from the couch, pads over to Holden, and starts winding herself around his legs. I can hear her purr from where I'm sitting.

Yeah, I'd purr too if I could wind myself around his body.

I close my eyes against the hideously inappropriate thought.

"Second of all, I'm not judging you, so get that out of your head."

"I'll try," I lie. Taking another sip of water, I feel only minimally better. My head aches, and I want to lie on my back and block out the world.

It must be evident from my expression. "Do you want to lie down?"

"Yes, but I'm not going to. You went to the trouble of answering my ill-advised texts and buying me chips, so I'm going to give you my best self." Even though it pains me, I rally all forty-two muscles in my face in an attempt at a wide smile.

He abruptly pushes his chair back, which makes a scraping noise on his polished wood. I want to bend down to inspect for scratches, but before I can worry about that, he's pulled my chair out as well and extended his hand to me. "Come."

I obey, feeling the weight of my shoulders fall when I exhale. He guides me over to the couch and grabs two fuzzy blue throw pillows from a chair. "Sit." He points to the couch and once I've sunk into it, he swivels my feet up so I can lie down. "Better?"

I nod, though this isn't the direction I should be headed. I shouldn't be making myself more comfortable and overstaying my already-overstayed welcome. I should be finding my shoes and hunting down my landlord, even if the thought of doing so feels depressing.

The couch is long enough for me to stretch out completely with my head on the pile of soft pillows at one end. Holden does the same at the other end. Our feet don't even touch, but facing each other seems so much more personal than the previous mechanics of moving in the same space.

"Okay, now once more for the people in the nosebleeds, you don't need to apologize to me, and you don't need to be your best anything. Except maybe be honest."

"You drive a hard bargain, but...fine."

"*I* drive a hard bargain..." he mutters. "Talk to me, Mare. Is everything okay?"

I debate how to answer his question without telling him the whole saga of my life. I decide on as much honesty as I can muster. "It will be."

He nods. "Guess that's a start."

"Pretty much ends there too. Tomorrow's a new day." I don't plan to unburden myself of my thoughts and feelings. And after puking on his doormat, I'm not about to cry on his shoulder about anything.

"Stubborn."

"Self-sufficient." It's easier to look at him when he's being his normal grouchy self. Only now, even his scowl looks sexy, and the furrow of his brow gives him a smoking hot intensity that I shouldn't be noticing under the circumstances.

He rubs a hand over his face, and when he looks at me again, I sense his mounting frustration. "I'm going to ask you this one more time, not because I'm super keen on sharing feelings or anything—I'm just trying not to be an unfeeling asshole. Do you want to talk about anything?" He folds his arms across his chest and sighs.

There's a warmth in his cool gray eyes that wasn't there the two times I saw him at the library. It makes me want to trust him, and I don't have too many people in my life who fall into that category.

Do I want to talk? Of course not. The last thing this man needs is my sad story about a guy I dated for years ago whose death freaked me out so much that I stay away from relationships.

Closing my eyes for a second to think without seeing his face, I come to a different conclusion. Maybe I...do want to talk.

Something about a virtual stranger who's done me a kindness makes me want to offer him something in return. Given that he's a famous athlete with a spectacular house, I doubt I can tempt him with any material gifts, so if he wants my honesty, maybe it's my greatest commodity.

So I answer honestly. "I'm not sure."

His lips quirk to the side and he studies me, eyes still inviting. "That's better than a no. Progress?"

I huff out a small laugh, which immediately sends a sharp

twinge of pain through my skull. At my grimace, Holden rolls off the couch to standing and goes back to the table where I left the Advil.

"Damn, you're stubborn. Take two of these. Drink the whole bottle of water." He hands me the round pills and I do as I'm told.

He disappears back into the kitchen, and I decide it's probably smarter not to move my head too much, so I rest my eyes while he rustles around. Greta chooses this moment to investigate me further, jumping onto the couch and slowly walking from my feet to where I can reach to pet her. She then moves back toward my feet and curls up in an empty spot next to my ankle. It feels like a victory.

Behind me, I hear bags of chips crinkling and cupboards opening and closing. In another minute, Holden returns with three wooden bowls, each with a different flavor of Doritos. He puts them on the coffee table and pulls it closer to the couch so I can reach them easily. Then he returns to his spot at the other end and faces me. Greta occupies the space between us, and after looking from Holden to me and back again, she curls into a ball and closes her eyes.

"Sustenance and water." He indicates the Advil. "Your head should feel better soon. So, let's talk." Even though his arms are crossed, his voice, both deep and soft, feels comforting.

I nod, trying to figure out a logical place to begin. "It's a little hard for me to do that."

"Because...?" He's patient, I'll give him that. When I don't answer, he waits me out, his gaze fixed on me. The smolder in his eyes just might engulf me in flames.

Swallowing hard, I feel my pulse flutter at the idea of telling him things. But some part of my brain urges me on, so I begin. Awkwardly, clumsily. But I'm honest.

"Today is the four-year anniversary of my former boyfriend's death. We only dated about ten times, but maybe it could've been something. And it's pretty much my fault he died, so there's that.

When the anniversary comes up, it hits me hard, but then I move past it. Like I said, tomorrow, it will be behind me. Mary Poppins will rise again." I try to mount a convincing smile, but my facial muscles feel worn out.

It's small, the flicker in his eyes, but I can tell he's taken aback. Who wouldn't be? I dumped nearly every taboo subject possible into one sentence—death, relationships, and alcohol. All that's missing is politics, money, and religion.

Since I'm feeling all the self-loathing right now, I debate throwing those onto the bonfire too and burning the house down.

He leans into the pillow behind him, putting a little more distance between us. I've shocked him, I know I have. He nods. "That's…a lot. I'm sorry."

"Right? It's too much. More than you bargained for, I'm sure." I'm already regretting my decision to blurt everything out. He was being nice, like he said. I should have taken that for what it was and politely kept my baggage to myself. "You think I'm this book fairy—everyone does. But I'm dark, Holden. You have no idea how dark."

For some reason, that makes him smile, and this time it annoys me how good-looking he is. It seems like an unfair advantage to possess such distracting qualities when a person's trying to wallow.

I want to hide in the closet. Or vaporize. Anything to get out from under his cool-eyed stare that both feels like a judgement and a soft caress of my soul. As much as I wish my body didn't respond to the mere sight of him, it's not a bad way to go out if I do end up embarrassing myself to death.

"Very, very dark," I emphasize.

Holden runs a hand over the stubble on his jaw, and despite the ache in my head, I can't help but focus on how striking his face is. Really, really pretty.

"I don't think you're dark."

"Then you weren't listening."

"What I mean is, so, you have baggage. That's because you're human and you live life and shitty things happen sometimes. Really shitty things, in this case. But it doesn't brand you. It doesn't make you dark. It makes you interesting." He lets his words sink in, and it surprises me when they do.

He shakes his head. "Kind of a relief actually. The image of you as a bright-eyed, chirpy book pusher was a little intimidating."

"Book pusher? Chirpy?" I feign insult.

"Sorry. My recollection of libraries was when my dad took me and my brother and tried to force reading on us when we really wanted to play video games. I guess libraries felt like a punishment for kids who'd rather be tearing up a patch of grass outside." He shrugs. "No offense."

His shrug doesn't feel very apologetic.

"And yet you brought your niece to the library. You must really hate her," I deadpan.

"Kath's the best." He doesn't elaborate. Pressing my lips together as though trying to ensure that no more words about death fly out of my mouth, I meet his eyes.

"Anyhow, that's my deal. Like I said, today was a rough one. I got all up in my feels thinking about the past, and then I drank too many margaritas after going for a run and not having water. Hence..." I point to myself. "The mess. But I'm done. Most of the time I live in the present and I'm happy that way." I lean over and grab the bowl I'm pretty sure contains the spicy nacho chips I'm craving.

He waves a hand. "Hold on. You can't just put this away and wait to torture yourself again in a year. I'm no therapist, but even I can figure that out."

I stall, then take a look around at what else I can see of his house from my vantage point. For starters, everything is some version of blue or gray or white, plus the brown wood floors. Neutrals. Very male.

The furniture all looks comfortable—from the cloud-like duvet cover on the bed and the overstuffed loveseat chair where Holden was sitting earlier, to the couch that wants to swallow me whole. The man has a taste for soft surfaces.

The iron-backed kitchen chairs are an exception. I'm about to ask Holden about them when I turn and catch his eyes fixed on me, challenging. He still has his arms crossed, and I feel like it's a war of wills.

I'm plenty stubborn. He was right about that.

Clearly, so is he.

Finally, he puts his hands up. "Listen, it's fine. You don't know me, you're just sitting in my living room. I get why it's weird to spill your guts. No pressure. Talk or don't talk, whatever."

"Okay, great." I could leave it at that. The death of a loved one is a reasonable enough explanation for getting stinking drunk. I don't owe him any soul searching.

Maybe it's the years of letting things fester, or maybe it's being in the presence of someone who's seen me at my worst and still wants to talk to me—I find myself wanting to tell him every-thing. Like a therapist. Or a priest.

"Well, so, here's the detailed version." I take a deep breath. Then it all pours out. "We'd been dating for two months. It was good, you know, the way the early days of relationships are? I liked him. I was… optimistic about our chances of being a couple. And then he got appendicitis. Normal, right? Happens all the time. Routine surgery these days." I take a breath. I need to breathe because I've said every-thing on a long exhale, so when I finally draw air it sounds like a gasp.

Holden scrubs a hand through his hair and nods. "Most of the time, from the little I know. Unless it ruptures. Is that what happened?"

I press my lips together, remembering. "No, everything was

fine. He had surgery, tiny little incision. Crazy how they can take an internal organ out through your belly button and leave a scar the size of a dime." I demonstrate with my pinched fingers. "Medicine. It will never cease to impress me."

I get lost for a moment recalling the aftermath of surgery and the almost invisible evidence that a scalpel was involved. Holden is watching me, and I don't know how long I've spaced out. He's waiting for the rest of my explanation, so I continue.

"After he came home, I stayed at his apartment for a few days to help out, you know, cook the soft foods and things you can have after surgery." I let out another harsh breath before admitting the worst part. "He was running a fever. So I brought him round the clock pain meds and anti-inflammatories, antibiotics, all the things the doctor prescribed after surgery." My voice catches on the last part.

If I had it to do over again, I'd be smarter. I'd do better.

Almost imperceptibly, Holden moves closer to me on the couch. Instead of stretching out opposite me, he inches closer to the middle, close enough to wrap a hand around one of my feet and give it a squeeze.

The reassuring gesture opens the floodgate of my hesitation the rest of the way. "He wasn't getting better, and the pain was bad, but I didn't know what post-surgery was supposed to look like. I googled appendectomies and read people's accounts where they felt horrible for days afterward. The doctor warned he might have a fever, so I kept giving him Tylenol to bring it down.

It wasn't until several days later that he removed the steri-strips and we saw that his wound looked swollen and infected. But good old Nurse Ratched over here had been like clockwork with the pain meds and fever management, so he didn't feel it getting inflamed. Of course, as soon as we saw how bad it looked, he went back to the doctor."

Holden's eyes don't break contact with mine, almost as if he's coaxing me forward with his entreaty to trust him. I admit the worst part, the thing a better person would have realized. "He had sepsis. It means—"

He interrupts, nodding. "It's dangerous. I've had a couple surgeries and it's one of the risks on the endless list they give you. It's why they prescribe antibiotics."

I shake my head. "Yeah, except they weren't holding back the infection, so he got really sick, really fast. They checked him back into the hospital immediately, but it was bad. He died the day after that. Twenty-six years old."

My breathing sounds ragged. I haven't ever uttered these words. It's an experience I buried four years ago in a box where I planned to keep it safe. I work hard to avoid thinking about it most of the time.

Holden closes his eyes on a long blink. Feeling my chin start to wobble, I work to push back the emotion that's had a grip on me for four years. "Look, I did see a therapist for a while. She thought Adam's death dredged up crap with my dad, who bailed when I was a kid—reinforced the idea I have that I'm not good enough. I don't know if that's right, but I do know if I'd gotten him to the hospital a day sooner, he might be alive." I barely get the last word out before my tears roll out in big, messy drops.

Why am I talking about this with a guy I barely know?

With the quickness of a panther, Holden has moved closer to me, taken the chip bowl from my hands, and lifted my legs onto his lap. He wraps an arm around me and lets me cry on his shoulder.

It's not like I haven't cried already today for Adam. I cried at the cemetery. But this is a different kind of crying. It comes in giant wracking sobs that I've never felt in four years.

I've done such a good job of holding everything in, holding myself together.

And now I'm having this cathartic experience with a soccer player from the library because it feels too good to be held and to let it out. I'm comforted by the idea that I probably won't see him again.

Holden says nothing, but he doesn't let go. He smooths a hand down my hair and allows me to cry until I have nothing left. And I mean nothing. My tear ducts strain with emptiness and I feel surprisingly better. Also very dehydrated. "I think I could use some more water," I admit, starting to untangle myself from Holden's comforting hold so I can find something in his kitchen and pull myself together.

"Nah. Stay there." He hops up and goes to the kitchen while I swoon a little from how good it felt to have his arm around me. I wasn't expecting that. Hell, I wasn't expecting *him*.

It baffles me that my alcohol-soaked brain somehow knew I needed him when I picked up my phone and sent that ridiculous text.

He comes back with a pitcher of ice water and a glass, two bananas, and a bowl of strawberries with the tops sliced off. He points. "Options."

After pouring water into the glass, he hands it to me and reassumes his position on the couch, lifting my legs so they rest on his lap.

Nodding, I take a long drink and put the glass down. Then I take a strawberry and turn it over in my fingers, studying the pattern of seeds because I'm avoiding looking at Holden. "Thank you." I bite off the end and savor the sweet taste before popping the rest into my mouth.

The one bite makes me realize I am hungry, so I grab the chips again and crunch through a few before daring to look at Holden again. When I do, I find him scowling.

Of course. He has listener's regret. People offer to lend an ear, but they have no idea what they're in for, and in my case, the spilling of information is accompanied by soul-baring sobs. I'm normally so much better at keeping it together. I have the urge to move father away, but I'm already leaning against the arm of the couch, so there's nowhere to go.

I consider bolting for the front door without my shoes—*where the heck did he put my shoes?*—and escaping the mess I've already made when Holden's arm wraps around my shoulders more firmly and he pulls me to his chest.

It strikes me for the second time that it feels absurdly good to fold myself into his arms. Over the past few years, my relationships with men have been pretty transactional—dinner, sex, maybe more sex, then goodbye.

I haven't let anyone hold me. That felt personal, and I didn't need personal. I didn't want it.

Now, with one embrace, this grumpy soccer guy has me rethinking four years of operating instructions that guided my life. I don't understand why, though later I'll blame the alcohol in my system, but for now, I sink deeper into his arms and sigh.

Any thoughts I have about leaving disappear.

CHAPTER 12

$\mathcal{H}$olden

Am I doing the right thing?

Absolutely not.

Is there a right thing when an angelic, somewhat-fucked-up woman evokes feelings I haven't let myself touch in two years?

Probably not.

Yet here I am, holding on to Molly like she's the steady beam from a lighthouse when I didn't even know I was the one lost at sea. I feel like she's the crutch holding me up. Instead of the other way around.

Yeah, I need to unpack that.

No doubt I won't like everything it says about me.

Scratch that. This isn't about me. She needs someone to lean on and I'd be an oversized asshole if I didn't volunteer. I'm not jeopardizing my commitment to my sport or my future unless I start to feel things, and I know how to keep a lid on my feelings. I've had years of practice.

Right now, I have something important to say. Turning to face her on the couch forces my arm away from her shoulders. I don't like that, but I need to see her. She immediately looks away, so I cup her chin in my hand and guide her face back.

"Hey." My deep voice comes out like a rumble but I keep it low. I think I scare her a little, even though I sense she isn't scared by much. I don't know what to make of that either. "I'm sorry about your dad. That one sucks and I'm not going to pretend I understand how that must've felt, but you were just a kid. No way can you put that on yourself." It seems obvious to me, but by the way she averts her eyes, hiding them beneath a fan of dark lashes, it's less obvious to her.

I keep my hand beneath her jaw because I like the way it feels there. She exhales, sounding frustrated. "Yeah, my therapist mentioned that a time or thirty."

"Sounds like you have a decent therapist, at least."

She rolls her eyes but leans her chin a little more heavily into my palm, and I take that as a sign she might be willing to entertain reason. "And as to the boyfriend, it's not your fault he died. I know I wasn't there, and I don't know all the details, but Mare, if you've been blaming yourself for this for four years…it's time to stop. Even I can see that and I'm about as stubborn as they come when an idea gets stuck in my head."

Her chest inflates with a deep breath and on her exhale, I sense some resignation to at least consider the possibility I'm right. "I know a world exists in which I am somewhat blameless, but that's not comfortable for me. I should bear some responsibility so I'm vigilant. So nothing like that happens again. Not on my watch. Never again."

Like she's slowly unwinding a spool of thread, Molly tells me about the scholarship fund and how she more or less keeps it afloat. Things start falling into place—the fear of losing her second job, even the fear of kids who look to her as a role model in their fragile-seeming years.

Understanding what she carries beneath her relentlessly bright exterior makes me want to gather her up in a soft blanket and shield her from it all. The feeling strikes me, like all the other ways she tugs on my emotions, as something I may be powerless to control.

Dangerous.

Exciting.

Inevitable.

I also have something bigger I want to ask, and it needs to come out the right way so I don't sound like a douchebag. It chafes at me, the hole in the information I want. It's begging to be filled. So I just ask. "Were you in love with him?"

I can tell she isn't expecting the question by the way her already large eyes widen. She opens her mouth and closes it again. "I-I mean, things were going well."

"And he got sick. That would scare the shit out of most people. It would also take a two-month relationship and ratchet up the heat to a thousand. Before you can even decide if you're his girlfriend, you're taking care of his health. Then it turns tragic."

She bites down on her lip, worrying it through her teeth. "But you can't control everything," I tell her quietly. "You know that, right?"

"I can control a lot. And the parts I can't control, I'll avoid." Crossing her arms against her chest, she seems to be girding herself against anything touching her deeply ever again. Her heart is locked up tight, and my own steely cage barters with me to open up a crack because I want hers to do the same. Even if it makes me a hypocrite.

How has no one helped her through this in four years?

I find myself wanting to know that, among other things. Oddly, I want to know anything she's willing to tell me, and I'm struck by that confusing emotion. This woman has gotten me past my dislike for libraries and challenged my ban on letting anyone get close to me in one fell swoop.

While the second part of that feels dangerous to my game and my emotions, I don't do anything to stop it. A part of me wants her to break through my walls and set me free, though I don't know why.

Why her?

The answer seems obvious.

Because. Her.

I notice that Molly has chomped through about half the chips in the first bowl, and while her single-minded devotion to this particular snack amuses me, the athlete in me needs her to eat something more nutritious. Plus, if she gets sick again, I don't really want to see red Doritos all over my couch.

"Let's get out of here." I lift her in my arms as I stand from the couch, and she squeals as she realizes I'm carrying her across the room.

"Wait, where are we going?"

"We're walking into town. The fresh air will be good to sober you up a little more, plus if you yak your Doritos, it'll save my upholstery."

She mock-gasps, "I would never."

"Not taking any chances. Then we're getting some real food into you. Did you eat at all today?"

She has to think about it, but then she shakes her head. "No, but I'm not going into any restaurant in basically my jammies."

"We'll get takeout and eat it here."

"Wow, you really are stubborn. Do you have an answer for everything?"

"Yes."

The only answer I don't have is how to keep her from infiltrating my heart.

It already feels like a lost cause.

Jesus, she makes me want to drop all my hard-wired rules and boundaries. No. Those are exactly the kinds of thoughts that will derail my game and, soon after, my career. I can't allow them in.

When we get to my side door, I put her down gently and retrieve her shoes from a bin near the door. "You have a mudroom," she observes. "Interesting someone built one in a place that doesn't get very much rain. Hence not much mud." Very little escapes her notice, and if she notices, she comments.

Normally, chatterbox types annoy me, but with her, unfathomably, I like it.

"I have enough putrid gloves and stained clothes after a game to make good use of it. At least the rest of the house stays somewhat clean."

"You're a neat freak." She's not asking a question. She's also not wrong.

I shrug and grab a hoodie from a hook and find the smallest zippered jacket I have. "It's cold. Wear this." She puts it on without argument or discussion and I almost laugh at how the striped sleeves of the team jacket hang off her arms. She swims in the blue dry-fit material, but at least she won't freeze.

Thanks to the Bay Area's evening fog, the air feels wet on top of the cold. When I notice Molly shiver, I pull her under my arm and stupidly set fire to ideas about boundaries. Walking so close together means we're walking slowly, more like meandering, and I don't feel cold at all.

To the contrary, I tug on the neck of my hoodie to keep from burning up. She pulls down the zipper of the jacket but makes no move to reclaim her space.

"You live pretty far from the stadium. Is that intentional?" Molly asks, looking up at me as we move through the near-silent neighborhood.

"I just like it here. It's close enough to the center of town that I don't feel stranded in suburbia." I chose Tiburon after selling the San Francisco penthouse I shared with Shyla—I needed a change and an escape from reminders of her, but

Molly's right—it's farther from the practice field and the Strikers stadium.

"Do other players live around here?"

"Nope. Just me."

The commute gives me time to sort my thoughts on the way to work, so I'm not a wound-up coil of unfinished business when I arrive, ready to spring on the wrong teammate at the wrong time. I also need the interval after practices or games—especially during our long losing streak—to cast off the negativity before I get home.

Since my concussion, it hasn't worked, and I've been pissed off day and night. A six-hour commute wouldn't be enough to cast off the stress of injury and irritation when we can't pull a win out of our asses to save our lives, but the separation helps a little bit.

I don't tell her any of it, even if she strikes me as someone who might care. Sharing intimate details about my life isn't going to help me keep my distance from her. Better to hide behind the stoic exterior most people associate with me.

I'm stuck in my head, so it takes a minute before I notice Molly's gone quiet after my last terse response. "You okay?" I ask, tugging her a little closer. If I'm honest, it's barely cold out, but I like holding her so I'm keeping my possessive hands on her.

"Yeah. I actually feel a little better since I dumped my whole saga on you." I can see the rueful partial smile on her face. "Though I'm still probably in margarita brain, so I may regret it later on."

"Oh, come on. What's a good dead boyfriend story between friends?"

She punches me in the arm. "Oh my God, are you seriously making a joke out of my dead boyfriend?" She's a little horrified, but thankfully, also a little amused.

"I'm not above a good dead boyfriend joke. You might as well know it about me—I'm an unrepentant asshole."

"You kind of are. And just when I was starting to think you were an okay guy." She shakes her head. I can't hide my grin. Despite myself, I want her to think I'm an okay guy. Even if I manifest that like the playground jerk who makes a girl cry because he's stupid in love with her.

Whoa. I merely like her.

A lot. More than I should.

"Well, as long as you're coming to terms with the real me, I'm gonna be honest—I find the real version of Mary Poppins Molly much more appealing than the relentlessly cheerful one you project all the time." The glimpses I've caught so far only make me want to strip the remaining sheen away.

"Relentlessly cheerful?" She squints at me and circles her finger. "I feel like there's a compliment somewhere in that insult, so thank you."

We've already walked five blocks, and I can see a small crowd in front of the Italian restaurant, which means the place is packed, as usual. Not a problem since we're ordering takeout, but it might take a bit longer if the kitchen is backed up.

"It's this way." I guide Molly down the street dotted with retail shops I never go into. Most of them are women's clothing stores, and one of them seems to sell nothing but printed napkins and tablecloths, if it's even possible to keep the doors open selling that type of shit.

Molly abruptly halts in front of a store window where she gazes inside like a goggle-eyed child in front of a Christmas display. I stop to see what has her so entranced. It's a bookstore.

Of course.

Typical of me that I never noticed it in the time I've lived here. "Hmph, didn't know this existed."

Not taking her eyes from the mesmerizing display of *Harry Potter* memorabilia that accompanies a stack of anniversary editions, she mutters as if in a trance. "Have you not lived here long?"

"Just under two years."

Eyes wide with shock, she wheels around and shoves my chest. "Two years? You've been here two years and didn't know you live a block from a bookstore?"

"It's more than a block."

"Not. The. Point!"

I shrug and rub a hand over my face, not sure if there's an appropriate excuse for my myopic state when it comes to books. "I realize this may be a dealbreaker for what little friendship we have, but even without a concussion, I don't have much time for reading."

The sharp intake of breath startles me, but only because I think I was expecting a greater form of violence. Then she nods, considering me, before dismissing my confession. "Fair enough. Is the restaurant this way?"

Before I confirm where we're going, she's walking, her strides surprisingly long for someone of her small stature. "Yes, up on the next block. With the striped awning."

"I see it." She plows onward with such purpose I have to make an effort to keep up.

"Why the sudden rush?" If she goes any faster I'll need to start jogging.

"I decided you're right. I didn't eat today, and the cool air feels good. I have my appetite back."

"Okay, but will you please slow down? This isn't part of my training schedule."

I intentionally slow my stride, forcing her to cut her pace if she doesn't want to shout at me from half a mile away. She slows down, making big, exaggerated strides at a pace that matches mine. "Better?" She gives me a closed-mouthed smile that looks like it pains her.

"Why did I ever think you were all sunshine and brown sugar? Turns out you're sassy, complicated, and human, with a ton of attitude." I give up on denying how much I like it.

She smiles and starts walking normally. "I think we agree I'm not Mary Poppins. Toldja you should've put me in an Uber and sent me home."

"With no keys? Sorry. Not happening. Besides, you're still plenty Mary Poppins, and this is way too much fun."

We reach the restaurant, whose door is barely accessible due to the crowd on the sidewalk, where the graying Italian owner holds leather menus over his head and ushers two people through the melee to their table. When the door opens, the aroma of garlic and oregano drifts outside and Molly groans. "That smells amazing. I'll have whatever that is. Two of them."

She peeks through the floor-to-ceiling front windows. The restaurant is packed to overflowing, with half a dozen people jockeying for spots around the bar and every table taken. "This place is either great, or it's the only game in town," she mutters.

"It's the only Italian, but it happens to be great also. The owner has a place in North Beach too, not sure if you ever eat over there, but people seem to know it. Vittorio's?" I point toward San Francisco, even though we can't possibly see the restaurant from here.

"Ooh, yes, I've been there. Do they have the same menu here?"

"Pretty much. There's a penne with vodka sauce that's amazing, if you've never had it."

She grabs her temples with her hands. "Ugh, just when my headache is starting to fade, you mention alcohol? No, no, no."

"There's no alcohol in the sauce. It cooks off."

"Doesn't matter. Even the name might inspire a courtesy hurl."

Chuckling at her dramatics, I grab a menu from the host stand and open it in front of us. "Tell me what you want, and I'll put in our order." After a minute of pointing and discussing, we agree on linguini with spicy marinara for her, penne alla vodka for me, and an arugula salad to share.

"Want to do a lap around the block while we wait? I can show you pretty much the entire town while they cook."

"Sure." She looks up and down the block in both directions, considering which way to go. Before we set off, I see the familiar dawning of recognition by a soccer fan when he tries to figure out if I'm familiar because he knows me personally before he realizes he's seen my mug on TV or on some sports blog. He drags his friend over. "Sanders. I'm a big fan of your game." He fist bumps me. So does his friend.

"Thanks, man. Appreciate the support." I'll never shortchange a soccer fan out of a meet and greet, a selfie, or anything else. I know I'm lucky to be able to play a sport for a living and we don't have a game without our fans.

"Saw the match where you went down," his friend says, shaking his head. "That hurt my head too, gotta say. Though prolly not as much as yours." He laughs and I nod along.

"Yeah, didn't see it coming, that's for sure."

"You never do, right?" the first man says. "Mind if we get a selfie?" He's already swiping on his phone and getting into position next to me before I agree. He and his friend flank me and we pose for a couple photos. Mindful of how Molly said she feels about people seeing her in pajama pants, I don't drag her in, but I keep my eyes fixed on her so she'll know I'm not ignoring her.

When the guys decide they're happy enough with the photos, they fist bump me and move away. Their interest stokes some more recognition from a few others in the crowd, and I go through the same drill with photos and fist bumps until I'm left alone.

Reaching for Molly's hand, I pull her back toward my side, conscious of how she steps closer to me but then drops my hand. I'm aware of subtle looks from a few of the people around us, and she folds her arms across her chest.

"I didn't think this through. I don't usually go out into crowds without a bra," she confesses. I don't tell her that under the giant cocoon of my coat, not a soul would be able to tell, because the image of her bare breasts immediately hinders my ability to form a sentence.

If she notices me choking on my words, she kindly lets it go. "When it was just the two of us back at your house, I kind of forgot you're a big soccer star. This is next-level fanboy stuff."

As much as I like that she didn't know who I was in the library, an unflattering bit of my ego wants her to see that I've gained the respect of fans. I'd like her to know I don't suck at the game.

"Does that happen a lot?" Her question pulls me from my mental preening.

I nod. "Sometimes. Just when I think the fans are sick of us for losing so many games, they restore my faith in their love for the sport."

She looks at the ground. "I'm sorry I didn't know who you were when you came into the library. Does that offend you?"

"Nope." I tip her chin up so she can't avoid my eyes. Or maybe it's just an excuse to touch her face. "I have a feeling I've offended you more by not knowing there's a bookstore in my neighborhood."

She smiles. "Not offended. Just...a little sad. I bet you could find a book in there that would change your life." For the first time since I picked her up from the stoop in the Mission, I see the hopeful glow she seems to get when she's around books. At least, I assume that's the reason, since I've only glimpsed it at the library.

"That's a pretty big statement."

"I stand behind it."

"Okay, then. I have a challenge for you. Next time I come to the library, find me a book you love that you want me to read. It doesn't have to be life-changing, maybe just enlightening. Or inspiring. I promise I'll find time for it in my schedule."

Her eyes sparkle. "I'm absolutely taking you up on that." She blinks rapidly, and I can only imagine she's mentally cataloguing the books she plans to find for me.

"Why do I think you're going to present me with a three-volume tome in old English?"

"Because you already know me well." She laughs.

The host brings our order out in a large shopping bag. "Good to see you, Sanders. Been worried about that head of yours," he says, mopping a sheen of sweat from his own head with the arm of a white oxford shirt.

"Don't worry. I've got a hard head."

"Good to hear. If you ever want a table, call me. I'll squeeze you in." His eyes fall meaningfully on Molly, and I pretend to ignore what he's implying. In two years, I've never brought a woman to dine with me in his restaurant and he knows it.

As we start the short walk back to my house, I can't deny the fact that Molly might have already changed my well-laid plans. I just hope I survive it.

CHAPTER 13

$\mathcal{M}$olly

I'M NOT GOING to sleep with him.

I'm *not* going to sleep with him.

Maybe if I tell myself the lie enough times, I'll start to believe it.

Would it be horrible to sleep with him?

No, definitely not horrible, judging by the taut pectoral muscles and the biceps that flex every time he spears a piece of penne with his fork. It shouldn't be a turn-on to watch a man eat pasta.

Oh, but Holden Sanders could start a fan club eating an onion sandwich.

To be clear, sleeping with him hasn't been suggested or even hinted at, but now that I've regained some of my senses, I can't deny the mountain of muscle beside me seems like a very good time. And I haven't had that in a while.

And my loopy exhaustion isn't helping matters. He's dreamy.

Maybe it's some kind of rescue fantasy I never knew I wanted, but somehow, the kindness that Holden paid me tonight, punctuated with the small, intimate gestures, the touches, the arm around my shoulder... I'm feeling...something. Something that could get me into trouble unless I shut it down immediately.

"How's your pasta?" he asks, mid-bite, surveying my progress on the noodles.

"Good. Great!" I nod enthusiastically, and he seems satisfied enough to focus on his meal for another moment. We've already finished every arugula leaf and shred of parmesan in the lemony salad dressing, and per his instructions, I've consumed approximately a lake's worth of water.

It seems important to him that I eat, and maybe if I wasn't so emotionally drained and physically exhausted from what I subjected my stomach to via margarita madness, I'd wisely agree.

Instead, I just obey. It's easier and kind of a relief to be freed from the possibility of bad choices. If he tells me to walk, I walk. If he tells me to eat, I eat.

If he ushers me upstairs to his incredibly comfortable bed, well, it wouldn't be the worst thing.

No.

I'm not going to sleep with him.

It's not even on the table. Holden Sanders surely has better prospects than a puking bookworm. The only reason I'm still here is that I stupidly flung my keys against a wall and until my apartment manager decides to return my call, I'm basically homeless.

Instead of worrying about the sex issue that isn't even an issue, I need to deal with that.

I look down at my pajama pants and the baggy concert tee, which does only a moderately decent job of hiding that my breasts have been left free and unattended.

Normally, I'd say down with the patriarchy and uncomfortable underwire cups. But with Holden, I mainly feel a self-conscious need to act like an adult and convince him I'm not a basket case. I don't like that he's seeing me outside of my librarian comfort zone, even though it's a situation of my own making.

"So, I should get moving on finding a hotel for tonight. I hate to make you drive me back to the city, but my landlord's still MIA, and I doubt I can afford the hotels around here," I tell him as a way of wrapping up his chaperoning responsibilities before it gets awkward. The food has done its job. I feel sober, if still a bit plagued by a headache that won't quit.

He stops eating and stares at me. "No."

"What do you mean, *no?*"

"You're not staying in a hotel. If you can't reach the landlord, you can stay here."

And there it is. The invitation to the sex I shouldn't be having with the man I shouldn't be liking as much as I do. Heck, I've already been in his bed. Nothing about this situation adheres to my normal rules about sex—get in, get out, no attachments, no future.

I *like* Holden. Sex with him would be a very bad idea.

Liking him is a bad idea in itself, which is why I need to leave and remind myself why I'm better off on my own—no attachments, no risk of being left behind. Thus, emotional security. It's been a solid plan for four years and I'm not messing with it now.

"I can't do that."

"You can. Stop being stubborn and give in to reason."

Reason, huh? That's a new euphemism for sex, but I'll give it to him.

I tilt my head and level him with my best stare intended to communicate that I'm onto him. Or maybe I'm shoring up my not-going-to-sleep-with-him determination. Might as well be honest. "I'm not having sex with you. I don't want to pile another regrettable decision on top of the existing ones. It won't end well for me."

His face contorts into the kind of uncomfortable grimace

accompanied by a blush that would be cute if I wasn't embarrassed—again. "No. That's not what I-I wasn't suggesting sex. Not at all. Even I'm not that big of an asshole. There will be no sex, absolutely not. I promise. But I have a spare bedroom—two, actually—and I'm not shipping you off to a hotel when I have perfectly functional accommodations here."

Now I'm the one turning pink with mortification, if only because his vehemence makes me a little sad about the absolutely no sex, even if it's for the best. And also because I incorrectly imagined he'd even want that. "Okay, well, sorry to assume. I guess I just—"

"No need to apologize."

"Okay, then." It's not okay.

"Okay."

I make a big, rather awkward display of yawning and Holden picks up on my cue and starts clearing our plates. "You should get some rest. The bed should already have sheets, but I need to check to see if there are towels in the bathroom." Dishes rattle as he rinses and stacks them, but he's back pulling my chair out a moment later, so I gather he's leaving them in the sink.

My mind goes to the bathtub I saw in his bedroom and the soft duvet on his bed, and I start fantasizing about the epic night of sleep I'm going to get in whatever spare room he has. I have a feeling it will trump my apartment tenfold, and I love my apartment.

"Come on, this way." Unlike earlier, when Holden rested a hand on the small of my back when he escorted me downstairs, he keeps his distance, walking next to me but maintaining space between us.

Great. I've made it awkward.

Scooping Greta up and cradling her against his chest with one hand, he guides me down a hallway I hadn't noticed earlier next to the stairs. It leads to a furnished guest room that I'd bet good money Holden didn't decorate himself. It has a black and green watch plaid comforter on the queen bed with about a dozen throw pillows in gray, green, and black patterns. The curtains match. The furniture, all distressed wood, matches as well. As if making the same observation I did, he admits, "My sister-in-law had a field day decorating this house."

Greta leaps from his arms and wanders around the room, eventually settling on a comfortable-looking chair like the one in Holden's room.

"Is she a designer?"

"Orthodontist. Decorating is her side hustle."

She's good at it. Holden surveys the room and nods before his eyes shift to me. It's the first time he's made eye contact since I stuck my foot in my mouth with the sex comment. When I meet his eyes, his gaze softens to the friendlier look he's been giving me all night. I feel relieved. At least I haven't screwed up whatever budding friendship we may have.

"This is perfect. Thank you again."

Frowning, Holden pushes past me and goes to the bathroom door, which he opens, setting off a motion-sensor light. I hear him rifling through cabinets and drawers and step closer to find him holding an armload of fluffy pastel blue towels and a new fresh toothbrush. He hands them to me. "Do you need something to sleep in?"

Gesturing at my comfy clothes, I shake my head. "Got that covered." I put the towels on the bed and glance toward him, but his eyes drop.

"Okay, then." He lingers, surveying the room as though assessing his hosting responsibilities.

"I'm good. Really. Thank you so much."

His eyes land on me again, and this time neither one of us looks away. It feels loaded, this moment—neither one of us knows what should happen next, but that whatever does happen will change things.

The gray of his eyes is tinged with a deep blue like the hot center of a flame. They heat my skin as his gaze moves from my eyes to my lips and lingers there. I'm a pile of kindling he could ignite with his stare.

I want to kiss him.

It seems reckless, but after the emotional roller coaster of the past twelve hours, reckless doesn't scare me much.

"Okay, then. Good night," he says quietly.

My heart feels like a pierced balloon, its air slowly leaking out, not so quickly to deflate it all at once. But the eventual emptiness is inevitable.

Which is why it's better not to start anything with him. "Good night," I tell him, my greedy eyes taking in the whole of him once more so I can dream about what isn't going to happen between us.

I take two big steps forward to hug him, but in my wound-up state, it manifests as encircling his neck with my arms in a bear hug like we're at the port and I'm seeing him off for a month at sea. Or like a grateful houseguest who doesn't know another way to say thank you. I hope it feels more like the latter.

It takes him a moment, but then I feel him return the hug, saving me from feeling like a desperate koala. When I loosen my grip to pull away, he surprises me by not letting go.

With one arm wrapped around my waist, he tugs me closer, so our bodies align against each other more completely. It feels good. Too good. I rest my head against his chest, incapable of retreating.

My arms hang limp over his shoulders until he reaches up for one of them and links two of my fingers with his own and brings our hands down by our sides. They stay intertwined as he takes a step back, the fire in his eyes singeing mine.

His eyes zero in again on my mouth, and I swipe my tongue over my bottom lip because it suddenly feels scorched dry. I watch his pupils dilate, turning his eyes a darker shade. He leans forward almost imperceptibly, and I have to fight to steady my breathing.

My legs feel wobbly beneath me and I'm grateful I still have his hand to anchor me.

He closes his eyes for a long beat, but when they open, there's a new resolution in them.

On a deep inhale, he releases my waist and takes another step backward. My arm falls from his shoulders and flops to my side like dead weight. All of me feels like dead weight, supple in his grasp, malleable into some new form I've never seen before.

He tips his forehead to mine. It stays there for a moment longer than I expect before he draws back and kisses me in the same spot. It's gentle and kind, the same way he's been with me all night. He's the same with his niece. And his cat. I shouldn't take it to mean more than it does.

He says good night once more and walks away. Greta leaps from the chair and pads after him, leaving me completely alone.

I take a deep breath and let it out slowly, still reeling from the effect he has on me. I'd glimpsed traces of it at the library, but he was so tightly wound there that I didn't really grasp the magnitude of his softer side.

Now that he's out of sight, my heart rate slows enough that I can put myself through the paces of getting ready for bed. I decide to shower, and the rain showerhead transports me to a tropical island in a summer storm. It does nothing to dampen the desire I still feel thrumming in my veins at how close Holden and I came to a kiss that I feel certain he wanted as much as I did.

Twisting my wet hair into a bun, I get back into my clothes and unwrap the toothbrush.

I decide I'm being ridiculous, letting my lust-filled fantasy carry me away instead of being grateful to have a place to stay tonight. I just need to brush my teeth and sleep off the remains of today. Tomorrow will be a fresh start.

The white drawers of the marble-topped vanity glide quietly

as I open and close each one, searching for toothpaste. I find one drawer containing a few more wrapped toothbrushes and another with hotel-sized shampoos and conditioners like the ones I found in the shower. Holden must travel a lot for games. No doubt he could fill every drawer with travel soap if he wanted to.

Closing the final drawer, I take one last-ditch look in the cabinets under the twin sinks, finding mouthwash but no toothpaste. I give my mouth a good rinse with that, but I'm a stickler for bedtime rituals and I want to brush.

Holden can't be asleep yet, so I walk upstairs and softly knock on his door. I hear his footsteps draw closer, and when he pulls the door open wearing a pair of sweatpants and no shirt, I swallow hard and stare at the floor. Well, first I check out his abs because they're spectacular. Then I stare at the floor.

"Mare? You okay?"

Remembering why I'm here, I look back up at his face, taking my time to appreciate the sculpted muscles along the way, and hold up the toothbrush. "Can I borrow some—"

I don't get to finish my sentence before his lips are on mine.

The gasp that escapes me gets lost against his mouth and the decadent, soft, commanding kiss that knocks all the remaining air from my lungs. He pushes his hands into my damp hair and pulls the rubber band away. His fingers comb through the strands as they tumble down my back.

"Better," he whispers before cupping my cheeks and claiming my mouth again.

Then we kiss like war-torn lovers who'll be separated at dawn.

Armies will march, towns will be destroyed, but for now, we have this kiss.

His lips are warm and gentle as they glide over mine, hinting at more and asking for permission to delve farther. I answer by tipping my head to the side in his hands, giving us a better angle to go deeper. He slides his tongue over the seam of my lips before sucking my bottom lip into his mouth.

He feels like a tide that pulls me away from the shore with a gentle but insistent beckoning to deeper waters. I may drown there but I'm willing to chance it, opening my mouth to taste more of him. Our tongues slide against each other's, and Holden pulls me tighter against him with a hand at the small of my back.

I drop the toothbrush and cling to him because it's the only way I can remain standing while his mouth invades mine. He's so thoroughly coaxed me into a swoon that I'm not sure I've taken a breath in over a minute. I don't care. Keep me here and I'll test the limits.

He pulls away and tips his forehead against mine like he did earlier. Only this time, I'm not questioning whether he wants me as much as I want him. It takes everything in me not to latch on and climb him like a tree.

"This might be a mistake."

"Holden, just kiss me again."

He nods, wheels turning in his head, eyes wild. Before he can analyze us too much, I pull his face to mine and relieve him of the ability to think. I'll kiss it out of him.

The delicate touches are gone. Now it's feral, needy, grasping, and hot. Holden grabs my hips and lifts me, pressing my back against the wall inside the doorway. I wrap my legs around him, closing any remaining space between us.

He's hard between my legs, hitting me where I need him badly right now. He circles against me as our hands roam, mine surveying every muscle in his back and down his lats. There's nothing under my touch that isn't taut and strong, well-toned from training.

Still holding me against him with one strong hand at my back, his other hand drifts down, under my oversized shirt. With feather-soft touches, his fingers travel up my side until he cups one breast in his hand, circling my nipple with his thumb until I shudder.

My involuntary motion has the effect of grinding the brakes. He lifts his face away and when I meet his eyes, I see them drift closed with something that looks like disappointment.

"Hey. What?" I trail a finger down his cheek and he opens his eyes. The disappointment is gone, and the corners of his lips finally admit to a smile. "Everything okay?"

He nods. "Fuck, yeah. Mare, you…you're going to ruin me."

"That doesn't sound very good." My brow furrows, and he smooths the lines with his thumb.

"It's the best kind of good." He exhales and shakes his head. "But we stop here. I made you a promise—no sex. And even if it was the stupidest thing I've ever said, I'm going to honor it."

"You're not serious."

"I'm serious. I keep my promises."

"A promise made under duress," I tell him, wanting him to abandon his principles but liking him more because he won't.

He huffs a laugh at my haste. "Nevertheless, it was right. You've had a hell of a day—and night—and I don't want to take advantage of that."

Take advantage. Please.

No. Don't.

I know he's right. If I follow him into his bedroom, it will be one night of fun, followed by me shutting down and shutting him out. It's that way with every guy I hook up with. Holden doesn't feel like a hookup to me, and as much as that scares the crap out of me, it also excites me a little bit.

"Thank you for being a good guy, even if it's killing me that you are."

His slow smile warms me, and he nods.

I grab both of his hands and intertwine our fingers, pulling them between us while I press our lips together. His mouth opens and it only takes a hot second before our tongues are twining together, wringing every bit of emotion out of this kiss.

We stay there for a long time. I think we end up kissing for an hour, maybe more.

Then he walks me back down to my room, places the toothpaste in my palm, and kisses me goodnight before I plunge into the best night of sleep I've had in a long, long time.

olden

IT'S BEEN a month since I got knocked in the head, and I still haven't gotten used to the deep fog that drapes my thoughts each morning. It takes twice as long to shuffle off the last bits of sleep and remind myself what's on my agenda each day. Fortunately, my days have been light, with physical therapy, doctor visits, and as much time with the team as the doctors and physical therapists will let me have.

It's why I don't immediately zero in on what's different this morning.

My body is smarter than my brain, however, and the smile creeps across my face before I put the pieces together that I'm enthralled by the scent of Molly on my pillow from when she passed out there earlier last night. I could wrap myself up in that scent, but I'd rather wrap myself in her.

The thought should send me into a panic, but it doesn't. Maybe it's because I've had to put a pin in training, but I feel like making room in my life for her won't destroy my focus—or what little I have with the brain fog.

So I'm lying here like a teenager reeling from his first fucking crush on the sugar-and-spice cheerleader who just might have a wild side.

After we stood in my doorway kissing for half the night, she permeated my body and mind, and I fell asleep enveloped in a cloud of her and the sounds she made when we kissed. My only thought upon drifting to sleep was how much more I wanted of both.

No question I dreamed about her, judging by the morning wood I haven't experienced in a while.

Now that I'm awake and thinking again, I'm in withdrawal from the heady feel of her legs wrapped around my waist and the soft curves of her body pressed against me. Would it be terrible to end last night's self-inflicted ban on sex right now in the downstairs guestroom?

No, nothing bad about that.

Except that the reality of a Saturday morning comes barreling in like an unwanted cousin with a spare key. My day is packed with a PT appointment I don't dare miss and a home game in the early afternoon. The last thing I'm going to do is rush things with her—she's not someone I want to rush anything with—which means I need to get myself into the shower, take care of business, and drive her home. Even if it pains me.

Fifteen minutes later, I'm a bit more awake, though the brain fog is still troublesome. No doctor will send me back onto the pitch until it's gone, which means my hiatus is already bleeding into its second month.

The depression flees when I jog downstairs and find Molly in my kitchen wearing a striped apron Jane gave me as a joke when I moved in. She might as well be wearing just the apron for the way my body reacts to her.

My kitchen smells like bacon, which is strange since I'm

pretty certain I didn't buy any, and she has several bowls and a cutting board loaded with items I don't recognize. We passed a market last night, and apparently she took note.

She bends and feeds Greta a tiny morsel of something and my traitorous cat looks at me like she's found a new best friend.

"Morning," I grumble because even after a shower, I'm not a morning person. Molly spins around at the sound of my voice, a smile on her face before she sees me.

"Hey! I hope you don't mind. I was up early so I decided to make you breakfast as a thank you for helping me last night." Her hair is piled on her head in a bun with tendrils falling out around her face. Without a stitch of makeup, her large eyes make her look hopeful and beautiful, and don't even get me started on how much I want her lips.

She turns back to the stove as though it's normal for her to be cooking breakfast in my kitchen, as though she does it every day. It surprises me how much I want her to do it every day.

It's not a conscious decision—I move as if I'm powered by a remote and close the distance between us. Wrapping my arms around her from behind, I bury my face in her hair and inhale. It's a different kind of relaxation than I feel after a full night of sleep.

Putting down the spatula, Molly turns in my arms and looks up at me, eyes questioning, smile still wide. "Hi," she says again.

"Hi." I don't bother with more small talk.

Nothing's worth saying that I can't communicate better by brushing my lips against hers...once, twice... I don't have to hint at what I want. Her arms run up the length of my chest and she tips her head back, giving me a better angle and allowing our lips to slide against each other like we have no other job in life.

I already have that addictive sense of wanting to devour her with every kiss, find the bottomless place where my senses will be sated. But it doesn't exist. I should walk away before things go any farther, but I don't want to.

I should. I need to be smart.

There's a hot stove behind her, so I hold myself back from what I want to do, which is to push her up against the closest object. Instead, I pull back a few inches so I can see her face again. Her expression is dreamy but there's a sharpness in her eyes that was missing last night.

"You really know how to greet a person in the morning," she murmurs against my lips.

I laugh at that. "Baby, I could greet you in so many more convincing ways." As I pull her closer, I know she can feel the hard evidence of my desire. Her gentle moan caresses my soul.

The blush on her cheeks is the only thing that could make her look even more beautiful, and the bloom of pink just about does me in before her lips fall hard against mine again. Our kisses grow fierce and deep, the heady sensation building in an instant.

The woman must have the willpower of a grown bull because she manages to pull away.

"I'll just have to trust you on that." She swivels back around to the stove, but I don't release my grip on her. Looking over her shoulder, I see bacon in a skillet, soft boiled eggs in the pot next to it and a bowl of what looks like hollandaise sauce. Two English muffins pop up in the toaster as if on cue.

"Eggs benedict? I'm impressed."

She nods. "I wasn't sure if you eat greasy bacon, being an athlete and all, so I got turkey bacon and I went a little easy on the yolks in the hollandaise."

"Looks incredible."

"Thanks." She turns off the burners and scoops the eggs from the pot with a slotted spoon I didn't know I had. Then she turns back around to face me. "Don't mind me and my hangover foods. I woke up craving eggs, so here we are…"

"Feeling okay this morning?" My eyes go to the Advil bottle on the counter. I hope she took two more before bed, but in my lust haze last night, I sure didn't remind her.

For a second, her face falls, then she recovers. "Yeah. All good. I'm really sorry about last night. I appreciate everything you did for me, and I swear to you, it was a one-time thing." She twists her hands together.

I reach down and gently separate her fingers, intertwining them with mine instead. "Stop. No more apologies. You ended up okay, yeah?"

When her grin returns, she releases my hands and reaches up to hold both sides of my face. "Yeah. So how about just 'thanks.'" She kisses me softly. The tender kiss turns deeper, and I don't hold back the things I'm feeling for her, wanting to show her through a kiss that she belongs here with me, even as my brain fights me on logic. She could undo me with those lips, and I can't mistake lust for something more.

When she responds by wrapping her hands around my neck and sighing into my mouth, logic gets smacked down hard, until…

Lingering in the back of my mind, today's full agenda pushes its way to the forefront. My focus returns. I reluctantly let her go so we can put the egg dishes together and bring them to the table.

Along with the hollandaise, she's made fresh salsa and sliced up a rainbow of fruits. "I'll make us some coffee," I say, but she points to my coffee maker, which has a fresh pot already made.

"Just sit. Let me do this for you."

I do as I'm told, and she layers the eggs, bacon, and hollandaise onto the muffins, slings on a side of fruit, and brings me a full cup of coffee. Before I can go to the refrigerator for milk, she brings over a small pitcher and puts it on the table.

"Is this something I own?" I ask, examining the small vessel I swear I've never seen before.

She laughs. "Allow me to introduce you to your kitchen. It's a chef's dream." In the time I've lived here, I've never been so grateful to have a nice kitchen.

Molly ditches the apron and joins me at the table, sipping her coffee but not eating. "I thought you were craving eggs."

She points to my plate. "You first. Chef insists." I take a bite, preparing to tell her it's great no matter what, but I'm not prepared for what I get in that first bite—rich, creamy hollandaise sauce that tastes like sin, perfectly cooked egg, and crisp, toasted muffin.

"My God, Mare," I say after I savor the bite and swallow. "This is fucking amazing."

She clasps her hands together, delighted. "Oh, yay. Okay, I'm digging in now." She slices off a bite from her own plate and I'm mesmerized by the scene before me. Twenty-four hours earlier, I drank coffee and ate a bowl of cereal standing at the counter in this same kitchen. There was no joy, no delightful bacon smell, no incredible woman.

And now…it's just better.

Molly puts her fork down after devouring one of the muffins on her plate. I love that she eats real food. My last frame of reference was Shyla, always on a diet or cleanse. As an athlete, I'm a pretty clean eater, so it didn't bother me much, but Molly's appetite is refreshing.

"So, tell me what you like about Tiburon. We got sidetracked last night when you were telling me why you chose suburbia even though it's far from work." She sips her coffee and leans back in her chair as though we do this every Saturday morning. I want to do this every Saturday morning.

I could lie and give her an answer that sounds straightforward —I like to hike, I don't like noise, something basic and explanatory. But I've asked her to be honest, so I don't want to lie. A tangle of memories grates at my nerves and I rake a hand through my hair.

"Simple answer is I needed a change of scenery, and I didn't want to run into…certain people." She's admitted to googling me.

Maybe she'll know I'm referring to Shyla, and the stern set of my features conveys how much I still hate her.

"You mean fans? The ones we saw earlier seemed harmless enough." She sips her coffee and regards me.

"No. My ex." I spear another large bite of the eggs benny and savor the mixture of flavors. Other than people I employ to do it, no one has cooked for me in ages. Jane and Edward invite me over often enough, but generally I leave before the breaking of any bread. I can't remember the last time a woman made me breakfast because she wanted to. And I like it.

"Ah." She gives me a rueful look. "Guess I'm not the only one who moved to escape the past."

"Guess not."

"You want to talk about it?" Her perky smile returns.

"Not particularly."

"Okay."

It surprises me a little that she doesn't force the issue, especially after I pressed her to tell me about her dead boyfriend. Guess she's nicer than me.

We're sitting in my uncomfortable iron-backed chairs, which I wish I'd never bought. Jane mostly did an A-plus job and didn't involve me in tiny decisions about fabrics that would have driven me bonkers. I came back from practice to find the house transformed into something worthy of a magazine spread. My only instruction had been to find furniture that was comfortable. She'd succeeded on all counts except for this damn set of chairs. One of these days, I'll replace them with something plush with a cushion.

It's nearly ten when Molly pushes back her chair and takes our plates to the sink. After rinsing them and placing them in my dishwasher, she turns back to me. "Okay. I should go, and I don't want you to have to make a round trip. Why don't I just Uber?"

"Because I'm driving you."

"You're so sweet, but really, it's not necessary."

"It is."

She stares at me, then swallows. I see the mental calculations going on, and I see when she concludes there's no point in fighting me on this. She nods. "Okay. Thank you."

"Any time. You don't have to rush off." The words leave my mouth before I have time to think about them. They're motivated by how much I want to carry her up to my bedroom and have a second breakfast of her. "But I do have physical therapy." I practically spit out the words.

"Aha, see? I've taken up enough of your weekend. Let's head out." She removes the Strikers jacket she wore last night from the back of the iron chair and walks it back to the coat rack. Then she fluffs the pillow on the couch where she sat earlier. As she puts everything back the way it was, it feels like she's erasing every trace of herself being here. I don't like it.

I also can't come up with a reason to keep her here longer, so I load us into my truck and drive her back to the city. First, we stop at her landlord's office to pick up a duplicate set of keys to her apartment. I want to yell at the guy for not having a better system in place when a woman gets locked out at night, but Molly makes me promise to keep my cool.

I grind through half the enamel on my teeth instead of shoving the small man against his metal file cabinets, and Molly's smile is my reward.

"You never told me where you live," I realize when she points me toward the Presidio.

She casts me a side-eye. "You okay there?"

"Yeah. Why?"

"You know where I live."

"I do?" I rack my brain, trying to recall if she told me last night. She did not.

Now, she turns her entire body in the seat and forces me to look at her. Fortunately, I've stopped at a red light, so I can meet her eyes. They're so pretty, a soft brown flecked with yellow that

I only see as gold. "You picked me up there. Tidy little box near the freeway? Ring any bells?"

"Wait, *that* was your goddamn building?" I don't mean to sound as aghast as I do, but as usual, I speak before thinking. I realize what a bougie jerk I've become as my salary rocketed into the stratosphere, because it never occurred to me she lived there.

A car horn honks behind me, and I whip my eyes back to the road, hopefully before she can read my thoughts in them.

She says nothing, and somehow I feel even worse.

We drive in silence for a few minutes. When I glance over, her head is turned to look out the window. We drive through Cow Hollow on Lombard Street, passing a Honda dealership and some two-story housing similar to where Molly lives. I can't help thinking I wished she lived here. It's safer, less industrial.

I turn onto Van Ness, heading toward the Mission. The longer she stays silent, the more I worry I've offended her with my disbelief that the crap hole where I picked her up is her actual place of residence. "I didn't mean—"

She puts a hand up. "It's okay. I know it's not Pacific Heights, but my apartment is really cute, and it's what I can afford."

"Because you donate most of your salary to the scholarship fund."

"Yes."

I want to tell her she's nuts to make that kind of sacrifice for kids she doesn't even know, in order to honor the memory of a guy she barely knew, but I can't. It's an incredible, selfless thing, and knowing this about her makes me want to do incredible, selfless things as well—for her.

But she's not asking, and from what I know of her fierce self-reliance, I doubt she'd accept anything from me anyway. So I deal with the things I can control.

"Is it safe to live there alone though?"

She quirks an eyebrow. "Now, who said I live alone?"

I'm pretty sure she's joking. She's holding back a grin, I can tell. So why does the idea of her living with someone—living with a guy, let's be clear—make it feel like a hot lava flow just tore through my chest?

"Do you?" My voice sounds like I'm chewing gravel. I clear my throat. "Have a roommate or whatnot?"

She shakes her head. "No roommate. No whatnot." She's enjoying taunting me. Whatever. I deserve it after my faux pas about her neighborhood.

"Then my point stands. Do you feel safe? The Mission has the second highest crime rate in the city."

Her lips twist to the side. I'm grateful for traffic lights so I can look at her. "You have all the crime stats memorized?"

"Not all of them, no."

What is it about her? It's not just that she's my physical type—petite with innocent round eyes, plush lips, and pale skin that immediately reddens at half the dumb things I say—but I like bantering with her. I like it when she throws a little sass back my way.

The traffic gets moving again, and we buy a bike tire from a shop near her building. A few turns later, my truck idles in front of the same spot where I picked her up last night. It looks a little better in daylight.

It also feels like much more than a handful of hours since then. "I'm walking you to your door to make sure you get safely inside, so don't argue."

As a protest to my bumbling chivalry, she pointedly opens her door without waiting for me to come around and do it for her. But when I extend a hand to help her out, she takes it. I feel like we're reaching an area of compromise between our two versions of stubborn.

She lives on the second floor, and the front door has iron bars in front of it. I breathe a small sigh of relief when I see that the entryway is newly painted and well-lit. She leads the way up a staircase that doesn't groan under our weight.

I'm clocking all these safety features before I'll feel willing to leave her here alone. I'm also unapologetically checking out her ass as it sways in front of me, and it takes an iron will not to cup it in both hands.

Jesus. I'm coming undone.

At the top of the stairs, she stops in front of the first door, and I nod at the deadbolt above the handle.

Rationally, I know she's survived here for however long before I showed up in her life. She doesn't need me to play body-guard. But without soccer in my life the way I want it right now, she's given me purpose—first at the library, and now, more inter-estingly, by bringing me here. I want to rise to the occasion and offer her something in return.

"Thank you again for the rescue," she says, unlocking the top bolt and sliding the key into the lower lock. "I'm still a little horrified I texted you. And threw up on your doormat. And told you about my dead boyfriend."

I grin at that. "See, the more you say it, the easier it gets."

"Probably not there yet, but thank you for listening."

"My pleasure." I reach for both of her hands and hold them against my chest, pulling her close. Kissing her now feels like second nature, and she responds immediately by tilting her head to the perfect angle so our lips meet seamlessly.

I can't get enough of her quiet sigh and the way her body melts into me as though she were a dollop of hollandaise. My physical therapy starts to seem unnecessary when this is all the therapy I need.

The thought rings loud enough in my thick skull to pull me out of my trance. With a series of kisses along her jaw, I shore myself up with a final taste of her and back away. "I don't want to, but I need to leave."

"I know. Thank you for the ride."

Her lips are swollen and pink from all I've put them through, and I can't help feeling proud of leaving my mark on her. I want to do so much more. She looks content, and I carefully wind the loose strands of her hair around my fingers and tuck them behind her ears. "I want to see you again."

She looks up at me from under her lashes and it's all I can do not to throw her over my shoulder, carry her inside, and spend the entire day finding ways to make her scream my name.

"I'm good with that," she says softly.

"When?"

"Tomorrow?"

"I have a meeting with my agent tomorrow night. I could cancel…"

"No, don't do that. Agent stuff sounds important." She's right, but I want to cancel.

It's exactly why relationships are dangerous for me, and it's why I need to stay focused on my sport the way I have been for two years. Even if this is just a distraction while I'm benched, I need to keep my priorities straight. "Yeah, I can't cancel."

"I'll see you Wednesday. At the library."

It's not the affirmation I was hoping for. Maybe last night was a one-time thing. Now, back to business as usual, me helping her at the library once a week, each of us going back to our lives. I don't want that, but I also can't articulate what I want.

"Wednesday, it is. Feels like a long way off, but…okay."

She laughs. "It's not that far off. We'll make it." She squeezes my hands and I let her go. She unlocks the door and slips inside. No invitation to see the place, no agonized need to linger. No indecision on her part at all. She's just…gone.

And hell if I'm not screwed.

Because after spending one evening with her, I'm gone too.

 olly

"YOU'VE GOT IT BAD," Preeta observes as I beeline for my car after school on Wednesday. For once, I plan to make it to the library on time. "I've never seen you walk this fast."

"I've got it bad," I confirm. There's no point in denying it. I want to see Holden. Three days have felt tortuous, and I have to keep reminding myself to take things slowly because my body, my heart, and my brain don't seem to be on the same page.

My body wants him in every way, right now, full stop.

My heart wants to shake off its four-year ban, let him in a little more, and learn to trust him now that he's edged open the rusty guard gate.

My brain is an exhausted referee at a wrestling match among toddlers, telling everyone to use their words, keep their hands to themselves, and have a time out.

My brain doesn't have a snowball's chance.

"Have fun. Full report tomorrow," she instructs. I nod before rushing off.

Holden and I have either talked or texted every day since Saturday—all friendly, flirty, maybe-a-little-dirty texts. Case in point, the exchange which made me choke on my water as I was walking to the teacher parking lot yesterday afternoon.

Holden: My abs want to know if you'll be wearing a dress tomorrow.

Me: Your abs and your other parts will find out when you see me.

Holden: Those parts hope you'll be wearing a dress.
Me: Why?
Holden: So I can remove it in one, efficient move against a bookshelf.

Score one for efficiency. My heart has been racing ever since.

And yes, I'm wearing a dress.

Who am I kidding? It's been racing all day, thinking about the ginormous elephant in the library—the sexual energy between us is white hot, and if we do chance upon a desolate corner of the library basement, the bookshelves will get a workout.

I made the mistake of mentioning my Saturday night escapades earlier to Preeta, who yelped loudly in the library and peppered me with equally loud questions about lingerie. Now I'm pretty sure half the student body knows I'm wearing a lavender lace bra and panties. Some of them seemed impressed.

Thanks to the traffic gods who seemed to like me today, I arrive for my shift early and get all my work done in record time.

Now, the closer it gets to the five o'clock reading hour, the more I twirl my hair around my fingers, anxiously awaiting Holden's arrival.

"Hey." The soft tenor of his voice behind me sends a chill along my skin. His chin hovers just over my shoulder, and my body warms without him even touching me. I'm filled with my usual relief that I don't have to face the kids alone, but also something else—I realize I missed him. Not only my body, but my heart too. My brain all but waves a white flag. When his hand lands on the small of my back, I feel an involuntary shudder. "Big crowd today."

"Hey." I turn to look at him and my stomach does a flip when my eyes take him in—all six feet two inches of muscle under low-rise dark jeans and a black T-shirt that hugs his chest. His face doesn't display his normal scowl.

"Yeah. The press seems to the like idea of a grouchy soccer star reading to kids." I point to a guy with a camera in the corner.

He rubs a hand over his jaw and rolls his eyes. "Team probably set that up. Sorry."

"It's fine."

Even when he folds his arms across his chest, it doesn't detract from how…content he seems to be here. It's a good look on him. It's pointless to tell myself to look away when my body and heart have mutinied.

Majority rules.

"They're restless." I point to the kids already sitting on the rug and try to seem normal and nonchalant, but my voice sounds strangled by the sudden thickness in my throat.

Holden's gray eyes have a lot of blue in them, mixed with the paler tones that look like ice. But the more I connect with his eyes, the more I see the warmth he hides with his grumbly personality. His lips are perfectly imperfect, the upper one pulling to one side above his full lower one.

Staring a little too long at his lips, I let myself fantasize for a moment, recalling them grazing the skin below my ear while he whispered things he wanted to do to my body in a low, urgent tone. He could whisper now, and I'd forget about the kids and let him undress me near the Urban Fantasy section.

Holden's mouth pulls to the side in a half smile, or maybe more of a smirk. He regards me as I continue to stare at him. "Everything okay?"

I nod like a zombie. He's got me in a trance, and instead of using my words, I'm busy noticing a scar above his left eyebrow. Before I realize I'm doing it, I reach up and run a finger across it. "Hazards of your job?"

From his sharp intake of breath, I can tell I've surprised him. Reaching up and touching a person's face is intensely personal, and I'm at work.

Eyes wide, I immediately recoil. Before I can pull my hand back, he captures it in his own and intertwines our fingers, which simultaneously calms me and sends my heart racing.

He answers my question like it's normal to be holding my hand in public. "Yeah, we get beaten up on the regular. That one was a cleat to the head a while back."

I want to tell everyone to leave the room. I want to be with him alone so I can learn more of his secrets, anything he wants to tell me. Meeting his eyes, I feel a firm connection between us. It's fragile, but it's there.

I give his hand a squeeze before letting it go.

"You ready for the kids?" I ask, looking over to the children's section, which is a mess of books pulled from the shelves. A lot of the kids have been here for an hour or more, curled up on the beanbag chairs, reading. It's my fantasy of how I envisioned the library looking once I lured more kids in with my baked goods and good programming, but clearly Holden is the draw.

"Sure, Mare."

I turn to walk us to the kids' area, but Holden stops me with a hand on my arm. "Hold up." I stop and look at him. He opens his mouth, then bites down on his lip. Then he starts again. "What time to you get finished here?"

"Seven."

"Have dinner with me. After."

Say yes.

My mind churns through questions. I start asking them in no

order of importance. "What about Kathryn? Will she come with us?"

He chuckles as though the idea is ludicrous. "No. My sister-in-law's coming to get her later, and I'm not in the habit of bringing my niece on dates."

I can't help but hang on one of his words. I feel my lips turn up into a stupid grin. "This is a date, is it? I thought you didn't date." But I want it to be a date.

Tilting his head to consider me, he doesn't hide his amusement. "Where'd you hear that?"

Caught, I press my lips together before admitting, "Um, the magic of google."

"You googled my dating habits?" Now he's smirking. I can't fault him for it. I walked right into this one.

"Purely as a soccer fan. I was interested in your stats, and your whole dating methodology came spewing out on all the channels."

The smirk morphs into an all-out laugh. "You're so full of it. I know you're not a soccer fan, but I fucking love that you googled my dating life." His eyebrows bounce and the smirk returns.

"So…what about that? Dating ban or not? It's fine if there is, since I don't do relationships."

He swallows hard and shrugs, but his words come out on a growl that sends fireworks blazing across my skin. "There is." He shakes his head, reconsidering. "There was. But now I'd like to take you out on a date. Do we need to alert the media?"

"We do not. Dinner sounds good. It's a date."

"Great." He grabs my hand again, lacing our fingers together. Then he leans in and whispers, "And maybe you'll rethink your relationship ban while we're at it."

Caught off guard, I feel my eyes go wide, but his willingness to lay down the gauntlet fuels me. "Maybe."

We walk to the reading area where I can't wipe the smile off my face for the entire hour.

 olly

ONCE MY SHIFT is over and every kid has gotten his or her ball or book or jersey signed by Holden Sanders, we exit the building.

Holden convinces me to leave my car in the library lot and ride with him. As we wind through San Francisco traffic, I notice plenty of good dinner options, but Holden drives on, single-minded. "You seem like you have a plan. Did you make a reservation someplace?"

"Not exactly."

"But you know where we're going?"

"I do."

"Interesting. Did you plan it while you were reading to the kids?"

"Nope."

"So you felt that confident I'd agree to a date?"

He puts a hand on my thigh, and I feel the heat spread in waves across my skin. My body responds to every touch, even under the fabric of my black maxi dress. I want him more, in more places.

"You know, I kinda thought we had a deal when I wore this dress." I tilt my head so I can read his expression. His eyes heat and he swallows hard.

"I did imply that, didn't I?'

"Mmm-hmm."

He inches his hand ever-so-slightly higher on my leg and my breath hitches with the pinpricks of pleasure that move across my skin. "I promise you…I will make that dress worth your while. Right now, it's covering far too much of you."

My voice catches as I struggle to reply, so I clear my throat and press my lips together.

He tries to hide his smile as he looks out the window.

By the time he's driven us through the Presidio and onto the Golden Gate Bridge, I have a fair idea we're headed back to his neighborhood. "You like your neck of the woods, huh?"

"Among other places. Is it okay to leave your car in the library lot for a while? I should have asked that before."

"It's fine. I have a gate pass, so I can leave it after it closes."

"Good."

I look out the window as soon as we drive onto the bridge. The looming orange spires always inspire me, and this evening the tops are shrouded in fog. In the distance, I see the container ships waiting to dock near Oakland, and after we crest the arc of the bridge, the tip of Sausalito comes into view.

Exhaling a deep breath, I feel myself start to unwind from my twelve-hour day. The long hours have never bothered me, and having two jobs has become so routine that I don't think of it as strange. Before I took the job at the public library, I worked the front desk at the Orangetheory fitness place closest to my apartment. The work was easy, but it didn't exactly relate to my master's degree.

"I'm starting to see the wisdom of living outside of the city."

"Right? It's calmer, quieter. All the better for being alone with your thoughts."

"Ha. Probably why I avoided the suburbs. I like drowning out my thoughts with city noise."

"Maybe we can change that." He doesn't explain and I don't ask. Not sure I'm ready to change.

Holden keeps his hand on my thigh as he drives, and my contentment makes me oblivious to our destination until we've exited in Sausalito. It's a charming town, and I've visited a couple times to hike in the Marin headlands, but mostly I avoid it—too romantic for my life.

"Did you move since Sunday? Second home here?" I ask, tipping my head to look at Holden as he navigates the narrow streets and looks for a place to park his truck.

"Neither one."

After he parallel parks, Holden hops out and rounds the truck to my side as I'm starting to open the door. He pulls it wide and extends his hand. When I place mine in his large palm, he escorts me and doesn't let go.

His hands are strong and masculine, capable. My mind briefly drifts to other places I'd like to feel his hands before I shove the thoughts away. He's behaving like a perfect gentleman and my mind is racing to pick things up where we left off on Saturday morning.

He catches me staring down at our clasped hands. New thoughts paralyze me. "You okay?" he asks, concerned.

"It just occurred to me what I'm holding on to." I lift our entwined hands. "These are billion-dollar hands, aren't they? If I squeeze too hard, I could ruin your career."

"Not underestimating your strength, but I don't think you can injure me, so hold on as tight as you want."

He chuckles and brings my hand to his lips, barely grazing my knuckles with the delicate breath of a kiss. I feel it deep in my belly. My brain gives up the fight against my body for dominance, but it's my heart that needs to be controlled.

Best of luck to ya.

I thought I'd lost the ability to feel the connection and closeness that comes from holding someone's hand. I grasp his a little more tightly.

We walk toward the yacht harbor—quiet, save for the soft slap of fiberglass boat hulls on water and the dull clank of metal. The mist of the sea air snakes around us and cools the heat of my face, which has flamed pink since Holden kissed my hand.

He punches in the code on a closed gate and pushes it open. We walk down the long jetty where boats are docked in every slip and it dawns on me, "Wait, do you have a boat in here?"

"I don't, but I have a friend who does. And I have a key." Holden holds up a single key attached to an orange foam keyring. "You up for an hour on the bay? We missed the sunset, but it's really peaceful on the water at night."

"Sure." An involuntary shiver reminds me that in my dress, I'm not equipped for nighttime foggy weather on the water where it's likely to be ten degrees colder. But I don't really care.

As though he knows what I'm thinking, Holden reassures me, "I brought blankets and jackets, don't worry." That's when I notice the canvas shopping bag slung over his shoulder.

"You come prepared."

"I do."

We stop at the slip where a beautiful boat bobs on the dark water. I don't know much about boats, but I know enough to see that this one is stunning. It sits higher on the water than the ones around it, with its gleaming white hull wrapped in a navy stripe that matches the sun shield over the captain's seat.

It's also the only one that doesn't have covers over the seating area and all the exposed wood on the deck, so I know Holden had someone prep the boat for us to go out. The seat cushions are a smooth white color with navy pillows against the backrests. "This is so pretty. Love that you have minions scurrying around to prep boats for you."

He tips his head to indicate a guy our age who I hadn't noticed before. His face is half covered by a baseball cap, and he wears a Strikers practice tee. "Molly, meet Tim. My minion."

He extends his hand. "Tim Cheltenham. Good to meet you. And just so you're aware, I don't show up at night and lend my boat to just anyone. This bloke's basically the only one I trust, so you're in good hands," he says in lilting English accent.

I know from the little bit of research I did on the Strikers that Tim plays left back and there's talk of him going back to his native England now that the new owner is trying to overhaul the team. "Thanks for letting us use it."

He waves a hand. "It's the least I can do. Holden will tell you stories, I've no doubt." He runs a hand over his clean-shaven face, which I can't see in detail in the dusky light. "Anyhow, you ought to have at it since you'll need to go slower at night."

Holden fist bumps Tim and steps into the boat before extending his hand to help me over the side. Tim has laid out cushions on the seats and a little spread of appetizers along with plastic wineglasses in drink holders next to the table in the middle. I look back to thank Tim again for setting all this up, but he's already moved to where the boat is tied to the dock so he can loosen the ropes as Holden fires up the motor.

I wrap up in a blanket and make myself comfortable on one of the seats while Holden takes the wheel and backs us out of the slip. "Careful, hard right…right, a bit more," Tim guides. Holden chuckles at him.

"If I go any harder right, I'm going in circles. Relax. I've got this."

"She's my love. I get nervous," Tim yells.

"I've got you, man. Thanks again," Holden calls as we glide

away from the dock, muttering under his breath, "Nervous Nelly."

"The boat is safer anchored at the port, but that's not the aim of boats," I observe.

He nods. "I know that one…Paul Coelho?"

"Bingo. *The Pilgrimage.* Someone knows his Brazilian lit."

Holden stands at the wheel of the boat, guiding it quietly toward the breakwater that divides the harbor from the bay. Small red lights flash on the edges of the rocks that line the breakwater, ensuring boats don't miss their entry point.

"English major, though I read a lot of British authors."

"Aha, so you just pretended to be anti-book." I feel a smile creep across my face at the relief that he shares my biggest passion.

"Not anti-book, anti-library. And I think you've gotten me over that one."

We motor slowly through the no-wake zone of the harbor with only the moonlight and the soft boat lights casting shimmering rays across the darkening bay water. We've missed the actual sunset, but the deep blue sky is striped by pink and orange clouds and the last hint of light.

The water laps the sides of the boat's white hull, and I lean back against the cushion and feel the evening wind blow across my skin. I know it's not warm out, but to me, it feels like summer.

Holden points to a wine bucket stowed next to the table. "Tim's all about the spread. I've only been out here a few times with him, and he always has drinks, snacks, the whole deal."

"Good host."

"Want to steer the boat?" He extends his hand, and I place mine in his warm palm. He pulls me to stand and join him at the helm of the boat. We're just passing the breakwater, but the bay is still at this hour, so there aren't really waves once we leave the security of the harbor behind. It feels like we're mostly floating, assisted by the gentle purr of the motor moving us along.

Pointing ahead into the distance, he eyeballs a tiny flashing light that's barely yellow in the darkening blue sky. "That's what you're aiming for. Just keep the top of the wheel pointed at the light and we'll stay on course."

He moves aside and I take the wheel, fixing my gaze on the light and getting a feel for the motion of the boat as I move the wheel slightly to one side or the other. He starts to grab the wine, but I panic as soon as he steps away. "Wait, don't go. I don't want to run into something."

His soft laugh is comforting. "There's only water out here, Mare. Nothing to run into. But I'm not arguing if you want me right here. The wine can wait."

"Yeah, maybe just to be safe, so I don't steer us into Alcatraz or something." Holden moves behind me and looks over my shoulder toward the light.

The second I feel his presence at my back, my body stills. I'm hyperaware of his large form and his breath near my ear, making me shiver each time he speaks.

He puts his hands on top of mine and guides me as I move the wheel. "There. A little more to the left." His touch is light, but it feels like a thousand-watt charge. I try to keep my breath steady with him so close. "Okay, you've got it under control. See? Easy. You're a quick study."

I relax into him, my whole body craving the way he shrouds me in comfort and security. He starts to move again to open the wine, and my arm darts out and holds him where he is. "No. Don't go. I like you here. I might lose my navigational mojo if you move."

Holden's hands drop to my shoulders, and he reassumes his position at my back, pulling me against his chest. We stay like that for a while, me tipping the wheel and feeling the slight change in course as the boat cuts through the water.

We don't speak. The moment is perfection. After a while, Holden wraps one arm around my shoulders, and I lean my head against the hard muscle of his chest.

With his other hand, Holden gathers my hair into a ponytail and lays it over one shoulder. When he leans closer and shares my vantage point over the dark horizon, I can feel the brush of his stubble against my cheek. My breath hitches at every miniscule contact which would be unnoticeable with anyone else. With him, every touch is a tornado.

"I like you here too," he says quietly, sending goosebumps along the back of my neck. "Do you want to go a little faster?"

At first, the only thing my brain comprehends is that he's asking how badly I want him.

More? Faster? Hot breath against my skin?

Yes, yes, and yes.

Then I realize he's talking about the boat. Which sounds fun too.

"Oh. Can we? I thought maybe it was against the rules at night."

He chuckles and drops one hand to the throttle, without letting go of me with the other. "The only rule is safety. We're not gonna go nuts because visibility isn't great, but we can pick it up a little. Have some fun."

The throttle kicks up a few knots or degrees or however boat speed is measured. All I know is it suddenly feels like we're flying. The boat slips though the water, which splashes more urgently against the hull, until Holden speeds up a little more.

It's as thrilling to fly through the darkness as it is terrifying. Lights dot Angel Island and the San Francisco coastline sparkles in the distance, but on the expanse of bay water where we are, I only see blackness in front of the boat.

I tense up against Holden's chest and he slows the boat a little. The noise level drops and I'm aware of the pounding of my heart. "Too much?" he asks.

"I was just worried we might not see something and run into it."

He shakes his head. "Don't worry. Anything we could run into has a light on it." He points to the lights on the bow and stern of the boat. "Unless it's a fish, but they're mostly under water," he teases.

"Okay, then, fire her up, Captain Sanders."

This time, we don't go quite as fast, but Holden steers us under the Golden Gate bridge, which illuminates the water a little more and streaks the top of the Pacific Ocean with its lights. We don't go too far in this direction before turning around because we're now in open water which carries a bit more current and a lot more unknowns if we venture farther.

Looping around, we sweep beneath the bridge a second time, this time hugging the coast of the peninsula, passing by Crissy Field and Fisherman's Wharf to our right as we make our way around the bay. I relax fully into Holden's chest as we rip through the water, a light ocean spray dusting my face.

He slows the boat near Angel Island and cuts the engine when we near a small cove where he can drop anchor. The water is virtually still, save for the wake we just created, and after a minute, the boat bobs so gently it's practically motionless on the surface of the water.

We move to the bench seat at the back and sit side by side. The easy drift of the boat feels like a rocking cradle. I can see why babies fall asleep with a little motion. "This is so nice. Do you come out here a lot like this?" I imagine him seducing women here. It wouldn't be hard.

He shoots me a glance and I return a steady gaze as if to say I'm not jealous, just interested.

"Sometimes," he says, not playing my game. He waits, watching me. Then he leans over and brushes a loose strand of my hair off my face. His fingers feel charged with electricity and my skin reacts instantly. I can't hide the shudder. He notices. "I've come out with Tim and some of the guys. They drink more than me, so I end up driving the boat most of the time. And then there are the many, many women I bring out here, if that's what you're asking."

"I was just making conversation."

He can't hide his sly grin. Or his wink. "Me too."

I like his flirtatious side. I also don't doubt he could bring a new woman out here every night of the week, if he wanted to, but he said he doesn't date. Yet here we are. If I'm going to let my heart out of its shackles for some supervised yard time, I need to know more.

"You still with me?" He has a concerned look when I pull myself out of my head.

"Yeah, sorry. I was just wondering about the reason behind your no-dating thing, if you don't mind sharing. I didn't push before, but I'd kind of like to know." I hold up my hands. "And no judgment. I don't really date either My dad was a relationship cautionary tale if there ever was one—after he left my mom, he was a serial adulterer."

He closes his eyes on a long blink and nods. "Fair enough. You were honest with me." He lets out a long exhale that sends a quiver of fear up my spine at what his honesty might reveal. "It's not that complicated. My relationship ended badly, and I let it get to me. Lost my Premier League opportunity. It nearly ruined my soccer career before I got back on track. Easiest thing was not to date after that. And it's worked great."

"So why risk it? We don't have to date. We can have fun and call it a day. Why put ourselves through something with the potential to dig up old pain, since we both have our share?"

He pulls me closer and wraps his arm around me. The second I feel the warmth of his body and the magnetic presence of him, I'm fighting a losing battle against my will.

"Because I'm getting tired of letting my past define my future." He brushes the strands off my forehead and smooths the skin as though erasing worry lines I didn't know I had. "I like you, Mare. I'm not saying I know where this will lead. Maybe it's temporary infatuation, maybe it's not. But I'd like to find out."

His fingers comb through my hair and trail down my back and I melt. I just melt.

"You would?"

His lips twist as though he thinks I'm funny. "I think you're worth the risk."

I let his body support me until I feel weightless. Almost carefree. "I find it hard to argue you when you're touching me."

The sexy tenor of his chuckle shatters the rest of my resolve. "You know you just gave me license to never fucking let you go."

He glances over at the glasses and points. "Would you like wine? I'm gonna assume the tequila-guzzling thing was a one-off and you don't have a drinking problem."

"Ha. Yeah, I think we've established I have a once-a-year drinking problem. I'm not a big drinker, but wine sounds nice. Thank you."

He smiles and opens the wine which has been sitting in its metal ice bucket all this time. The condensation runs down the neck of the bottle as he works the corkscrew into the top. I hold out the two plastic wineglasses while he pours. Then he holds his up for a toast. "Thank you for agreeing to a date."

We each take a sip. The cold white wine goes down easily, and I turn the bottle in the bucket to see its label. "I like this."

He moves so his body faces me more squarely. Watching me, he brushes a finger underneath my chin. I can feel my cheeks heat, and I know he notices. I also know he likes it. "I've never brought a woman out here. Never wanted to."

"Thank you for making an exception for me." My voice sounds breathy and hoarse. The air around us is silent, only marred by the soft, rhythmic lap of water against the boat.

"I'm getting the impression you *are* the exception. In every possible way." His gray eyes are hypnotic and dark, their intensity almost too much. I take in the other parts of his face—the high cheekbones, a day's worth of stubble, the quirk of his full lips as he gives me an almost-smile.

Unsure how to respond to his assessment of me, I take a sip of my wine. The thickness in my throat makes it hard to swallow. Looking at him now through my lashes, I find his gaze hasn't wavered from my face, but it's moving from my eyes to my lips.

I feel the presence of him in every part of my body—quivering in my limbs, heat in my belly and between my legs. The sweet anticipation of whatever will happen next hits me like a drug, humming in my veins and making me feel hyperaware of every sound, every shift in the wind.

I'm certain Holden can hear my heart, which thunders in my chest like someone's just used defibrillator paddles cranked up to a million. His hand falls over mine where I'm holding the glass. He takes it from me and slides it across the table, off to the side. His already sits there on a slip-proof coaster.

He brings my knuckles to his lips like he did earlier. His soft kiss and rough exhale of breath on my skin have my nerves feeling raw. But that's all he does. Bringing my hand down, he holds it in his lap.

I almost can't take it. I want to climb into his lap and wrap myself around him. His lips press together in a patient smile, and for a moment I think maybe I've gotten it all wrong. Maybe this is going to be the kind of date where we do a lot of holding hands and hug each other goodbye at the end of the night.

That sounds like a stupid date. I don't want that kind of date.

Then I see it, the fluttering pulse in his neck. And it's ratcheted up like mine. Just to test it out, I slowly move toward him, leaning close to his face until I can whisper in his ear. I want him to feel the whisp of breath on his skin, just like he's been torturing me for the past hour.

"This is the best date I've been on in a long time," I say softly. Before backing away, I hear a low groan rumble from his chest and then I know for certain that holding himself back and taking his time is killing him, just like me.

I meet his eyes again, challenging.

For a moment, he doesn't move. Then he picks up my wineglass and hands it back to me. He grabs his own and takes a long sip. I do the same, even though I want him so much I feel like climbing out of my skin.

Our eyes meet again.

"Oh my God, Holden. Just kiss me." I pluck the glass from his hands as the questioning is replaced by a fierce smolder that floods my veins. I put down both glasses before his hands push into my hair at the temples. I fist his jacket and tug him closer.

When our lips draw close, I breathe him in. And I'm gone.

The crash of our mouths is needy and rash. My hands move up Holden's chest to where I can slide my fingers along the hard planes of his chest.

The feel of his pecs underneath my hands makes me sigh, but the sound is swallowed up by the boat slapping on the water. The initial fury of exploration winds its way down into a long, hot kiss.

Holden's tongue slips along the seam of my lips, teasing, tasting. Then it melds with mine.

The boat's slow motion starts to mirror our own, as Holden pulls me onto his lap so I'm sitting sideways. He holds me closer, and I wrap my arms around his neck, running my fingers through the soft hair at the nape of his neck.

One kiss morphs into a hundred long, slow kisses that I sink into. A dream on a feather pillow.

When we finally break for air, I'm lightheaded. It takes me a minute to articulate a thought. And even then, all I can come up with is, "Wow." Tipping my forehead against his, I feel dizzy.

"Fuuuuck, Mare. I'm going to smash every one of my

goddamn rules with you," he growls, demanding my lips again for another long, breathless kiss.

It feels different with him. And if it also feels scary, maybe that's because he's the first person in a long time who makes it impossible to see what would end us.

CHAPTER 17

Holden

Two years.

For two years, I've kept my head down and my emotions locked tight. Maybe denying them space to breathe is the reason my body is shaking right now, literally vibrating with desire I've never felt before. I don't want to live like an unfeeling robot. I want soccer, sure, but I *need* Molly.

To hell with my dating ban.

It was stupid, shortsighted, and absolutely unnecessary if it keeps me from spending the rest of the night on top of, beneath, and—heaven help me—inside this woman to my right.

The only thing I care about right now is how fast I can drive this damn boat to the harbor so I can get her back to my house or hers and taste every inch of her skin. I'm not about to do that in the berth of another guy's boat.

The spray hits my face and cools my libido only slightly, but with Molly tucked against my side nuzzling my shoulder, my concentration is barely sharp enough to steer the boat properly and keep an eye out for the tiny lights indicating something in our path.

It only takes twenty minutes or so to get the boat back inside the breakwater and another fifteen to motor it to the slip and hand everything off to the deckhand I hired from Tim to put stuff away.

I tip him and thank him, but I can't get us out of there quickly enough. I like us better when we're alone, and even the momentary intrusion of a helpful worker feels like a burden.

Once we get back on the road, I'm less antsy. "Where to?" I ask, my one-track mind calculating which of our places is closer so I can get finish what we started. My athlete's brain is trained to calculate efficiency and lowest energy expenditure to achieve the goal. I'd also be fine with the back of my truck.

I'm so lost in my metrics that it surprises me when Molly's hand lands lightly on my thigh. "How about Café Med? You need to feed me, soccer star, or my blood sugar will drop and I'll get hangry. I promise, you don't want to see that."

It surprises and delights me when Molly suggests we stop at a fast-food Mediterranean restaurant where we can get shawarma and falafel plates. I like that she doesn't pretend she's not hungry.

"Pretty sure I've seen worse from you, Mare."

"I thought we agreed not to discuss it." She doesn't look offended.

"I agreed to no such thing. I intend to use your embarrassing incident for maximum entertainment value whenever needed."

"Great. And here I thought you were a nice guy."

"I'm not nice. Not at all, and I'll prove it in just a few minutes," I say, slipping my hand along the curve of her thigh to let her know how not nice I'd like to be right now.

We pick up the food and I drive like a madman because I have a one-track fucking mind and I want her. Now.

I don't even wait until we're at the top of the stairs in her building before I press her against the wall and cover her mouth with mine. I want the plush feel of her bottom lip against my tongue as I suck it into my mouth. Every part of her is soft, pliant, willing, nimble.

Her moan tells me everything I need to know, and I'm glad we had the conversation on the boat about risks because now I know we're in this together, wherever it leads. I can't dwell on it for more than a second the way I'm straining against the zipper of my pants.

She fishes in her purse for her key, and we tumble into her apartment, her moving backward and guiding me forward. She tosses the food bag on a table. Meanwhile, I'm not breaking the goddamn kiss for anything.

We land on a couch, and she gestures around the room with one hand. "Welcome to my apartment. All four-hundred square feet of it."

"It's perfect."

"You didn't even look."

"I'd rather look at you."

I also don't want to offend her, and this is her home, so I glance around. The room is dark, save for the moonlight beaming through a window next to an equally bright streetlamp outside. For safety reasons, I'm glad she doesn't walk into pitch blackness, but for my seduction purposes, the lighting couldn't be more perfect.

There's a kitchen area off to one side and an open doorway to a second area too dark for me to see inside. We're wedged next to each other on the small couch. "I don't usually have people sitting here with me," she explains.

I have no problem pulling her onto my lap so she's straddling me. "Problem solved."

Grabbing my face with both hands, she drops her lips to mine again. Our pace slows now that we're finally out of the library, out of the car, and off the goddamn boat.

Kissing her feels so fucking good. With my hand wrapped around her hair, I tug until her mouth is angled right where I need her.

I didn't want to want her, but now I can't stop.

Her lips move across my cheek until I feel the exhale of her soft breath next to my ear and the gentle hum in her throat as I move my hands up her thighs and massage my fingertips into the curve of her hips.

Everything about this woman is worthy of savoring. "I thought my heart was dead, Mare. You're my proof of life."

My confession results in the loss of her lips against my neck as she pulls back to meet my hungry gaze. I have no doubt my eyes mirror the swirling dark embers I see in hers. It's lust, sure, but there's something deeper between us.

There has been since moment one. Since the day she rammed into me in the library when I was looking for my classic movie fix—yes, I noticed her then. Since the moment she chased me down under the tree and challenged me to be a better guy.

I don't dare try to put a name to it because it scares the hell out of me, but she's like nothing I've ever experienced before. There's no bullshit, no games. It's right and good and I'm not about to let her go out of fear. I've faced down bigger mental roadblocks and prevailed.

I'm thinking all of these things instead of taking the plunge into whatever we'll be once we get our clothes off and I lose control over my impulses. Now is the time for thinking, and I can't come up with a single reason why I shouldn't take her into my arms and show her how fucking turned on she's had me since the second I saw her today.

And while I'm lost in my head, our eyes stay locked on each other's. I see her swallow hard, waiting me out, probably thinking I'm playing some kind of game.

I'm not.

I wasn't doing that on the boat either. But every time I looked at her and wanted to kiss her with every fiber of my being, I had an equal desire to take things slowly.

"Fuck, Mare. I gotta be honest. My self-control is hanging by a thread. I want you so much it hurts, but I also really want to take it slow because we only have one first time, and I don't want to miss any of it."

Eyes moist and sparkling, she reaches for my face and cups my chin in both hands. "That's maybe the sweetest thing anyone has ever said to me. I want you too, Holden, but you're killing me with this slow thing. Killing. Me."

My laugh breaks the tension I created with my grandiose sentiments. Thank God. Because the only thing left to do is let our bodies take over. And they do. My mouth crashes onto hers, muffling the gasp that barely escapes before our kisses become bottomless and searching.

I work my hands up along the contours of her waist, feeling apologetic for the roughness of my hands on her soft skin but she doesn't complain.

"If you're not going to make use of this easy-access dress. It's gotta go." She whips the long thing over her head and I can't help but laugh.

"Please always wear clothes that can be taken off that quickly." My hands continue their tour, feeling every inch of her skin and wandering higher until I reach the delicate lace of her bra and greedily run my fingers over the full cups.

I'm harder than I've ever been, at least that's the way it feels, and she knows exactly how to move against me so it stokes my desire to a fever pitch, rolling her hips and circling above me until I'm paralyzed with need for relief.

From the way she grinds her hips I can tell she's enjoying it too, and I love that she isn't afraid to move in the way that makes her feel good.

She pushes my shirt up, and I gladly throw it over my head and onto the floor next to her dress. Her nails drag along my abs and across my chest, and I hear a satisfied hum that stokes my desire in ways she can't possibly understand.

Our kisses slow to a more languid pace, our hands still moving across each other's exposed skin with more urgency.

"Holden," Molly breathes when we break the kiss. "This couch is too small."

"It's perfect." I'm not about to criticize any aspect of her apartment because it's working just fine for me.

"No, come with me." She wrestles off my lap and presents me with her hand. But I can't move a muscle because she's standing there in the moonlight and all I can think is how gorgeous she looks. The lacy lavender bra highlights just how creamy white her skin is, save for the light smattering of freckles on her stomach that make me think she spent her childhood on beaches in the sun.

She has a petite, taut body she never lets me see in those over-sized sweaters she wears. The curve of her waist and the swell of her breasts over the cups of her bra beg me to run my tongue over every inch of her.

"Mare..." I say in a daze. She looks at me quizzically as though she's worried something's wrong.

"Yeah?"

"Just...you're beautiful."

A small smile curls on her lips and she takes my hand. "Thank you," she whispers, drawing me toward her and wrapping her arms around my back until we're flush against each other. Then she walks us into the kitchen area where a wooden table takes up most of the space.

The backs of her knees hit the table and she lays on her back, scooting up and pulling me with her until we're a tangle of limbs splayed on the hard surface.

"I know you're taking your time, and I love that." She bites down on her bottom lip and it's all I can do not to bite it myself. I reach up and free her lip from her teeth and run the pad of my thumb over it until she opens her mouth.

Sucking hard on my thumb, she pulls me against her with both hands and I shudder out a breath, feeling my will slipping away. I can't take this any more slowly, but she's just told me how much she likes it. Then she lets go of my thumb and finishes her thought. "I want you too much for slow."

"Honey, you can have it any way you want…" My voice sounds like the growl of a caged animal because that's how I feel. "If you want me to fuck you hard and fast, I'm all yours. But the next time…it's going to be slow and deep and it's going to mean something, even if that scares you."

Inside my arms, I feel Molly inhale a deep breath that seems like it requires effort. When she exhales, her eyes close, and for a moment, I know she has thoughts brewing beneath the surface of her words and actions, and I wonder how closely they mirror my own.

She presses her lips to mine, just a brush, and backs away enough to rub her nose against my cheek. "Thank you," she says again, her voice thick with emotion. "Now, quit thinking so much and fuck me, soccer star."

I was wrong. She's not the exception.

She's the whole goddamn rule book.

olly

TRUE TO HIS WORD, Holden unwraps a condom in one swift motion, rolls it on, and takes me hard and fast the way I want. My apartment may be small, but there's something glorious about a well-placed kitchen table for when a gorgeous man needs to fuck a lady in a hurry.

After the tender touches and lingering kisses, I need the release, and I can tell he does too. All the talking and kissing and hand wringing about our fears was making everything feel too heavy. Or maybe I'm just not ready for sex to be meaningful yet—I need one round where it can just be fast, hard, and fun.

It *is* fun. So fast and fun, I barely get a chance to take in the glory of a naked Holden, and when he hurls us both over the cliff of a fist-biting orgasm, I'm still wearing my lingerie. His deft hands shove my panties aside and give me every inch of his rock-hard length until I prove I can swear like a sailor.

It's a one-bite appetizer before a four-course meal.

And now the angst and tension are gone.

Ahh.

"Good idea, right?" I gasp when I can finally draw breath.

He blinks stars out of his eyes and works to form words. "Great idea."

"Come." I beckon with one finger, guiding Holden into the other area of my charming studio apartment. He recovers his composure quickly, kissing my neck and digging his fingers into the flesh of my hips. By the time my back hits my baby blue comforter, the look in his eyes makes it abundantly clear that the appetizer course is finished. I am the meal.

After a quick trip to my bathroom to dispose of the first condom, Holden returns with a fresh one. He sits back on his heels and his eyes survey every inch of my body. As the heat of his gaze moves over me, every place he looks warms another ten degrees. He could burn me alive with just his eyes.

His slow smile turns wicked, and his hands trail up my sides until he's cupping my breasts over the lacy bra. "You ready for slow?"

"I'm ready for anything."

I finally get the opportunity to see Holden, head to toe, and the sight alone makes me gasp. I can't imagine what sounds and feelings will escape when I get my hands on him. But first, I'm going to look.

Holy crap.

He might as well be carved from marble, for how defined his chest and abs are. The hard V of muscle directs my eye lower to where he's impressive and hard, and now I'm done looking and all about touching.

My hands travel over his pecs, appreciating them just as he still seems to be appreciating me in the Little Lingerie That Could. I knew it matched. I did not know it could bring a man to his knees, but that's where he is, sitting back, surveying how and where he'd like to have me for dinner, dessert, and a midnight snack.

"Kiss me, sexy man," I demand, lying back, pulling him over me.

"Mare." His kiss is commanding, insistent.

I slide my tongue from one corner of his lips to the other and bite down teasingly on his bottom lip. He smiles against my mouth and angles my head for a deeper kiss.

When he says slow, he means beautifully, luxuriously slow. Pulling me to sitting, Holden peels down the straps of my bra. He reaches behind me and undoes the clasp, and I wriggle free. Reverently, he ducks his head to take one breast into his mouth, circling my nipple with his tongue until I'm shaking and leaning back on my hands for support.

He moves to the other breast, giving it equal attention and trailing his fingers along my skin. "I think I'm going to enjoy slow," I manage to exhale as my hands explore every ridge of his abs and dip lower to wrap around the length of him. My moan turns into a whimper.

His eyes meet mine with a smug gleam. "You and me both."

He groans as I stroke him harder, tipping his head back and letting me have my fun. But then, he slides out of my reach and I'm a prisoner of his tongue once more. Tiny licks on my stomach, a trail of wet kisses along the edge of my panties and a hard suck at my center.

Then he pulls the meddlesome scrap of lace from my body and gazes down on me like a smug winner-takes-all champion. "You are…fuck, Mare. You're gorgeous. And so, so wet."

I can't even form the words to respond because his tongue renders me speechless. He licks and sucks every inch of me until I'm quivering in his mouth and under his hands.

I'm all on board with the slow plan, but he's building me to a new peak and my body's not holding back. When he slips two fingers inside and curls them to hit me in a perfect spot I didn't know I had, I'm undone.

"Holden, my God," I gasp, as my field of vision fills with light and darkness all at once and I tremble beneath him, pitching over the top and falling into an abyss of pleasure.

He's watching me as I come—at least, I think he is—I don't know. I'm not paying attention to anything except the exquisite feeling he's still pulling from my body. "Holy…wow," I'm finally able to utter once I know I've survived him. *Him.*

"Not done with you, Mare." He places the condom in my palm and moves up my body for a deep, lingering kiss. I taste myself on his lips and I've never felt so desired and appreciated.

No, worshipped.

He's quickly moving me past the question mark of whether to date him and pushing me to an exclamation point of knowing he's the right decision.

When he teases my entrance, it's all it takes for another orgasm to begin building. The tease turns into a taunt. "Holden, please." I'm putty, but I'm trying to assert some sort of will.

Reaching down, I stroke him, wanting to get him as desperate as I feel. It only takes a minute. I slide the condom over his hard cock, enjoying the groan it elicits from deep within his chest. Then he's steadily pushing inside until he fills me.

He moves slowly at first, circling his hips, building us to another peak of oblivion. Then we're cresting the peak together. He's groaning my name on a curse. I'm moaning and begging him not to stop. We're gripping each other, nails biting into skin, thrusting.

Then, the mind-scrambling, dizzying release.

And that's only the beginning.

olden

TWO MORE WEEKS of concussion protocols under my belt, but this two weeks has felt painless. Wonder why?

Spending every night with Molly has taken the angry edge off of my sidelined status and replaced it with a beautiful distraction that feels like something I want in my life all the time. All the fight has gone out of me because she's different from anyone I've ever dated. Generous. Complex. Kind.

There's no point in arguing against the truth—I'm falling in love with her.

I know it, just like I know I'll fucking kill the next teammate who asks how it feels to be on vacation.

"Don't know how you spend your vacations, man, but if you're off getting CT scans and looking at eye charts, you're more wrong in the head than me," I tell Weston when he's dumb enough to ask.

"Too bad the docs didn't give you a personality transplant

when they had the chance," he mouths off before heading to the field, knowing I'd give anything to feel the turf under my cleats. Asshole.

"Keep working your left foot, Weston, maybe you'll stop hitting the post," I call after him. It's a low blow after he missed a key shot that could've given us our first win in a while on Sunday. Instead, we ended in a draw.

The rest of the players take the field, and as usual, I take a spot in the bleachers.

It may not be a full practice, but the time spent at the training facility watching the team feels one step closer to getting back on the pitch. A small, agonizing step because watching my teammates train and having to sit on my ass almost kills me.

"Builds fortitude." The voice coming from the bench behind me startles me because I didn't know anyone was there. Turning, I see the new team owner, Charlie Walgrove. "Watching your teammates play and jonesing to be out there, it's ultimately good for your game. Even if you hate it right now."

I nod, still a little creeped out that he's been sitting there for however long. Watching the team? Watching me?

"Just got here." So he's a mind reader too.

Nevertheless, I'm glad to see him out here because I hope that means he's busy using his robot brain to figure out how to get the team out of the slump we've been in for the past year. Charlie's a tech guy—a billionaire computer scientist—who left his virtual reality company with the express intention of using computer algorithms and analysis to build a better team. Everyone's a little uneasy because that will no doubt result in trades, but it's part of the game.

Our slump doesn't have a clear source. Every player on the pitch is top rate, at least in a vacuum as a series of stats and skills. But somehow our chemistry is off. We get all this talent together and it implodes rather than lifting the team.

I've pestered Charlie a little bit, trying to understand what he has in mind. I'm also trying to suss out who has job security here, but Charlie's poker face has never given any indication. My time away from the game certainly isn't going to help things. How can I prove my worth when I can't even play?

"How's it going up in the executive offices?" I look over my shoulder at Charlie, but it's awkward, so I move up one row to where he sits, leaving a few feet between us.

Charlie's face briefly twists into a frown before he raises his eyebrows as if to wipe the slate clean. "Much happier down here."

"You and me both. I mean, I'd be even happier in goal, but that'll come, or so they tell me."

"I heard you're looking at a few more weeks." I don't know why it surprises me that Charlie would know exactly how much longer the doctors are keeping me off the field. He probably knows more than I do since he essentially owns me.

"Yeah. Sticking to protocol, don't want to stretch this detention out any longer than I have to."

He leans back and reaches his hands out to grasp his knees. He nods, but his eyes have a faraway look, and he's not watching the players running drills. I get a pit in my stomach. Is this where he tells me I don't need to worry about my recovery because I no longer have a position with the team?

My skin feels cold and clammy at the thought that I haven't impressed him enough to merit a spot. Intellectually, I know my track record will leave me with options. My agent always says as much. But it's better to get scouted before a team thinks about dropping me, and I've never enjoyed surprises, so I flat out ask him.

"I'm very invested in the team's success, but I also have to stay a step ahead of any talk of a trade. Do you mind filling me in?"

For a moment, his expression is blank, but I can tell he's thinking about how to answer because he looks away. It's been his tell for as long as I've known him, so I wait for him to finish. "I'm hearing there's some interest from the Premier League, depending on how you do after your recovery, but that's your decision to make if you get an offer. I don't see trading you as any part of a winning strategy."

I nod. It's a relief to hear, but I hold my emotions tight. No reason for him to know this conversation makes me sweat. It's also heartening to hear from him that there's still potential in England, though I know it's a long shot.

"I did want to talk with you, though, so I'm glad to see you out here today." He squints off into the distance again, giving me the impression whatever he needs to discuss is producing heartburn. "I'm told by our PR team that you've been making waves on social media with some volunteering you're doing."

My brain quickly runs through what I recall of my contract, which isn't much because my agent only gave me the high points, in other words, things that involved dollars. "Right. Am I not supposed to be doing that? I'm pretty sure it's just people taking selfies and posting shit. I haven't made any implications that reading to a few kids has anything to do with the Strikers."

He waves his hands. "To the contrary, that's what the publicity folks are on about. Your volunteering is shedding positive light on the team, which is great, given all anyone seems to want to write these days is that we're a Cinderella story in need of a prince."

"You need a prince, I'll put on a fucking crown," I mutter. Even the fear of being canned five minutes earlier doesn't blunt my need to be a smartass.

"I hate to ask because I myself am not a fan of publicity stunts, but if the PR folks want to send more media your way..." He holds up his hands defensively. "This isn't coming from me. But I said I'd ask."

"You own the team, Charlie. You can pretty much tell the PR people or whoever you want around here to fuck off."

"True, but I happen to think they have a point." He inhales and nods. "Moving on... As team captain, I'm going to need your help once I have the data and roll out some proposed changes. It's going to look a little radical at first, and I'm telling you this in confidence, for now. I'm suggesting some players move to positions they may not have played in since they were kids, if ever. Tim Cheltenham is a warrior, but he doesn't always make plays up top. Making a few key changes are going to breathe new life into your game out there."

The word *radical* has me a little worried, and so does the idea of asking players to shift positions. Or teams. We play where we play for a reason. "How radical?"

Charlie rubs his hands together and watches the players on the field for a moment. Then he points. "McKenzie. I've run analysis on his last thirty games. He runs more than anyone else on the field in sheer miles and speed, which is unusual for a defender. He's a second late every time he takes off for a run and has to compensate to catch up. It might be showmanship…it might be habit. But it's wasting energy, which means he's getting close to depleting his glycogen stores toward the end of a game. Do you know that the past three losses occurred after a goal scored after the eightieth minute?"

I blink a couple times, digesting his words. This is crazy. From my position at the back, I see the whole field, every player. I know more about what they're doing and why than the coaches sometimes do. I've never thought of McKenzie's Energizer Bunny running as something that could be hurting us, but now that Charlie mentions it, I can see his point.

"Have you looked at every player with this kind of thing in mind?" I can barely form the words because my jaw is hanging open.

Charlie nods. "Every single one. Once you're cleared for more screen time, I'd like to have you watch all the game tape I've compiled of the players, and you'll see what I mean."

I cock my head to the side. These are guys I know well, since we've been playing together for years. "You mean tape of the games since I've been out?" I'll admit I haven't kept up on the last few games. The shitshow was too painful to watch.

My eyes drift to the drill Coach Derry has the team doing now. My quads twitch with the desire to be out there running. I'd even settle for walking. I want a ball in my hands so badly my palms sweat just thinking about how I'm losing muscle memory and hand-eye coordination with every day I sit out.

"No, I'm talking about all of this season and last. Plus some of the European league games because there are a few guys there I may want."

My head snaps from the field to Charlie. Did I hear him right? "Wait, you're saying you've compiled tape on every player in the entire league, plus some from Europe?" That's hundreds of hours of footage he must've gone through, if not thousands. He nods like it's normal for every owner to do that.

It's not.

"I'm a data guy. Most teams hire data managers to do this kind of thing, but it's my wheelhouse, so I tackled it first."

It's then that I realize the team is in the hands of the one person who may be able to analyze us out of our slump. Our problem is not the talent roster we have assembled—we all agree on that. It's the chemistry.

If this guy thinks he knows how to fix us, I'll be the first to line up behind him.

"Absolutely, Charlie. Count me in for watching all the footage you want. I'll back your methods up with the rest of the players, and I really hope you're right."

He exhales a long breath. "I have a pretty good feeling about it. The last time I felt this optimistic was right before I started my company, so it feels right."

The man built a multibillion-dollar company from nothing. Feels right to me too.

olden

Two news vans sit outside the library and the crowd of parents and kids—many of them teenaged boys—winds around the block.

The children's section of the library appears to have made the nation's list of trendiest places to be in the after-school hours. Is there an official list? There should be. I'd boast about it on my social media. Molly should be proud of how much her reading program has grown in a month.

She now holds kids' circles every night of the week. Even though I still only attend on Wednesdays, she's stopped worrying so much about whether the kids like her, mainly because they love her. As she's gradually let go of her guilt and self-blame for her ex's death and her father's shortcomings, she's gotten less fearful of the kids.

On the plus side, I think Molly has the job security she wants. On the negative, having me there has created a monster, and now we need to sit in front of hordes of gawking sports fans and news cameras each week.

For once, I arrive on time, and I find Molly wringing her hands near the go-back pile on a large rolling shelf of books. I know her well enough now to understand she'd rather spend the next half hour re-shelving all the books than read in front of the several dozen kids already sitting on the rainbow rug squares.

In a yellow-striped dress and brown sandals with a wedge heel, Molly looks like a spring day.

She doesn't see me when I slip behind her and rest a hand on her hip. When I lean in and whisper hello, she audibly sighs. It's butter melting on toast.

"Who knew this many people could read?" I deadpan, assessing the crowd which has to have topped three hundred. I'm not especially intimidated about reading or spinning facts in front of this many people, but Molly is near-hysterical.

"Do you remember how I always say children make me nervous?"

"Yes. I think it's adorable."

"Great, because you're about to find me as cute as a baby lizard because this crowd is giving me hives."

I take both her hands in mine and pull them against my chest. Leaning in, I whisper, "I don't know what kind of pets you hang out with, but reptiles don't really do it for me. But I'd be more than happy to take you into the stacks and show you just how fucking adorable I find you right now."

Her eyes drift closed, and I feel her shudder at the closeness of my mouth next to her ear. I give her earlobe a little nip and she lets out a ragged breath. "Oh, that's tempting."

"Might take the edge off your nerves when you're sitting there if you're remembering how I made you come next to an aisle of books. I'd even let you stroke the pages of your favorite memoir while I devour you with my tongue."

With fortitude greater than mine, she pushes herself back

slowly and opens her eyes. A slow smile drifts across her face. "Oh, I will be taking you up on that one. Count on it."

Seems like the mere suggestion is enough to put a little sway in her stride. She waggles her ass as she walks away and tosses me a sultry look over her shoulder. If there's anything hotter than a sassy librarian, it's this sassy librarian who has all kinds of secrets buried beneath her sunny exterior. I love it.

And heaven help me, I think I love her.

HOURS LATER, we've had dinner and shared a bottle of wine, courtesy of the PR department, which compensated for the barrage of press by sending me to the library in a nice town car and having it drive us around all night.

We have at least a half hour drive until we make it back to my house, and two things immediately become clear to me—as much as I've learned about her in the past few weeks, I want to know her better, and she's way too far away from me. I tackle the first issue first.

"What kind of books does a librarian love?"

Her look tells me she thinks I'm kidding. "Right. Good one." The eye roll and smirk don't come with a verbal answer, so I'm confused about why she thinks it's a joke.

"Does that mean you won't answer my question?"

Now she looks confused. "I'm not sure I understand the question."

The fact that we're in a face-off with equally baffled expressions forces a laugh from me. "And I don't understand what's confusing about the question. Just answer it."

"What do I love to read?" she repeats as though making sure she heard me correctly.

I nod.

"Everything."

"Seriously? You love every book you read?"

Nodding soberly, her expressive eyes grow even wider, as though she's puzzling through one of nature's mysteries. "I love something about each one. There's always value. Isn't it amazing I get paid to read? I have the best job on the planet. It should be illegal, but I'm not telling anyone, and if you blab, I won't hesitate to hurt you, soccer star."

I feign fear. "You'd never get away with it. The soccer fans would demand their bounty in books."

She mock-gasps. "No! Not the books." She laughs, but I'm pretty sure a part of her isn't entirely kidding. The town car snakes through the traffic-filled streets, and the way Molly's turned toward me with her back to the door leaves a halo of city lights around her head. She looks angelic, as though saluted by a parade of insistent fairy fireflies demanding I not take my eyes off of her.

I can't.

I wouldn't even if I could.

"Tell me more," I say, reaching for her hand and intertwining our fingers.

"More about books?"

"About anything. Sure, tell me about books. Name one book that changed your life or made you think differently. Can you come up with one on the spot?"

"Ha. I could come up with ten. Or a thousand. Honestly, I could make a case for almost any book I've read because they've all made me think in new ways about something, even if it was small. So they've all changed me in some way." Next to her smile, the bright flickering lights around her look like runners-up.

"You're getting philosophical on me. No such thing as an easy answer to a question where you're concerned, is there?"

"At least not when it comes to books. How about this? Name a book, and if I've read it, I'll tell you how it influenced me."

While I'm thinking of a book that might challenge her

premise, I glance down at our hands on the bench seat between us. I like the way they look linked together.

But something doesn't feel quite right.

Reaching over, I unsnap her seat belt. Her gaze jumps to mine, questioning, but before she can ask what I'm doing, "Come closer." I point to my side and she slides over so I can pull her in with her back against my side.

I buckle the center belt over her lap and keep my arm around her. Wordlessly, she settles against me, and I feel her contented hum—a good, satisfying sound that hits me deep in my chest.

I don't want to let her go, and the feeling surprises me for how unplanned and unexpected it is. Just makes it all the more genuine that my heart pushed its way through my stubborn rules that govern my life.

"Okay. I'm going to say the Stephanie Plum books by Janet Evanovich."

Her jaw drops. "Really? I was expecting you to hit me with some kind of sports reference book or something."

"Now, where's the challenge in that? All sports reference books are life-changing."

"Right. I forgot that kernel of truth. So really, Plum, huh? I like that you're a fan."

Shrugging, I admit, "Years ago, when I stayed with my brother and his then-girlfriend, now-wife, I had some time on my hands and Jane had a whole shelf of her books. They're fun to read."

"They are fun to read." Tipping her chin so she turns to look at me, I assess her expression for whether she's going to take the bait. Her serious demeanor gives nothing away. "Okay, I'll bite. You're talking about the whole series or one book?"

It shouldn't shock me that she's taking my proposal seriously, that she's prepared to explain the great wisdom behind an entertaining series that's one nut shy of a screwball comedy.

"Up to you. Can you do it?"

She nods soberly. "Totally." Her grin twists into a smirk. "Did you doubt me?"

"Mare, I'm learning never to underestimate you. Even though I assume you're more inspired by the Jane Austen ilk, or maybe Hemingway."

"Oh, well, sure. They're on the list, and the list has way more than ten, by the way, but I'm accepting your challenge."

A low chuckle erupts from my chest, and I pull her a little tighter against me. "Okay, tell me how Stephanie Plum changed your life."

"Well, she's a badass, for one thing. Department-store-lingerie-buyer-turned-bounty-hunter? That's a heroine I can get behind. She gets fired from a dead-end job and goes after the big money with a little side of vigilante justice. Stark reminder to never, ever underestimate your capabilities. That's inspiring to me."

"Do you also harbor secret desires to quit your job at the library and bust criminals?" I drag my finger along her cheek and brush a few loose strands of hair behind her ear so I can see her face better.

She bounces her eyebrows. "Never say never, soccer star. If duty calls, I'd like to think I'll rise to the occasion."

"I'm a little afraid to pursue this line of questioning much farther. Which one's your favorite book in the series?"

She looks to the roof of the car, eyes moving back and forth as though the books are displayed there and she's reading passages. "I haven't read them all, but that's easy. Number four."

"Why?"

"Two words, Joe. Morelli. Number four has the epic steamy love scenes. And they have a messy past, and their attraction is on a slow burn for three books. Ah, Morelli."

The way she says his name—twice—makes a red-hot flare of jealousy roil my insides. It's crazy. He's fictional. But I can't help my reaction to her wanting any other man, real or made up.

I shift a little on the seat so I can face her more squarely and watch her until she realizes I'm staring. When her eyes meet mine, I lock on them, daring her to look away. She doesn't and after only a second, her pupils dilate a bit, and her eyes grow cloudy and unfocused. Still, I don't break contact with her gaze.

I slowly caress her cheek with one knuckle until I see her shiver under my touch. Her eyelids drop subconsciously. Leaning in close, I whisper into her ear, "Don't say his goddamn name again."

"Whose name. Morelli's?" Her voice is dreamy, but she winks, taunting me.

"Yes."

"Holden, are you threatened by him? By Joe Morelli?" Her voice is a husky whisper, and she knows she's driving me crazy. Her hand brushes my thigh, and she adds a scrape of her nails.

I graze the skin beneath her ear with my lips and feel her shudder as I breathe one word. "No."

Her back arches against me and I don't withdraw, holding her tight. "Good, because Morelli—"

I don't let her finish. I don't care what else she has to say about a goddamned fictional man. "Say my name, Mare, only mine. And tell me how our epic steamy love scene plays out." My voice is low, almost a growl in her ear. She gasps as I brush my lips across the soft skin of her neck and trail my tongue down toward her collarbone.

"Holden," she pants. I tip her chin so I can lick her jaw, moving slowly and letting my breath linger over her wet skin until I feel her whole body shudder.

I love that I can whip her into a frenzy like this. I love that I have the same effect on her as she does on me. "Tell me, Mare."

Her head leans back on my shoulder, and I trail one hand down the front of her body, slowly, slowly, taking note of each breath, each sigh of appreciation as I go. Waiting for the loss of control. When my hand reaches between her legs, her back arches almost imperceptibly more, and she sucks in a sharp breath. "What's the fantasy, Mare? Tell me about the epic love scene."

It's my possessive, fucking competitive side that won't settle for being outdone by any man, even one she's romanticized in her head. I want to be the only name on her lips.

"Holden," she gasps. "This." She swallows hard, then clears her throat, making sure I hear every word. "This is the love scene."

She turns in my arms and her lips land on mine, kissing me with deep, tender reverence. I push my hands into her hair and cradle her head while one of her hands comes up to cup my jaw. It's an epic kiss fueled by a fictional adversary.

Molly's lips move away from mine, tracing a line from the corner of my mouth and down along my throat.

She pops off the seatbelt again and slides down my body, knees landing on the carpet, doe eyes looking up at me from under a fan of dark lashes. "Just hold onto me, make sure I don't fly out the window." Her voice is soft and husky. So fucking sexy I can barely keep my eyes open, but I don't dare look away. I'm riveted by her blond hair spilling around her face as she watches me watching her.

"Soccer star, Morelli's got nothing on you." Her pink rosebud mouth curves up into a mischievous smile and she digs her teeth into her bottom lip. My dick strains against my suddenly too-tight pants, and I inhale a rough breath.

I don't know what she's planning, but I'm getting a damn good feeling, and I'm sure glad I put up the privacy partition between us and the driver.

"Mare, baby, whatcha doing?" I reach for her face and cup her flushed cheeks in my hands. The most beautiful sight imaginable, my girl on her knees for me.

She grabs both my hands, kisses each palm, and places them on my thighs. "My first time in a chauffeured car. Don't want to waste it."

Untucking my shirt in one rough pull, she drops her lips to my abs, sucking on the skin as her tongue trails downward. I groan and slouch down in the seat.

Her sweet gentle licks set every nerve ending on fire as my fingers dive into her hair and smooth it back from her face.

With steady hands, she unbuckles my belt and yanks the zipper on my jeans. I lift my hips to help ease them down, greedy for more of her mouth everywhere.

Her hands find my aching dick first, gripping it and giving me a few hard pumps. Then, I'm enveloped in the perfect satin and gentle wet lap of her tongue. She takes me in slowly, like she's savoring every inch. Like I'm her favorite dessert.

Always surprising me. Always more to her beneath the surface.

I love how much she seems to be enjoying it, taking me deeper until I nudge up against the back of her throat. Fisting her hair, I start to lose my grip on everything else.

Is there anything else?

Pretty sure this is the entire world right here.

"Mmm, Holden," she hums while she unleashes gorgeous fucking torture with her hands and her tongue up and down my shaft. My hips buck and I lose my goddamn mind in the dark unspooling of hedonistic pleasure that nearly pulls me under.

"Fuck, Mare." I know I lack for more interesting language, but she's reduced me to caveman levels of communication.

She tips her head up to meet my eyes. "You okay?" she asks, more flirtatious than concerned. She knows I'm a hell of a lot better than okay. Her gentle laughter pushes me right to the edge.

"I'm close—" I want to give her warning. Maybe she wants to stop.

"Good." Her mouth draws me in again, and I'm past the point of no return.

Flying. Diving. Maybe dying.

She keeps going, licking and sucking right through my spine-twisting release.

By now, I'm sure the driver can hear me shouting her name on a curse, but I don't give a goddamn flying fuck as long as he doesn't crash the car.

So far, so good. When I'm able to open my eyes again and grasp some semblance of reality, the car is gliding along quietly. Molly sits back on her heels and presses her lips together, her amusement at my torn-apart state abundantly clear.

I tug my pants up and she scoots onto the backseat next to me.

With two dainty fingers, she wipes the corners of her mouth and leans her head against my chest.

Fucking Morelli. I owe him one.

CHAPTER 21

 olden

THE SUN STREAMS in through the high window of the medical facility making everything in the room look especially bright. White countertops on the lab tables that remind me of my high school science classes. White walls with generic-looking photos of islands at sunset. White paper covering an exam table where I perch on pins and needles, awaiting this week's prognosis.

I've done everything correctly. Held myself back from how fast I wanted to walk or run on the treadmill, even though the adrenaline burned my veins so intensely I thought I might combust. Limited how much time I spent looking at my phone and virtually abandoned my computer for the past month.

Of course, spending time with Molly has made the time bearable. More than bearable.

I'd forgotten that I could actually enjoy life if I wasn't playing soccer six days a week and immersing myself in game footage, physical therapy, and teambuilding during all remaining hours.

Fortunately, since we're midseason, there are fewer team-building sessions because we're connecting on the field, and I've been present for all the post-game analysis and strategy sessions. Not to mention time spent watching training days just to convince my brain I'm still a player.

While I wait for the doctor to read through the results from this morning's battery of tests, I realize for the first time that I'm okay not playing soccer every waking minute, which is…unnerving. For a guy who lives in fear of what life looks like on the other side of professional sports, it feels equal parts hopeful and terrifying.

I hope I'm not losing my edge.

"Okay, I'm going to give you the official go-ahead. You're cleared." Doctor Sanchez has his nose buried in my chart when he speaks, so for a second, I'm not sure he's talking to me.

Then the words sink in.

"Wait, for real? I can get back on the pitch?" It's a full two weeks before I expected to be cleared to play, and if I'm honest, I still have lingering headaches. I point to the computer screen of his laptop, which contains calculations from the battery of tests we've just run through. "All the data looks good?"

"Better than good." When he looks up, he must see something he doesn't like in my expression because his forehead creases beneath his shock of thick, black hair that stands up like brush bristles. "Why do you not seem happy about it?"

"Oh, no. I'm thrilled. It's just sooner than I expected, and I still have headaches."

He looks in the chart again. "I don't see a note about headaches. Did you tell the medical assistant when she did your intake earlier?"

I shake my head. "No. I told her nothing had changed. I've had headaches for weeks."

"Okay, let me run a few more tests and get another head CT, just to dot every I and cross every T for the third time."

I feel embarrassed to seem like a whining baby. "You don't need to do that. It's probably nothing—dehydration or something."

He closes the chart and levels me with a dead-eyed stare. "We're getting the scan. You want to go back out and have balls and cleats flying at your head every day, I want to be absolutely sure."

He also doesn't want to be sued. The last thing he needs is to miss something and have me take a lighter hit in a couple weeks that triggers some unnoticed issue and takes me out of the game for good. It's the last thing I need as well, which is why I'm not setting foot on the pitch until I'm doubly sure everything checks out.

It has nothing to do with wanting to spend a little more time with Molly before I'm officially back in training twenty-four-seven.

Nothing at all.

Get your head on straight.

If I'm cleared to play, nothing's taking priority over getting back to the sport that's been my sole purpose all my life.

Maybe I can do that and be in a relationship. I should be able to, right? People do it all the time.

So why am I worried I'm the outlier?

CHAPTER 22

*M*olly

"YOU'D THINK people would get tired of hearing me read," I say, sitting on Holden's couch and leaning against a stack of throw pillows. The crowd this afternoon was standing room only, and most of the kids return week after week, even when Holden isn't there.

We're eating dim sum I picked up in Chinatown on my way over, and Holden set everything up on the coffee table in front of his extra-long couch so we could watch a movie while we eat. Then we couldn't agree on a Bogart noir film or a Depression-era comedy.

"Never. I could listen to you read all day long." Pulling me against his side, Holden stretches his long legs under the coffee table.

"Yes, but you like me."

"No, I love you." He says it so naturally, I just may have imagined it.

My head whipsaws so I can look at him. "What?" I turn my whole body to face him because I'm not sure I heard him right.

His brow furrows and he looks a little uneasy, like maybe he didn't mean to say it. And it's fine if he didn't because—love— that's a big deal and we're new and fragile, and I still thought we were temporary.

Holden swallows hard and his gray-blue eyes soften. "I love you, Mare. I'm fucking crazy about you. I'd be lying if I pretended I'm not."

I feel a surge of emotion that threatens to overwhelm my senses, followed by a confluence of thoughts crowding my brain —I'm happy, I'm touched, it's too soon, I want this, he'll leave, I love him too. "I-I'm happy."

Let's start with that.

He lets out a nervous laugh, but his face is colored with relief. "Okay, well, that's good. Because I..." He seems to lose his train of thought, something that's happened a few times since I've known him. He says it's a side effect of the concussion, but it's been weeks since it happened, so I wonder if it's something else.

"Are you okay?"

He doesn't answer immediately and my concern morphs to worry. "Holden? What just happened?"

Shaking himself out of whatever trance held him a moment before, he gives me a forced smile. "Sorry. Mind drifting."

"Where to?" I run my hand over his chest, feeling the contours of muscle under my fingers.

He stares at the ceiling, his voice hollow when he speaks. "Docs cleared me to play yesterday. All the scans came back normal."

It takes me a few seconds to digest the meaning of his words. He's going back to work. Our fairy tale vacation is coming to an end. But...he loves me?

I focus on his good news. "That's incredible! I'm so happy for you. Weren't you expecting to need another couple weeks of rehab?"

His eyes meet mine. "At least. Frankly, I thought two weeks was optimistic since I was out longer than this the last time I had a concussion."

"Do you feel ready to go back? No lingering issues that you somehow forgot to tell the doctor about?" He's mentioned headaches, lots of headaches. I know I have PTSD after missing the signs that Adam needed medical attention, and I'll be damned if I do it again.

Pulling my chin toward him, he kisses my lips. Gently at first, then deeper. "I know why you're worried, but trust me, if the doctor clears me to play, I'm good to go. And he's telling me I can suit up for practice on Monday."

Monday. Four days from now.

"Wow. So why aren't you jumping for joy? Isn't this what you've been waiting for? Why don't you seem more excited?"

"Because, Mare. I don't want anything about us to change." He looks away, and I get the feeling he has more to say, but he's silent.

"Okay. Does it have to?"

"I hope not."

Reaching for him, I cup his cheek in my hand. "What aren't you saying?"

"The sport has a way of taking over my life. I hope you'll be patient while I try to find a balance."

I believe he wants us to be together—at least for right now—so I don't panic, even though it feels like a warning. "You can't scare me away with that, soccer star. You cracked my heart open and there's no going back. I'll be patient."

Another kiss. And another. Then Holden wraps his arms tightly around me. "Don't worry, Mare. We've got this."

He moves us so he's stretched out on the couch and I'm lying next to him. We're face to face. "Are you free this weekend?" I tangle up my legs with his, but I can still look at his face. Tracing a finger down the strong line of his jaw, I smile at him. "I love that you're making plans to see me again even though you're with me right now."

"You didn't answer my question."

"Such a one-track mind."

"Nah," he says, grabbing my finger in his hand and guiding it to his mouth where he gives it a slow, seductive suck before flipping us over so he's propped on his elbows, hovering above me on the couch. "I'll show you a one-track mind." His lips find mine in a deep, hot, mind-scrambling kiss.

Our mouths meld into one, exploring, tasting, as though it's new territory every single time. I can't get enough. It feels like I'm falling into a deep cavern of desire and I'll never hit bottom.

I feel myself melt beneath him and as my brain turns to mush, I can't remember his question.

I've never been as thoroughly kissed, caressed, and cherished as I am with this man, and I feel like an addict whenever he's not with me. My body craves him and my emotions twist and hang in the wind, wanting him near.

And I'm pretty certain I love him too, though I'm not ready to admit it.

His hand comes to my forehead as he pulls back enough so we can see each other. He brushes the crazy tendrils of hair off my face and splays my hair out on a pillow beneath me. "You look like a goddess." His voice, gruff and deep, sends a chill down my spine as his eyes survey me appreciatively.

I know I can't possibly look good, with my crazytown hair and my swollen just-kissed lips, but I love that he sees me better than I see myself. And I appreciate him for it.

"So. My question. I'll ask once more, but if you don't answer this time, I may get a complex and spend the weekend with Tim."

"You and Tim make an adorable couple, but yes, I'm free, and I'd love to spend time with you. What do you have in mind?"

He bounces his eyebrows in a way that tells me exactly what he has in mind, but I sense there's more, so I wait. "Tim said he'll lend me the boat, and I thought we could take it out toward Stinson Beach for the day."

Biting my lip in anticipation, I nod fervently. "Oh, I've never been there by boat. Can we do that? I'd love it."

He laughs at my enthusiasm. "Yes, we can do that. I'm glad you're into it."

"So into it." He could have told me he wanted to drive to a landfill and watch garbage trucks deliver their loads all weekend long and I'd have said yes. But a few hours on the boat, heading up the coast? Yes, please.

"Great." He rolls off and lays down next to me, so I prop myself on an elbow so I can still see his face. "Mare, the day we met, I told myself not to fall for you. Then I ignored all of it and fucking dove off the cliff."

"You took me with you," I whisper.

It's all I feel ready to tell him, but it's the truth.

olden

My first game back feels like my first time playing for a pro team all over again. The same rush when I hear the lion's roar of fans cheering us on. The same sense of ownership when I dive for my first save and smash the ball away from the goal with my fist.

The crowd goes nuts, chanting my name and rallying in a deafening united cry that surrounds us. Tim Cheltenham catches my eye and shakes his head. We haven't had this kind of fan support in a while, even from the diehards who've been cheering us on through a series of losses. He points a finger at me. "You," he mouths.

My ego isn't big enough to think he's right. I know the fans are happy to have their starting keeper back—what fan wouldn't be? But the mad shouting from the stands is more about the potential of this team with a new owner at the helm and the promise of something good to come.

Okay, and it was a great save. I'm not gonna lie. It feels good to know I'm back, and I've never been happier for the grueling workouts I've endured to get here. I'll work myself to the bone to make more saves like this one for my team.

Charlie has already started implementing some tweaks based on the data he's analyzed and if this game is any indication, his ideas seem to be working. For the first time in over a year, the team is playing as a unit, not a gathering of individuals. It may be imperceptible to the fans, but it's noticeable from my position at the back.

Moving to the top of the box, I hurl the ball to our left back who takes two touches and passes the ball up the pitch. Our team plays well from the back, and part of my job is to see the entire field and direct my players since I have a better vantage point than anyone, even the coach. It's partly why I earned my captain's spot.

As much the game and the crowd support pushes me forward, I'm focused on one particular fan. I know exactly where Molly is since I put her in one of my seats. And I can't help it—I want to impress her.

It's stupid—and potentially deadly—to glance up in her direction during a match, but I do it anyway. I want to believe I can see her face, that smile that sends me over the moon.

I know she didn't give a flying fuck about soccer before we met, but she's started watching game footage with me in the evenings, partly as a way to spend more time together, partly as a way of sharing something that lives deep in my bones.

Our team loses possession on a pass that Weston should have made a second earlier. He's done this twice so far in this game, and now that I understand how Charlie is logging these types of stats, the more I worry for his future on the team. Maybe it's just a timing issue that can be fixed. Maybe it's a pattern he won't be able to break.

I can't think about that now. I need my head one hundred

percent in this game. And yet, I can't stop thinking about Molly and telling myself to remember details so I can share them with her later.

Our team regains possession and takes a shot, but it's from too far out, and it lofts way over the top of the goal. The keeper sends the ball toward me, and I watch the clean passes from player to player as our defenders try and fail to disrupt the play and get the ball back.

It only takes about four seconds for the Red Bulls to advance the ball to the front of the box. All my senses are on high alert the closer the players and the ball gets to me. I'm watching everyone, light on my feet and ready to dive or jump as soon as someone takes a shot.

The ball moves quickly, and the Red Bulls' center mid kicks the ball low to the right side of the goal, and I deflect it with my foot. Easy.

A few seconds later, it comes back at me off a header, and I catch it. The crowd noise ratchets up to a million. This is why I've spent most of my life training. I kick it to midfield and let my teammates take it from there. They're on fire, rushing toward the goal, getting past the Red Bulls' defenders until Weston sees an opening to take a shot.

From where I stand, it looks perfect, his timing right on the money. It soars through the air, slips past the keeper, and hits the back of the net. Goaaal!

If I thought the crowd was raucous when I made my earlier saves, they've gone certifiably insane now. Horns blast and a chorus of cheers erupts from every corner of the stands. I have no idea what they're shouting, but the din carries me to another plane.

I'm back.

Nothing else in the world could ever feel this good. Except that I'm knocked sideways by a second set of emotions.

It's not quite enough.

Now that I've felt the visceral pain of sitting on the sidelines, I can't let chances slip away. If an offer from a Premier League team is a possibility, I want it.

It's a sobering realization in the middle of a game, right after our team looks like it might pull off a win. I can't think about what else it means right now, but I sure as hell will later.

It only takes a second for the errant thought to evaporate. My eyes, heart, and mind are fully locked on this game. And we're so close, everyone can feel it.

A few minutes later, the clock is out on regulation time and we're into three minutes of stoppage time.

The Red Bulls can't make anything of their possessions and soon the ref blows the whistle on a Strikers win.

The stadium explodes, and I stride away from the box to a chorus of fans cheering my name. It feels great.

"That was…oh my God, it was the most exciting game I've ever seen!" Molly flies at me when I leave the pitch and jumps into my arms. I dip my head into her hair and inhale the sweet goodness of her. I haven't showered yet, and I know I smell atrocious, but she's burying her face in my jersey like it's made of roses.

"Isn't it the only game you've ever seen?" I point out.

She kisses me hard, wrapping her hands around the back of my head. "Shut up. I watched lots of footage, and this game was the best! You killed it."

I love hearing those words from her. Objectively, I know I had a great first game back, and sharing the victory with my team always leaves me on a high.

But this is different. It hits me with a wallop how much I care about her opinion. She's infiltrated every part of me, including my game.

Aware of paparazzi snapping photos of us, I shift so her face isn't caught directly on camera. I'm not sure how she'd feel about ending up on ESPN's social media feed. It's enough that there will be questions about my dating life now that it's obvious my self-imposed dry spell is over.

I push the thoughts aside because the win feels too good.

~

"OH. MY. GOD." Molly looks dazed and very pleased. "Not gonna lie, soccer-win sex is a whole other level."

Raising myself up on my forearms above her, I spare a moment to take her in, this complicated, sweet beauty who gives of herself every day to other people, mostly to avoid worrying about herself. She pulls the breath right out of me.

"Why are you looking at me like that?" she asks, licking her lips.

"Because I love you. Like that."

She grins and reaches up to kiss me again. I could leave it at that, bury my face in her neck and work her body to a fever pitch that will make her forget her name. But she deserves more than, and I really should tell her what I'm thinking about the Premier League, but without a concrete offer, there's no sense in rocking the boat. We're too new.

"Mare, I had no idea what I was in for when you stormed out of the library that day, looking to kill me for skirting my parental responsibilities."

She squints, then her expression turns wry. "I'd never kill a person." She tilts her head from side to side, considering. "Well, unless you burned a book."

Nodding, I kiss her softly. "I respect that. And I want you to know you can trust me. I know people have left you behind in your past, but I hope you believe me when I tell you I'm not going anywhere. I'm here for you." As I say the words, I believe they're true. If I move to England, I hope she loves me enough to come with me. Even if she hasn't said the words.

I don't know what I'm expecting. Maybe relief or acknowledgment that she's not going anywhere either. I want to believe she feels the same way.

I don't expect her forehead to crease and her eyes to glisten with tears, which swell until they can no longer be contained and roll down her cheeks before she buries her face in my shoulder.

Turning us to the side, I wrap her in my arms, as the flow of tears turns to quiet sobs. I smooth her hair and give her the outlet she needs, even though I feel guilty for making her cry.

With a sniff, she leans her head away and meets my gaze. Her wet eyes glisten above pink cheeks. I wipe a remaining tear away with the pad of my thumb and rub her back gently.

"I'm sorry. I didn't mean to make you cry."

"You didn't," she whispers, wiping her eyes. A moment later she laughs at the lie. "It was stuck inside me. You just let it out." She exhales, tucking the emotions away.

"You okay?" I want to tread carefully until I know where she is in her head.

Nodding, she reaches for my cheek and cups the side of my face. "Thank you for saying that. I'd never ask that of you, but thank you. I love you. So much."

I've been waiting to hear those words. For a moment, I'm convinced that everything between us can stay this easy. We're both cautious, but we can cross each new line together. It feels powerful to be able to do that with her.

"I know you'd never ask. That's why I said it. I wanted you to know."

"I'm not going anywhere either."

I'm struck by a foreign but welcome feeling, a realization that I can't go backward now. I can't be okay without her in my world. I need to tell her about the Premier League, but it can wait another day. She likes to live in the present.

She loves me.

Everything between us is still so fragile and new and good. I don't want anything to change us.

One more day won't hurt.

CHAPTER 24

*M*olly

OUT OF A TWENTY-FOUR-HOUR FRIDAY, I can pinpoint my happiest twenty minutes.

It's early dismissal day at school, which leaves me an extra hour to get to the library for my shift. Ordinarily, I grab a cup of coffee, eat a healthy snack, and catch up on emails or internet memes the girls have convinced me to check out.

Now, Fridays are different. If I time it right and the traffic lights run in my favor, I have enough time to drive to the Strikers practice field for a quick visit with Holden. And a better than average chance of some kissing. Okay, a whole lot of kissing and maybe lightning-fast quickie up against a wall in the back of the press room. Well, that was last week.

I feel certain I'll keep my clothes on today—at least pretty certain—but a girl needs to be flexible, so I'm not ruling anything out.

When I get to the practice facility, I park in the lot and walk through the small main building which takes me on a shortcut to the field through a side tunnel. The bright afternoon sun blinds me when I return outside so I can't immediately pick out Holden on the field, even though I know roughly where to look.

My eyes adjust and I see the players lined up to take penalty kicks against Holden, and he's told me he loves this ritual when he gets to face down his teammates and try to improve his average number of saves against each of them. The team's winger, Hayden Daley, has the best record of scoring on Holden in these shootouts, so he's the one Holden always wants to beat.

Hiking up the low set of bleachers closest to the goal, I take a seat and watch. My eyes greedily take in Holden's form, arms to the sides, bouncing on his toes. His massive quads flex as he jumps and the muscles of his back ripple as he moves his arms around, trying to distract the kicker.

Donovan Taylor takes his shot, and Holden dives right, body stretched long, arms extended. He easily deflects the high shot with his hands before he lands on the turf. I'll never understand how he can dive to the ground time after time and not end up battered and bruised, but he's well-trained, and each time he hits the ground, he's only there for seconds before he pulls himself to standing and goes back to the center of the goal.

Due to the direction the field faces, afternoons mean the sun blazes across the turf from end to end. It was built that way intentionally, to give the team practice playing in conditions where they're facing into the sun, which happens during most games.

Right now, the sun that blasted me in the face when I walked out of the building is shining directly into Holden's eyes, but he stays focused on Hayden Daley, who steps up to the line and prepares to take his shot.

I know how competitive Holden is, even against his own teammates, so I feel myself holding my breath in anticipation of Hayden's kick. What I don't expect is for Holden to glance furtively to where I'm sitting and shoot me a gorgeous smile. It melts my insides and I grin back at him like a groupie.

At the whistle, Daley takes two steps for momentum and drills the ball to the left side of the goal, which is the side Holden chooses, but the ball sails high and Holden reaches for it but can't get his hand on it. The ball hits the back of the net in a whoosh and Holden hits the ground, sliding near the post.

I can't tell if he connects with the post or not, but something makes a disconcerting thudding sound. It chills me, even though I know it's probably a normal soccer noise. Somehow, being this close and seeing the way Holden goes down evokes a sickening sense of déjà vu.

It looks clumsy, like he lost his footing going for the exact shot he blocked two minutes earlier from Donovan Taylor. I can't help feeling a little guilty that he glanced my way beforehand. I hope I didn't distract him.

A surge of bile hits my throat before I swallow it down, sorting through the reasons behind my reaction. I don't like seeing Holden fall to the ground, sure, but it's his job and I've watched enough game footage now to know how keepers dive. They do it hundreds of times per week, but maybe I'm not used to seeing it so close up because it looks painful; I can't help but worry.

Daley runs back to high-five his teammates, who whoop and holler, but my eyes are still on Holden and the way his body looks limp, but only for a split second. Then he rolls to his knees and sits back on his haunches, dropping his fingertips to the turf while staring into the sun.

He doesn't pop onto his feet the way he normally does. He takes a moment, leaning on his hands and knees as though he's catching his breath. It seems like he got the wind knocked out of him, but it didn't look like that kind of blow.

Two of his teammates stand over him, extending hands to help him up. After a couple more seconds, he sits up and lets them pull him to his feet. The coach watches this all play out but doesn't go to the field, which reassures me. The team medic calls to him, "You good, man?"

Holden waves him off and goes back to his position, but Coach Derry blows his whistle and calls for the team to take their break. It bodes well for me since I only have a half hour at most before I need to leave for the library. But while the other players file off the field, headed for the physical therapy rooms and the sauna, the coach calls Holden over for a quick conference with the team trainers and medic.

There's a lot of nodding and after a minute, the coach claps Holden on the back and sends him on his way. Instead of going through the side door where the rest of the team went, he strides up the bleachers to me.

"Hey!" His bright eyes and smile wipe any evidence of injury from my mind, at least for a second.

"Hey there, soccer star." He wraps his arms around me, and I breathe in the intoxicating mixture of athlete sweat and his pine-scented soap. Sighing in contentment, I marvel at how much I missed him after only a handful of hours since he left my apartment this morning.

"You want to hang out here or should we find somewhere with more privacy?" His eyebrows arch suggestively, and his wicked smile looks delectable. I catch Coach Derry looking up at us on his way into the building and feel self-conscious.

"Do they mind that I'm here? I don't want to be a distraction."

Nuzzling my ear, Holden's words are a growl. "You're the best kind of distraction. Besides, you can't go anywhere when you're not wearing panties."

"I am wearing panties," I whisper.

"You won't be in a minute."

I shudder at the image and my head drifts back, giving Holden access to my neck, where his mouth ignites a firestorm against my skin. His tongue innocently slips along a spot beneath my ear, and I'm reduced to a quivering mess.

"How can a person go from this to cataloguing books?" I sigh.

"She can't. Call in sick and stay here." His wicked smile alone could pillage entire towns.

I laugh. "I don't like to call in sick unless I'm actually sick. Feels like bad karma. Besides, don't you have a few more hours of training?"

His smile dims only slightly. "Yeah, I do. And actually…" His brow furrows, smile dimming a few watts. "I need to get checked out by the trainers before the next session. They're worried about the fall I just took."

The concern must show on my face because he reaches for my cheek and smooths the skin. "Don't worry. It's probably nothing, but after my last go-round, everyone's being extra cautious." He looks like he wants to say more, so I wait. Instead, I see a tiny muscle in his jaw pop as he works to school his expression.

"Are you sure? I saw you hesitate before getting up. I was worried I'd thrown you off. Maybe I shouldn't come out here."

He holds up a hand. "You won't throw me off, Mare. Unless you leave before I get you alone in a room. Then…you'll shoulder all the blame for my blown concentration. I don't think you want to risk the consequence." He waggles an eyebrow and is so damn sexy I'm about to tell him I'll risk pretty much anything where he's concerned.

I do love him. Despite my sturdy walls and warnings, he's broken through them all.

I glance at my phone. We don't have a lot of time. But we have enough. I lean in and whisper, even though no one's around to hear. "Better find that room, then. Your concentration isn't what I want blown."

He swallows and his eyes flame, dark and determined. He kisses me hard, his tongue sliding against mine and knocking the wind right out of my lungs with his white-hot intensity. He pulls away, leaving me breathless. "Do I kiss like an injured man?"

"Hardly. But I can't help worrying about you."

"Then I will fuck those worries right out of your mind." The quiet rasp of his voice lights a torch between my thighs, and I feel my muscles clench.

Before I can react, Holden scoops me up and carries me down the three steps of the bleachers and over to where he knows the locations of *all* the rooms.

CHAPTER 25

olden

CHARLIE LURKS at the fieldhouse after practice, his eyes lasered on me.

"Sanders," he says calmly as I pass. I tip my head in his direction and see an urgency in his eyes that makes me shiver. It's the kind of look that means I'm either fined, censured, or…traded?

"Charlie, what's good?" I fist bump him and take a seat next to him on the bleachers. Looking around, I see no telltale notepads or any other indication he's using his data to make decisions about the future of the players. At least not today.

My heart, still thudding after the cooldown jog Coach just put us through, kicks up a notch. I don't panic, not yet. I've learned enough to listen first, react second. Finally.

His demeanor is so cool, it's impossible to tell what he's thinking until he says it outright. It makes him a good owner and probably a phenomenal poker player, but I'm not here to guess his hand. I want facts.

When Charlie taps a finger against his lips, why does it feel like the grim reaper sharpening his scythe?

"You settle on a winning roster?" I ask.

He continues tapping his lip, and I want to crawl out of my skin for some relief from the heat. "Have you fielded any official offers from the Premier League?" he asks, emotionless. He's blunt, but I appreciate that he doesn't suffer fools. If he has something to say, he says it.

In all the scenarios my paranoid brain was painting, this question didn't enter my mind. "What? No. Why?"

"I've heard from two different coaches in the past week alone. You came back swinging after your injury, and it hasn't gone unnoticed."

The burning streak of pride feels like redemption. But I only let it flare for a few seconds before I bring myself back down to earth. Charlie doesn't have me here to talk about a couple compliments from European coaches. And they're not calling him because they're buddies.

"That's nice to hear."

"You have some options if you're interested."

My pulse speeds up. "You know this for a fact?"

He nods.

I can't settle my heart rate down to anything manageable. Rubbing a hand over the sweat across the back of my neck, I try to run through scenarios I haven't considered in over two years. "Anything specific you want to share?"

Charlie nods. "I've heard from Aston Villa. And Tottenham's a possibility, though they've proven to be fickle in the past, so only you know whether it feels right to start talks with them again. Your agent can advise you better, but I wanted to give you a heads-up since they came to me directly."

"Shit." Now I rub a hand over my two days' worth of stubble. I'm going to run out of nervous habits in another second, and I'm still amped and uncertain how to process all of this.

"I'm going to assume these are opportunities you'll seriously consider. Most players don't get a second chance like this."

"Never thought I would, that's for sure."

I feel like a two-hundred-pound bag of sand sits on my chest. There's no question it's because of Molly and the fact that another week has gone by and I've never breathed a word to her about the possibility of playing in Europe.

Initially, there was no reason to mention what felt like a one percent chance I'd get a new offer to play in the Premier League. Maybe I'd already given up the hope. Maybe I didn't want to shatter the fragile trust she was building in me when the previous men in her life had let her down. Maybe I didn't want to rock the boat with her when things felt so good.

Doesn't matter what my reasons were. My lie of omission is as good as an intentional one. Even if I never dared to believe I'd get another shot at Europe, I hoped for it. I can't deny that I did. It's a pipe dream, but a part of me wants to circle the sun at the slimmest chance of playing on a global stage. It's what I've always wanted.

For the first time in two years, I feel like someone's turned back the clock on all my bad decisions and given me a do-over. No one fucks with a do-over.

I have to tell her.

I'll do it tonight.

Charlie slaps a hand on my thigh and stands. "Listen, you need to do what's best for your career, I know that. Just please do me the courtesy of letting me know as soon as you've decided. As you're aware, I have big plans for this team, and I need a top-rate keeper. If that's not going to be you, it leaves me behind the curve."

"Of course, Charlie. Of course. I can't thank you enough for letting me know about this. Truly. You're one of the best I've ever worked with, and that means a lot. Any decision I make won't be made lightly."

"Good to hear." He extends his hand to shake mine and I exhale all the air I've been holding in my lungs in a whoosh. Then I start thinking about everything he just told me, and I let out the world's loudest holler with a fist pump in the air. It feels great, even if not a soul is there to see it. I've earned this moment, and I'm going to embrace it.

olly

MY PHONE DINGS with another news notification from some gossip site. "I've got to turn the notifications off," I mutter. "I feel like one of Pavlov's dogs."

After pictures of Holden and I started getting plastered all over social media, Preeta helpfully put a hashtag of his name into my phone so I'd get alerts each time something was posted. I meant to delete it and forgot.

"You can put it on silent if you want to scroll through them on your home screen later. At least you won't hear them."

I'm swiping and tapping at my phone to silence the damn thing when I see another alert come through. The mention of Holden's name and the word "trade" catches my eye.

I've gotten used to seeing his name in my feed since he started back up and the team has been on a winning streak. People can't get enough of Holden the Hero, and it only stokes people's interest more that we're dating. I'm tempted to put the phone down without reading it since it's probably breathless gossip ahead of the upcoming game against LA Galaxy.

But something makes me read the headline, and when I do, my stomach drops to my knees. "Sanders in trade talks to Premier League."

"Holden."

"Yeah? You need help silencing it?"

"No, I've got that part." My voice sounds hollow and strange to my ears. "Um, hey, people are saying you're in talks to transfer teams. Just so you know."

The rational part of me knows he'd have told me if he was talking to coaches in Europe about playing for them. He'd have let me know he was thinking of moving to another country. On another continent.

But judging by how the color drains from his face, I start to believe I'm wrong. He looks over my shoulder at the headline and grimaces. "Can I?" He takes the phone from me and scrolls through the whole five-line article. I read it over his shoulder. When he hands the phone back, his jaw is set in a line. I don't like the way it looks.

"What's going on?" My stubborn brain won't let me accept that he's made plans to move to another country without mentioning it to me. He knows I have lingering abandonment issues from my dad.

Holden rubs a hand over his face which looks like he's trying to wipe off his anguished expression. He fails. Walking me over to the couch, Holden folds into the soft cushions next to me and pulls me close against his chest. For the first time in five minutes, I have only a fragile sense that everything will be okay.

I almost manage to let out a full exhale before he says the words, "It's true. Nothing's been decided yet, but...there are offers. My agent confirmed it earlier." I see defeat in his face, and even though I'm upset, I don't want to begrudge him his comeback victory. So I smile. That's how big a masochist I am.

The rock that hit the depths of my gut wells up into a nauseating lump in my throat. I feel like crying, more out of a feeling of betrayal than sadness.

At the same time, I know how important soccer is to Holden. It's his life, regardless of how he feels about me. "Congratulations. That's amazing."

"You don't have to say that." He looks at me and something in my expression must reveal my complicated feelings because he blinks a couple times, as though he's seeing me in a different light.

I don't know what he sees, but internally, I'm a whirlwind of thoughts and feelings, dominated by one that manages to struggle to the surface amid chaos. "I'm not saying it because I have to. I'm saying it because it's right. You should go if you get the chance."

He looks like I've sucker punched him even though the feeling's mutual. "So…just like that, you're ready to ship me off?"

"Isn't that what you want?"

He exhales a long breath. "Wow. I thought we had more between us than a quick send-off at the first mention of an offer."

"That's not what I'm saying."

"Sounded like it."

He's right and I know exactly why I'm pushing him away. It's been lingering in the back of my mind since I saw him take the hit at practice, and all the fears about trusting in the permanence of a person in my life are rising to the surface. I can't fight the shouting chorus of voices telling me to run before I'm left behind again—either because he moves on or gets injured or…worse.

"Maybe it's for the best," I say quietly. "Before either of us gets too comfortable thinking this is permanent." His face falls, and I know it's a hurtful thing to say, but I can't stop, now that I'm starting to verbalize everything that's been eating at me.

"Fuck, Mare. You really know how to throw ice on a moment." He looks more shocked than angry, but it proves to me that our relationship only works on his terms. He thought I was being dramatic when I told him I was dark, but I was talking about a deep lack of faith, and this is how it looks.

I reach for his hand, needing some connection between us so he'll understand that what I'm about to say comes from a place of love, even if it doesn't seem like it. He squeezes back for a second, but then his hand goes limp, even as I continue to grasp it.

"What I mean is that seeing you on the ground today scared the hell out of me. I heard the thud of bones against turf and saw a moment of hesitation before you got up, and even if I couldn't verbalize it or even admit it to myself at the time, it brought back memories of Adam."

His expression softens and I see he understands. "Mare, nothing's going to happen to me. I won't let it. I'm really careful. That's why the trainers checked me out. No one is going to let me get hurt. I'm not going to leave you like he did."

"But you are." I hold up my phone as proof. "Tell me I'm misunderstanding here." It doesn't matter if it's from a physical ailment or a career decision or the temptation of another woman. He'll leave. Unless I leave first and retain a shred of the self-preservation that keeps me going.

He inhales a deep breath, but instead of denying what I've said, he exhales and shakes his head. "You're not."

My vision clouds but it takes me a minute to realize it's because of my tears. I feel more betrayed than sad. I also feel stupid.

What kind of naïve woman doesn't see the obvious? Holden is a soccer player. He told me that when we met. He told me that's why he doesn't date. So what if he loves me? He loves soccer more. It's his life.

"How long have you known it was a possibility?"

"It's not even an official offer yet. I—"

"How long?"

"I started hearing rumblings of interest a couple months ago." His voice is a dry pile of tinder.

I nod. "So, before you told me that you weren't going anywhere. You didn't have to say it, you know. You didn't have to make me believe you."

You can do this. You're a badass librarian-turned-bounty-hunter.

I turn to face him, still wrapped in his arms. "Holden, this isn't going to work."

He looks shocked, eyes wide with deep furrows in his brow. "You won't even consider that maybe it could?"

It's hard to swallow and I don't want to lose my composure. "No."

"What the fuck, Mare? What are you saying?"

"I'm saying you had me believing in love. You had me even believing in forever. That scared the hell out of me, but I was willing to see it through because that's how much I love you. But you're not even planning to stick around."

"I know that's how it looks, but I didn't want to say anything until I knew for sure."

"That's not how it's supposed to work when you're in it for real. You say something."

"I could say the same to you. If you were in this with me, you'd stay at the table and talk about it. Instead, you're shutting down and bolting the second things get complicated. You're so afraid of being left behind, you're not even giving me a chance to stay." His eyes are pleading, but I steel myself against the rush of feelings.

"That's not fair. I'm not the one who said he wasn't going anywhere."

"I fucked up. I admit that. But there has to be more to us than that."

My heart is begging me to abandon my cautious instincts and

sign on for whatever unknown he's offering. "I don't think there is."

I love him so much, but my heart can't have the reins right now. My brain needs to be the cool dictator over everything, and it's telling me to walk away.

I have to listen.

olden

IF IT'S POSSIBLE, I'm playing better now than before I got knocked in the head. And I'm doing it despite my utter agony over the way things ended with Molly. I've been a miserable wreck of a human, ready to bite the head off the next sorry son of a bitch who wants to congratulate me on my Premier League prospects.

Life is stupid that way.

After a brutal three hours of training, I stand in the locker room bathed in sweat. The clang of lockers slamming shut and the din of voices feels like a salve to my jangled nerves. I'm trying my damnedest to shut out the image of Molly's face when she walked away or the giant hole in my heart that has me training even harder to exhaust my brain. It isn't working.

For now, I focus on the banter between my teammates. Danny Weston is giving our backup keeper shit about the PK shootout we had at the end of practice. "Dude, you let your emotions get the better of you. Me and my evil eye strike fear in the hearts of keepers nationwide, but I didn't expect it from you."

Caleb swats him with a towel. "Bullshit, Weston. You don't scare anyone with your pansy-ass stare. You just happened to kick right, and I chose left."

Weston shakes his head. "Naw, it was the stare. Gets 'em every time."

"Yeah, then how come it didn't get me?" I pipe in. Not going to lie, it felt good to see that my penalty kick average hasn't dropped at all. I know the players on our team, though, so I anticipate what they do more often than not.

"Lucky, you chose the right side."

After we clean up and head upstairs for some food, I pack my gear and leave out the back entrance to the facility, close to where I parked my truck.

The last person I'm expecting to see is Shyla leaning against it, but there she is wearing a skin-tight black dress that has no business anywhere but at a cocktail party. But she has it paired with spike-heeled ankle booties and a lot of funky tangled necklaces that probably cost a fortune but look like they came from a yard sale.

Her long, blond hair hangs straight down her back under a brown bucket hat with a wide blue stripe. Her lips are pink and puffy and covered with lip gloss.

Looking at her now, I can still recall how flattered I felt when she picked me out of a crowd of thousands at an event for the team. She'd headlined the entertainment at the stadium, and every guy on the team was dying to get close to her at the after-party. She worked the room with a majesty that dazzled me at the time, along with everyone else in the place.

When her gaze landed on me and she slipped between the bodies in the room to talk to me, I felt like a king. She knew just how to pin her stare on me so I felt like a million bucks, the hottest thing on or off the pitch.

Only now, she's leveling me with the same stare, and I feel so many other, far worse things. The humiliation stands front and center in my mind, even after more than two years. But seeing her in person, my anger fades to disinterest. Exhaustion.

Problem is she's blocking the door to my truck. "I need to go. Do you mind?" I ask, not interested in pleasantries. I don't owe her anything. Forgetting the fact that she cheated, she never apologized for the lies she told about why we ended.

She has the nerve to look aghast. "What kind of a hello is that?"

"The kind that means goodbye. I need to get out of here, and you're blocking my door." I'd like her to move of her own volition, but she seems rooted to the spot. I'm not above lifting her off her feet and placing her down a couple yards away, but I don't even want to touch her. And for all I know, some fuck face paperazzo is lurking around here somewhere just waiting to get photos of the two of us together.

Hell, it's even possible Shyla told him to come.

Folding her arms across her chest, Shyla succeeds at pushing up her cleavage so it spills out of the top of her dress. She smiles in a way that used to do something for me—a seductive look that says she and I are the only ones who really understand how it is between us. It used to drive me wild. Now, nothing. "When did you become so rude?" she asks, blinking her long lashes.

"Shyla, we've got nothing to say to each other. I'm just acknowledging it. You should too." I don't want to get into it with her. Two years is a lot of water under the bridge, and I'm over it. "Listen, I hope you're well, but I really need to go."

She pouts. "What if I have something to say?"

I roll my eyes. She's a drama queen if I ever met one. She's also not going to budge until she says her piece, so in the interest of leaving, I indulge her. "Okay, I'm listening."

I see regret on her face. I see someone who just wants people to like her, and it makes me sad. And relieved that she did me a favor by bailing out when she did. It may have messed with me at first, but my life is so much better for it.

Or at least it was.

She doesn't move from in front of my door, and it's starting to annoy me. Putting my hands on my hips, I keep a good four feet of distance between us. No chance this looks romantic in the slightest. My angry stare challenges her to move out of the way or explain why she won't.

She watches me, her eyes roaming over my frame until she's ready to speak. "I saw you're dating again."

And there it is. "Right. So I'm with someone else and now you're interested in me?" It's such a cliché, and I want no part of it.

"No, that's not what this is. I'm here because I know how it was with us back when you were waiting on offers from the Premier League and you had one foot out the door. The sport came first. I could see that even if you never said it."

"Shyla, what difference—?"

She cuts me off with a raised hand. "You're in the same boat now? I read about the new offers to play abroad. Same thing all over, and you're gonna fuck it up again. Just like with us."

I'm not sure I'm hearing her right. "What are you saying…that it's my fault you cheated?"

"No. I mean, not entirely."

"Not entirely? Not at all!" I feel done with the conversation. No way I'm standing here and listening to how I'm to blame for her infidelity. I start for my door handle. Now, I will push her out of the way if I need to. I've heard enough.

"Holden, stop. I know I was wrong, and that's on me, my timing—I didn't do things in the right order. And I'm sorry for that. But Holden, we were over long before I even met Peej." Hearing his name still makes me want to bash my hand through the window of my truck, but I try to hear what she's telling me through the angry din in my brain.

Why is she dredging all this up after two years? She says nothing, and I throw my hands up and make a go again for my truck. I don't need a lecture today.

"Wait, will you listen?" She puts her hand on mine, but I pull away. "Holden, I'm just saying we were never going to work out. Let's be honest."

Her eyes plead with me to hear her words at face value, so I summon some strain of zen calm I didn't know I had to slow my heart rate and listen. "You'd have left me either way," she says quietly. "Tell me I'm wrong."

But I can't. I know she's right. She's right, and I never had the guts back then to say it to her face.

She nods. I return the gesture. "You're not wrong."

"All I'm saying is if it's good this time, do better. Be a better guy." Her words ring in my ears, the same thing Molly said to me outside the library. I heard the words, but I didn't heed them.

I nod, suddenly choked up by the way she's laid it all out when my stunted neanderthal brain couldn't do it. "Okay."

She smiles and adjusts her hat. She's always loved being right. "Okay, then. If you love this girl, don't fuck it up. I've said my piece. Don't let her think you love this game more than her."

I don't bother telling her she's too late, that I already fucked it up beyond belief. She doesn't need to know.

I'm still in shock that she came down here and waited for me in order to…try to help me? I've been harboring a hatred for her all this time because it was easier than looking at myself in the mirror and taking ownership of my part in a relationship that wasn't strong enough to withstand Peej Tinselman.

When I think about it that way, hell, it wasn't very strong to begin with.

In two years, it never occurred to me that I owed her an apology, but I'm not too proud to do the right things now. "I'm sorry I didn't make you feel like you were important enough to belong in my future."

Her eyes soften. She blinks a couple times, but that's the closest she'll get to emotion when she's not on stage. Or maybe that's not even true. Maybe I never looked far enough beyond the surface to really know her. "I think I thought... The thing with Peej was supposed to be a wakeup call. I figured maybe you'd get your priorities straight if you thought you were gonna lose me to someone else. But you just...gave up."

She's right. I did. Didn't want it as much as I thought, even if it took her antics to show me.

"Truly, I'm sorry for my part in it," I say again. Shyla nods.

"I swear I didn't come here to make you feel guilty. But I couldn't watch history repeat itself either."

Turning to go, Shyla adjusts her bucket hat again, pulling it down a little more so it partly shields her eyes.

"Thank you," I grind out.

"You're welcome. Take care, okay?"

She opens her arms for a hug, so I relent. It's a short, friendly hug, and her hand comes to pat my cheek. "You're a good guy, Holden. Don't believe everyone who says you're an asshole." It's almost funny coming from her.

Leaning over, I give her a quick kiss on the cheek, and she steps aside enough for me to open the door to my truck. As I fire up the engine and drive away, I watch her in the rearview as she walks back to her car.

I really haven't had a fucking clue. About anything.

olly

I SHOULDN'T BE BOTHERED by the photos. I'm the one who pushed Holden away and told him to live his best life. I guess I just didn't expect that his best life would include his ex-girlfriend who broke his heart and wrote about it in an album's worth of songs.

The pictures of Holden and Shyla are everywhere. I keep telling myself not to look—and I forced Preeta to turn off my notifications entirely because the constant one-liners on my home screen are relentless—but I'm human, and I still love him despite myself.

From what I can see, it's versions of the same photo posted over and over again—Holden kissing Shyla on the cheek, Holden and Shyla in an embrace, Shyla touching Holden on the cheek— and they're all in the parking lot of the Strikers' facility, most likely on the same day because their clothes are the same.

I'm social media savvy enough to know that the breathless headlines and speculation that they're getting back together don't translate to fact. But what does it matter, anyway? He's free to date Shyla or anyone else. He'll probably have an exotic European girlfriend inside of a month once he moves, now that I've helped him get over his fear of relationships.

It all just shows me I made the right decision in protecting my heart.

"You've made the wrong decision, love." Preeta leans on my desk, her long fingertips tapping together as her pink-painted lips form a scowl.

Rolling my eyes, I pretend I have loads of organizing to do on my desk. As I move one pile of books from the right side to the left, I remind myself of Seth. Maybe all his absentminded organizing is his way of masking avoidance. I'll have to talk to him about that.

Meantime, Preeta's searing gaze bears down on me and demands an answer. I've avoided talking to her about our breakup, but she knows about it. For the past two weeks, she's seen me at work with bags under my eyes, no makeup, and the baggiest sweaters I own, along with my I've-given-up pants.

She's a good enough friend to have left me alone to sulk on my own at first, proving to me she knows me better than most people. But now, apparently, she thinks it's time for a conversation. Or an intervention.

I can't say I blame her. I probably resemble something near death. It's how I feel.

"How can you say it's the wrong decision when you can see how happy I am?" I answer, feigning a smile.

She reaches over and flicks her fingers on my forehead. "Dimwit."

"Ow."

"Oh, stop. I could do so much worse. Come with me." She beckons me out of my seat with a tilt of her head, but I don't budge.

"Where?"

"The lunchroom. My treat."

"Ugh. I have no appetite, and besides, I have loads to do. There are books to sort, recommendations to make, readers to inspire." I gesture lamely to the three girls working quietly in study carrels as though they're apes climbing the zoo walls.

"Jesus, only you could still be shoveling brown sugar during a crisis. And you're in a crisis, Mary Poppins."

At the mention of Holden's nickname for me, I feel a pang of sadness tear at the carefully constructed wall around my heart. I don't want to feel it. I don't want to feel anything, but my resistance is flagging. "Who'll keep order around here?" My protest lacks conviction. Even I can hear it in my voice. Preeta pounces.

"Your intern." She points to the student behind me who earns community service credit for sitting there, doing homework, and shelving the occasional book. She has a point. "Come." Done beckoning, she loops her hand under my armpit and yanks me up.

I'd protest, but staring at books all day only makes me depressed that I'm not a character in one of them. I need an author to write me an alternate ending to my depressing life.

"Fine." I follow her out of the library, noticing that the hems of my wide-leg blue pants are dragging on the ground. Every couple of feet, I step on my pants and almost trip. Preeta keeps her arm looped around mine and holds me up without judgement. For a minute, at least.

"How many pounds have you lost? Your clothes are swimming on you."

I shrug. "I haven't stepped on a scale."

"Have you eaten anything in the past two weeks?" She shoots me a sideways glance, but I keep my eyes fixed on the ground, which pitches and rolls beneath my feet. Preeta probably has a point, I concede. I can't remember when I last ate a meal, unless Oreos count.

We pass groups of students chatting and eating at outdoor

tables on the terrace next to the lunchroom, which is a converted classroom where a catering company sells premade hot food and boxed salads, along with fruit and chips. It's a low-frills operation, but it suits the four hundred high schoolers who need sustenance throughout the day.

Preeta keeps her grip on my arm, working us through the roped-off line until we get to the front. "Two chicken Caesar salads, two Diet Cokes, and a bag of brownie bites." I start rifling through my pockets until her glare sets me straight. Not going to mess with a headstrong math genius when she's on a mission.

"Thank you," I mumble, looking around the small space for an empty table. Preeta piles the food and Diet Cokes into a canvas tote bag I didn't notice she was carrying and pilots us out the door and around the corner toward the patio of the teachers' lounge. As we walk, my eyes drift to the soccer field, and I let out an audible whimper. Preeta follows my gaze. "Sorry, I should have taken us the other way."

"No, I can't spend my life avoiding things that remind me of him. I'll get there. Eventually."

"Yeah, we're going to talk about that, don't you worry."

The patio is crammed with faculty members, but we find two empty chairs and drag them to a corner, next to a potted Ficus tree, and sit with our salad boxes in our laps. Having food in front of me does nothing to stoke my appetite. I stare at the box, lost.

"Eat," Preeta instructs, brushing her long hair over both shoulders and watching me instead of opening her own plastic container. When I don't make a move, she takes the salad from me, opens it, pours on the dressing, and stirs the contents with a fork.

She hands it back. "Seriously, love, if you don't start eating, I'm going to get rather mean."

"This isn't you being mean?"

She cocks an eyebrow. "You have no idea. So you'd better eat some salad and tell me why you're being so bloody stubborn about wanting to stay miserable."

I start to protest her characterization, but she puts a hand up and points to the salad. I grudgingly stab a fork at some lettuce and a piece of chicken and shove the bite into my mouth. The chicken tastes like Styrofoam, but at least the dressing gives the lettuce some flavor.

Under Preeta's watchful stare, I take one more bite, chewing slowly because my jaw seems to have forgotten how to work on anything that isn't round and made of sugar and lard. I sip the Diet Coke from the can, liking how the bubbles burn my throat—a welcome pain that comes from someplace other than missing Holden.

"Good girl. There's more color in your face already."

"Feel better, do-gooder? You're worse than my mom."

She wags a finger. "I'm better than your mom. I don't see her here feeding you."

"That's because I haven't told her," I sheepishly admit, anticipating the daggers Preeta's eyes shoot my way next. I know I'm stubborn and needlessly self-reliant, but I've being doing it for so long, I don't know any other way.

We eat in silence, which allows me to relax and stop bracing for an interrogation. Maybe she'll just feed me and send me back to the library. After a few more bites, I concede that Preeta was right to drag me out of the hovel where I've spent the past two weeks trying to lose myself in publisher catalogues. Anything to keep myself too busy to think.

It's also mid-semester, so most of the students have term papers to write, which means research. They've been coming to me for source materials because their teachers only let them cite Wikipedia one time as a reference and the rest of their data needs to come from books.

For some students, it's the first time to figure out what the library is for, other than a gathering place when it's too rainy or cold outside to sit on the terrace. Normally, I relish this time of year because a few students inevitably fall in love with a new area of literature.

Not now. Not when I feel like I'm missing a limb since Holden and I broke up. I don't see an end in sight for my misery.

"Okay," Preeta says, ditching her lettuce in a nearby trash can. "Let's get you sorted."

I throw an arm over my eyes, dreading this part. "I'm good, I'm fine. I'm happy."

She barks a laugh. "No, not when you aren't letting anyone talk sense into you. I volunteer as tribute."

I can't help smiling. Preeta knows I'm almost as big a sucker for *The Hunger Games* as I am for *Pride and Prejudice*. I secretly believe Elizabeth Bennet and Katniss Everdeen are literary twins, separated at birth, but that's a discussion for another time. A long discussion.

"Fine. Sort away." I lay my hands on my lap and look her in the eye for the first time, a shred of my stubbornness blunted by the fact that she cares enough to be here for me. Even if it means she'll make me talk about uncomfortable things. "Can we at least dig into the brownie bites?"

"Once I'm satisfied with you."

"Wow, tough crowd."

Her pink lips twist into a smile and her long lashes flutter. "You better bloody well believe it."

I look around the patio, amazed at how many teachers leave their offices to eat lunch together. It makes me realize how anti-social I am, sitting at my desk most days during lunch. My excuse is always that someone needs to be there for the students, but there's always an intern backing me up. The only one to blame is me.

When my eyes land back on my friend again, I see only concern. "You look awful."

"Thanks," I deadpan.

"Why'd you let him go? You two seemed perfect for each other, but more than that, I could see the love between you. That wasn't temporary infatuation."

"You only saw him once," I protest. Holden had convinced me to take a personal day and skip my afternoon library shift. I relented as long as it didn't mean lying about being sick, so he came to the high school to pick me up. Fortunately, most of the students had left for the day so it didn't cause a sports fangirl meltdown, but Preeta was around so I introduced them. "For like ten minutes."

"Exactly. It was obvious to me in ten minutes. That man adored you, and you seemed…really happy, Molls."

After two weeks of wallowing, I can't say why that particular combination of words drives me over the edge, but I feel all the air leave my lungs. When I finally inhale, it comes in the form of a sob, followed by a cascade of tears.

Preeta doesn't hesitate. She pulls me in and pats my hair and rubs my back and does all the things I didn't know I needed until she forced a salad on me and proved to be a good friend. "I was happy. I-I don't know what I'm doing," I admit when I can finally take a breath without breaking down.

She continues rubbing circles on my back and nodding, but most of her efforts seem to involve positioning the tree in such a way that none of the other teachers seem to notice me weeping in their midst.

"I also don't know why it feels so good to cry, but it does," I admit.

"Because you never let yourself have an emotion that isn't whitewashed with happy dust. I love you for your bloody cheer and your infernal optimism, but there has to be a limit, even for you."

I want to be mad at her for belittling my cheerfulness, but I know she's right. Partly because Holden told me the same thing, though the grumpy soccer star was nicer about it.

The tears keep rolling down my cheeks and after a while, I stop wiping them. Preeta doesn't push me to talk, which I appreciate. I notice she's busying herself dividing her hair into sections and starting a French braid. But once I've finished blubbering into my lap, I look up at my friend and blink away the tears blurring my vision.

She hands me a napkin, and I wipe my drippy nose and pull myself together a tiny bit. The cascade of tears and wracking sobs seem to have exhausted my emotional well, so I start telling Preeta things in no particular order, filling her in on how bad it felt to think about him leaving.

"I think I pushed him away to protect myself. Like if I did it first it would somehow feel better."

She nods, flipping the braid over her shoulder. "Did it, then?" she asks, as if she doesn't know the answer.

"Nope. It felt awful. I wasn't doing it as a ploy to get him to stay here. It wasn't some kind of test."

"I know, love. And I'm betting he knows too. But you didn't even give him a chance. Maybe he wanted to find a way to make things work before you shoved him off."

I swallow hard, recalling how shocked and hurt he looked when I told him to take the job if it was offered to him. "It was the right thing to do. Soccer is his whole world. He's been working to get to the European league since he could dribble a ball and he may get that chance. And then he'll go."

"Proving that everyone you care about leaves you. I know it's happened in the past, but you can't let it define you."

I shake my head. She's wrong. Why can't she see that? "That's not it. Him getting that offer was a wakeup call. We were only a temporary thing while he was laid up with a concussion."

"You really believe that in your heart?"

I nod because I'm almost too choked up again to form words. Then I blurt, "I don't belong in a relationship."

Preeta takes the bag of brownie bites from her canvas tote and holds them in front of me like a peace offering. I see it as her concession to my logic. But when I reach for it to take one of the gooey chocolaty squares, she whips the bag away. "Are you kidding me? No! Not when you're acting like an arse."

"I'm pretty sure you're the *arse*. I need a sugar fix."

"Don't test me, love. You have no idea what I'm willing to do to get you to see the truth."

"Which is what?" I shout so loudly that a few teachers look our way. Preeta waves at them and moves the plant a little more squarely in front of me.

"That man loves you, full stop. Maybe soccer was his world, but I'm telling you this one more time, and I hope it sinks in," she says, tapping against my temple. "What I saw between you for ten minutes was the kind of love you read about in your embarrassing books—not the trashy ones, the classics. The swoony ones. If I'm lucky enough to have what I saw between you for even a heartbeat, I'll consider myself one of the greatest love stories ever. So if you don't make something of what you have with that man, I don't know what to say to you other than… you're a twat, undeserving of great love."

With that, she opens the bag of brownies and stuffs two in her mouth.

It's the final punctuation on her benediction, and as much as I fear that I really am a twat, undeserving of great love, I kind of hope we're both wrong.

CHAPTER 29

$\mathcal{H}$olden

"I THINK THAT WENT WELL, don't you?" my agent, Ken Johnston, says in his clipped all-business voice that he sometimes forgets to turn off when it's just the two of us. We've just left the Aston Villa office suite where a very generous offer was all but handed to me on the spot.

"They said they'll be in touch," I remind him, well-trained never to get excited about a win of any kind until the ref blows the final whistle—or the papers are signed, in this case.

Ken loosens his tie and waves a hand. "Just a formality. It's the twenty-four-hour cooling-off period. They'll make an official offer tomorrow."

My tie feels like a noose around my neck. I loosen it, but until I can get out of my suit, I'll be uncomfortable and irritable.

Yeah, that's the problem—the suit.

I'm ready to go home, and we still have the second half of our trip—ostensibly, the more important half, where I earn some redemption from Tottenham after they pulled my offer two years ago.

I can barely gather enough enthusiasm for it. It's probably the jet lag and the relentless schedule I've been keeping up the past few weeks.

Now, I'm starting to see things a little more clearly. Maybe because I've been walking around for two days like earning a spot in the English Premier League is the next best thing to a death sentence.

Ken has kept me busy since we landed, so I haven't had much time to think about why I've been in a crappy mood from the moment we left California. I was so damn exhausted from working myself to the bone in double practice sessions that I passed out on the plane and woke up across the pond with a strange sensation that felt like homesickness.

"Let's hit the pub, catch a game." Ken pivots us down a smaller street to Old Contemptibles Livery Street Pub near our hotel in Birmingham. "I'm superstitious about celebrating too soon, so let's just call this me buying you a pint because we're in England."

"Good enough for me," I say, dropping onto the red leather banquette under a row of framed portraits, while Ken goes to the bar for our beer. I figure I have about three minutes to get my head in order before he comes back and asks what's wrong with me.

I know I was quiet in the meet with the team brass, but he'll chalk that up to nerves.

If I'm quiet here, he'll ask why, and I don't have a good answer for him.

Tell him you're worried this trip was a mistake.

I work to silence the voice in my head because it's unproductive to think that way, for one thing, and because it can't be a mistake to see through a dream I've had my entire life. But if I'm honest, I think coming here may have been the wrong decision.

The Strikers have a bye week, so the timing was perfect to fly to Europe to meet with the two teams that expressed interest in signing me. My agent insisted I do everything by the book, in person, and as soon as possible.

Not going to lie, it feels good to be appreciated for the work I've put in for the past eleven years. And who am I kidding? I've been working hard at soccer a hell of a lot longer than that. It's all I've wanted since my dad handed me a ball and prayed it would keep me occupied for five minutes or more.

It's kept me more than occupied for twenty-five years. And I'm a certifiable idiot for not feeling thrilled to be here. It's everything I've ever wanted and after today, I feel this close to achieving it all. To be here after thinking it would never happen two years earlier is the kind of fairy tale I can get behind.

That thought immediately makes me think about Molly, which I've been trying my damnedest not to do. For the most part, I've succeeded because I stayed focused on training, watching footage of the teams hosting me here, and making sure I pulled together all the cat supplies needed so Kathryn could take care of Greta while I'm gone.

And who am I kidding? Jane is doing all the work, so I really need to bring her back something nice.

I work hard to focus on souvenir ideas so my brain doesn't go south and start thinking about Molly and ruin the rest of the night. Not when Ken is walking back over with two full pints and a bowl of crisps. The last thing he wants to hear is that I have cold feet.

And I don't. I want this.

But I miss Molly, and I know it's not fair to try to woo her back when I can't give her what she needs—a promise that I'll put her before soccer. It would be disingenuous of me to try. Despite Shyla's wakeup call, I can't make promises about anything until I finish all the meetings on this trip and find some time to sort my thoughts.

"Cheers, mate," Ken says in a cockney accent that's not half bad, dropping a pint glass on a coaster in front of me. He clinks my glass with his and sips the foam off his dark beer. "Been a good trip so far, yeah?"

"It has. Thanks for pulling it off on such short notice."

"We have people in the office who do the heavy lifting. I just showed up at the airport, same as you."

"Well, even so, thanks."

His normally tidy, gelled hair is a mess, so he must have shoved his hands in it a few times while he waited for the bartender to pour our beer. With his tie now off and the top button of his shirt undone, he looks like any other local forced to wear a suit during the day and eager to shed the stiffness once meetings are done.

He somehow still looks clean-shaven at the end of a day, whereas the rough sandpaper on my jaw probably makes me look as dead fucking tired as I feel.

I've stripped off my jacket and tie as well, and with my sleeves rolled to my forearms, I almost look casual. I'd really like a soccer ball at my feet, but I'll satisfy my urges by watching the Chelsea-Arsenal game on one of the multiple TVs. My pulse kicks up a notch just seeing the green of the pitch and observing how the players move the ball. No question, playing here is a level up.

Ken reclines in his high-backed chair facing me, tipping it onto two legs and resting his knees against the underside of the table. The creases I thought he had permanently etched into his forehead have disappeared now that he's no longer sitting next to me in a meeting wearing his game face. My stats and reputation only take me so far. He's good at his job, negotiating terms and giving the team owners a subtle hard sell on why they need me.

Now that he's off the clock, however, I see a less intense side of him that appears somehow heartening in a guy who always seems glued to his job.

If I saw glimmers of the less intense side of myself with Molly, it's long gone now, the workhorse returning by default. I don't mind—it's the devil I know, and it's gotten me pretty far in life. It's gotten me here.

"Don't tell my quarterbacks and first basemen, but your sport is my favorite," Ken says, not taking his eyes off the screen.

"Your secret's safe with me." I start to relax with the hypnotic movement of the ball between players.

"When you watch a match like this, does it get you amped up, stress you out? Or can you watch it like any other fan? I always ask my clients that."

He's turned his chair sideways so he can see the TV screen, which means I only glimpse the side of his face as he talks. When I don't answer right away, he turns. "You still with me?"

"Yeah, sorry. I was thinking about your question. No one's ever asked me that before."

"That mean you don't have an answer?" He turns back toward the TV.

Rubbing the back of my neck, I try to come up with an answer that sounds halfway reasonable. "Mostly, I'm pumped like any fan of the sport, but I probably analyze the play a bit more. Not stressed, unless it's my team and we're behind and I'm on the bench," I answer ruefully.

"Yeah, say no more. It stressed me out seeing you on the bench as well, not gonna lie." Nothing else needs to be said about that. We both get wrapped up watching the match, where the score stands at nil-nil with ten minutes left of regular play. Even though neither team is from around here, every pair of eyes in the place is focused on the game. It's the beauty of the sport in England, and the blood pumps hot in my veins at the idea of being a part of it.

Ken pumps his fist when the Chelsea striker goes up for a header, but the shot hits the post and bounces back to a midfielder who takes a clean shot, but not before he's fouled in the process. The crowd in the pub lets out an audible groan, with a few people yelling expletives. Ken gets to his feet, craning his head to see the replay.

"Not a foul, if you ask me. It was all ball." A vein in his temple throbs, and he's no less invested in the game than the locals who live and breathe the sport.

"You ever think about repping only soccer players? You could carve out a niche over here," I ask Ken, wondering if he'll continue to rep me or pass me off to someone local if I make the move. Some agents have clients overseas, but his are all based in the States.

"Oh, don't even tempt me. Like I said, it's my favorite sport. Ah, it'd be great to have a roster of only footballers." He purses his lips and tips his head to the side. "In another life, maybe." His eyes don't leave the game, but he blows out a breath.

"Why not this life?" I don't know what I'm asking him. Am I looking for a pal to move here with me and hold my hand? Not really. Maybe I'm just making conversation. My brain has been so scrambled since I got on the plane; I don't know which end is up.

"Got everything I want back at home. Love my wife—seriously love her, and not just because she puts up with my bullshit. Though that certainly helps." He laughs. "We make a good team, shuttling the kids around, working at jobs we like. It's all good, man. Nothing's going to tempt me to leave it."

In the four years Ken's been my agent, we've never talked about his personal life, maybe because I've never spent a week with him. Or maybe because I never asked. I guess I'm that big of an asshole because I didn't even know he had more than one kid.

"Good on you, you've got it all working for a nice smooth ride," I tell him, hoping the sentiment doesn't sound as lame to him as it does to my ears once I've said it.

"You've got the work part right, anyway."

"Meaning?"

"I dunno. Who really ever has a smooth ride? There are bumps for sure, but I wouldn't want it with anyone else." He huffs a laugh and drains his pint. "Not gonna lie, it takes a hell of a lot of work. You want another one?"

"Yeah, in a sec." I tip my glass back and finish the rest. Looking around the pub, one of so many in what could be my new home, I think about how it would be to live in England. I've never given it much thought over the past two years because it felt like a pipe dream, but now that I can almost touch it, I need to get straight in my head.

Something's preventing me from going all in. I want to think it's nerves, but I can only live in denial for so long. It's Molly.

I fucking miss her, and being this far away only drives home how much. I never imagined I could want a woman so much that my career goals might come second. In fact, I did everything in my power for two years to make sure it didn't happen.

"How about you? I know you're seeing someone. How's that going?"

He doesn't know we broke up. No need for him to know anything about my personal life, especially if it takes me away from the sport. At least, that's what I've always told myself. Maybe it's okay to let him know me better, given that he's been nothing but open with me. I huff out a laugh and roll my eyes. "It's work."

"The good ones always are, but lemme say it if you don't already know. So worth it."

"I'm starting to see that."

Finally peeling his eyes from the screen, Ken surveys me. "You don't sound convinced."

I'm not, but it isn't in the way he thinks.

Do I really want to play in England?

I can't believe I'm having doubts.

The coaches and technical director at Aston Villa could not have been nicer. They invited me out to a team training session yesterday, where it became clear someone tipped off the sports paparazzi because I caught a few cameras pointed my way, in addition to some reporters waiting outside the stadium to push a mic in my face and ask if I'd like to comment on my plans.

It's an open secret I'm being considered by several Premier League teams, but I answered with a swift, "no comment." Rule One when I started professionally was never to comment on rumors.

I carry our empties to the bar and buy the next round, despite Ken's insistence that everything's on him this week. I know he'd gladly pick up the tab when his ten percent from repping me nets him seven figures, but it's the principle of the thing.

By the time I get back to the table, the match is over, tied with no score. "I hate a scoreless game," Ken grumbles.

"For a keeper, no score is a win," I remind him.

"True. All a matter of perspective."

I still don't like the way Molly and I left things. Her insistence that I follow my professional dreams without her smacks of her self-preservation. I get it, but I wasn't in a position to do anything about it when everything went sideways between us.

I lift the beer to my lips and taste the bitter pale ale as though it's my first ever sip of the stuff and close my eyes for a moment, letting the fact that I've made it here with two potential offers on the table wash over me. Then I drink about half the pint and put it down.

"Ken, I think we need to talk."

He turns his chair back around to face me, and we get into it.

 olly

THE LIBRARY CROWDS have died down a little bit since Holden stopped coming to read to the kids, but a lot more people show up in the afternoons now, so I owe him something for my current sense of job security.

We still have a fair number of people waiting outside when I arrive on Wednesday, late, as usual. I'm too preoccupied with the thoughts that have been churning in my head for the past few days to pay much attention to them. Preeta's words have been echoing in my brain on repeat: "You're a twat, undeserving of great love."

I don't want to be a twat. I do want great love. And I want to deserve it, but I worry that I haven't made a very good case for myself.

Even if it scares me not to know how everything will play out, I want Holden in my life. Somehow, some way.

It's time to leave the safe haven of my tiny studio apartment and safe, steady jobs and fight for a relationship I want to see through. I want more than two months. And if that means going to England with him, I'll get on a plane. I'm so preoccupied by thoughts about how and when to do it that I don't notice a few differences today at the library.

Apparently, there are news vans parked out in front. Apparently, the crowd is bigger and louder than usual. Apparently, Judy's smile is so wide, a boat could sail through it—a nice one, like Tim's. The thought of the boat reminds me of Holden, which pulls me even further from reality as I skulk through the children's section, oblivious to my surroundings.

But then I stop short because something's different.

The crowd is huge. Standing room only. Dozens of six-year-olds on the rug, parents standing around them. And they're all quiet, even though I haven't started reading yet. It's strange, but I keep walking over there on autopilot, convinced that I must be later than I thought. That's the only explanation for why Judy had to send someone over in my place to hold court in front of the group.

Not just someone.

Holden sits in the chair at the front and he's talking quietly to the group. I can't hear exactly what he's saying until I get closer, but when I approach, I'm met with a dead silence as every pair of eyes in the room turns toward me.

At least, I think they do. I'm too focused on one pair of eyes in particular, sending an unspoken request for some sort of explanation. Instead, Holden smiles—that joyful, impossible-not-to-return smile that rarely slips through his grumpy façade, the smile I normally find irresistible. Today, I find it confusing and worrisome. I don't think I can bear to see him if he's only here for a media stunt no one even thought to tell me about.

I won't do it to myself. Which is why I shake my head at him and whatever cute plan he has and turn to walk away. I just need to get out the front door of the library—then I can fall apart. But I won't do it here.

"Mare." His voice slices through the silence only marred by my insistent footsteps. Even though I know I'll probably regret it, I stop and look at him. He's standing, one arm outstretched, beckoning me back. "Please? I'll explain why I'm here. Just…please."

"Fine." I walk back over to the group, which immediately breaks into a round of applause when I approach. It makes no sense. And even though I have no clue why he's here or what he wants me to do, I walk toward him like a zombie moth in front of a shining torch.

"Hey," he says quietly when I get close enough to hear him. His palm slides against mine and he interlaces our fingers as though ensuring I won't bolt. But he doesn't understand. The moment I feel the warmth of his skin against my hand, the butterflies in my gut stop their genteel waltz and begin jockeying for position in a mosh pit befitting a rap star.

I don't want to walk away from him again. But more than that, I don't think I'll survive it. So I hope this isn't some kind of goodbye tour because I want there to be a next chapter for us despite what I told him the last time we spoke.

"Hey," I reply, reading his face for clues to explain what he's doing here. "I thought you were in England."

He shakes his head, then nods. "I'm not. I was." He doesn't offer more of an explanation, instead seeming to lose his train of thought as his eyes move over my face. They meet mine, searching at first, then they soften and roam over my cheeks to my lips and back to my eyes. It feels like we're the only two people in the room, and I have to work to remind myself there are others—most of them children.

I have so many questions. Even if it might make me sad, I want to know if he made a decision about which team to play for next season. I've scanned my social media feeds, but I've found only speculation and no definitive news. Is that why he's here? Does he want to tell me to my face where he's going?

The roiling flood of emotions drowns out the butterfly dance and replaces it with a confusing urge to hug him mixed with an equal desire to run from the room. As though sensing the latter, Holden's grip on my hand tightens. I meet his gaze again and find that he's laughing quietly. "What's funny?"

"The wheels are cranking in your head so furiously, I'm shocked you haven't turned back time."

In a daze, I mumble, "I don't think time works that way."

"I wish it did." His words snap me out of my reverie, as does the sincere look on his face.

I swallow hard and ask a question I'm not sure I want answered. "What would you do differently if you could go back?"

"So much." The emotion in his voice catches me off guard. My eyes lock on his, and I see determination but also vulnerability. It's clear I hurt him as much as I hurt myself, but we both need to leave it behind if he's moving to England alone.

It's not that I haven't seen him emotional before, but he keeps his feelings on a tight leash, and we're here in front of several dozen people, some of whom have taken out their phones and snapped a photo or two. "Will you?" He gestures to the chair next to his and I nod, still unsure why he's here.

"Sure, but Holden…what is this? Your farewell reading group before you pack up for England? Is this some kind of goodbye photo op?"

My words land like a blade. I can tell by the way he reacts that I'm misunderstanding something, but for the life of me, I can't figure this out. "Will you just sit? I'll explain."

Our chairs are pulled close to each other, closer than they normally are when we do our tag team of reading and engaging the kids with stories and facts. I wonder if it's a coincidence or if Holden pushed them together. When I sit, I'm hyperaware of him, the presence of his body, the scent of his woodsy soap, the heat that seems to be radiating from his skin.

Oh wait, that's just me, perspiring like I'm wearing a parka in June because I'm nervous and confused about what we're doing here.

The kids sitting on the rug haven't quieted down enough for our voices to be heard over their chatter, but I can tell we've caught the interest of the adults in the room, even if they're accustomed to seeing the two of us sitting here together.

It's then that I notice a third chair at the front of the room. It's empty, but Holden stands and beckons a slim Black teenager over from the crowd. "Molly, meet Troy." We shake hands, but my confusion must show on my face because Holden assures me, "He'll explain."

Troy faces the crowd and quiets everyone down with the self-assuredness of a teacher. "Hello. My name is Troy Higgans, and I'm a senior at Whitney Prep over in Oakland." The name of the school rings a bell, but I'm too focused on Holden to let my brain wander.

"When I finished middle school, I got a scholarship to Whitney. I'm gonna be honest with you all. I probably wouldn't be here today without it. My older brother was in a gang, and I was set to follow in his footsteps." He pauses for emphasis. "He died in a gang-related shooting three years ago. I have no doubt I was heading down the same path."

He's charismatic, comfortable in front of a crowd, so well-spoken for eighteen. The kids are all riveted. He might as well be handing out candy for how fixated they are on him.

I can feel Holden's gaze on me, but I'm too transfixed by Troy's story to look at him. Boys like him were the reason I wanted to start the reading program here. I feel Holden squeeze my hand, but I can't look at him. It will hurt too much.

Troy continues. "Anyway, I'm here today because I didn't go down that path. Like I said, I got a scholarship to Whitney, which is the kind of school that means business. I couldn't cut classes. I couldn't show up late. I had to work. So I did. And I figured something out about myself. I figured out I'm hella smart, and with the hard work and the education I got at Whitney, next year I'm going to a four-year university. First in my family to go."

He pauses and looks at me. I nod, encouraging him to keep going, if encouragement is what he's looking for. "I wouldn't be here today without that scholarship, I have no doubt. Four years of school. Paid for by someone who works here at the library. And she doesn't just work here, this is her second job. She only has this second job so she can put more money into the scholarship fund, so like I said, I wouldn't be here today without her."

I inhale a sharp breath when I realize he's talking about me. I look at Holden. How? He smiles and gestures to Troy who's still talking.

"Scholarships are anonymous, so ordinarily I wouldn't have any idea who to thank. But her friend invited me here today so I could meet her and thank her in person. So, Miss Molly, I'm here for that. Thank you doesn't even cover it. Truly, I owe you my life."

He opens his arms for a hug, and I stand and step into his embrace, partly to hide the well of tears in my eyes. The room erupts in applause, and I probably hug him for too long, but he lets me stay there until I've composed myself.

When I take a step back, I see his eyes are wet too. I don't dare look at Holden. I'll break down completely if I do. "Thank you, Troy, for coming." I inhale a deep breath and calm myself on the exhale. "You know, it's funny. All the years I've been donating, they never told me the scholarship was going to one person year after year."

He points at himself with both thumbs. "I'm the one person. I can't thank you enough, truly. I never thought I'd get to meet you, so I'm really grateful to Holden here, for reaching out."

I can't not look at him. When I do, he nods. "You make a lot of sacrifices for other people. Thought you should at least know how big a difference it makes."

"I can't even..." I nod. "I'm glad it's you, Troy. I'm glad you got to go to that school. You'll make your parents proud."

The crowd is getting restless, and Troy wheels around and commands their attention instantly. "You all, I completely forgot the other part. I worked it out with the librarians to start volunteering here in the afternoons. Would you guys come read with me?"

A chorus of cheers and hollers erupts among the kids. "Yeah? How about I start right now? That okay with you, Miss Molly?"

I nod, still too choked up to say much else. Full of swagger in a button-down shirt and tie, Troy goes back to the rug and picks up a big stack of books, getting right down to it.

"Can we talk?" Holden gestures toward the front of the library. I nod and follow him outside. He stops under the tree where we first met and spins to face me. "I'm sorry. I should have told you there was a chance I might get an offer and leave. I know how hard it was to trust me, and I broke that. I'm so, so sorry, Molly."

I hear the words, but there's nothing surprising in them. He's not saying anything I don't already know. I appreciate the honesty and the apology, but as far as I know, he's still leaving. As much as I want to offer to go to England with him, I start to lose my nerve. We've only been together for two months, and like he reminded me when I told him about Adam, two months is barely a relationship.

I sit on the bench and tuck my legs underneath the long black skirt I'm wearing with a baggy gray sweater. "Okay. I understand." I can't let myself see him coming here today for something that it's not. Bringing Troy here was sweet, but it doesn't change anything between us. I hold tight to my heart. "And thank you for bringing Troy." There's nothing left to say, so I look down.

He holds up his hands and stands in front of me. "Hang on. I'm not nearly done."

Swallowing hard, I meet his gaze. His eyes are the fierce gray I've seen when he's resolute about something he wants. "Okay."

"I've had two weeks to think about this, and what I didn't figure out until now is that there's no debate. No weighing of the scales." He puts his hand on my knee and the warmth of it radiates across my skin through the fabric of my skirt.

When he turns it over, I hesitate. If I put my hand in his, I'm not going to want to let go.

I do it anyway.

Because that's how little I'm able to resist him. I'll take one more small touch even if it makes it harder to get over him.

Laying my hand on his, I'm surprised when he grasps it tight, the expression on his face equally intense.

My heart floods with the warmth that's been missing for the past two weeks. I didn't realize how cold I've been until now. Icy. Arctic.

"When I was in England, you were constantly on my mind. Every damn second. I realized I can't be a continent away from you when I can't even bear to be separated by one fucking foot."

He sits next to me on the bench and reaches gingerly for my face, running two fingers along my cheek. This gentle caress, this reverence, it grounds me. I lean into him—it's what I need, his body, the connection that's bigger than us.

I close my eyes as my body starts to shake—with laughter. He looks at me quizzically. "You found that funny?"

Reaching to touch his lips with my finger, I continue up over his nose to smooth the crease between his eyes. "Just that even when you say the sweetest possible thing, you can't do it without swearing."

His face relaxes, and a small smile plays on his lips. He closes his eyes. "You better fucking believe it."

The silence that hangs between us now feels comfortable, unburdened.

"I love you as much as I love the game. It's the truth."

I hold up a hand. "You don't have to say that. I respect your love for your career. I admire it."

He nods. "I know. I value that, but Mare, soccer is one part of my life. You—you're all of it."

Emotion wells in my chest. "Even after only two months?"

"Two amazing fucking months.

My heart leaps so abruptly at his words that I feel short of breath. Before I can recover enough to say more, his words continue pouring out.

"I'm not going anywhere without you. I'm not doing it. I won't. Fuck England. You're it for me, Mare. You're the one."

"You're it for me too. I know it in my bones. But I don't want to be the reason you don't take the job you've dreamed of. I could...I'd move to England with you."

His face registers surprise and he closes his eyes. When he opens them, he smiles. "Or don't."

I flinch at that.

"What I mean is, I want you more than I want to be a global soccer player. I want you first. Everything else, we can figure out together. If I go, I do it with you. If I stay, I'll be happier than I deserve to be. Honestly, none of it matters without you. I wish I'd said so two weeks ago, but I still had my head up my ass, unfortunately."

"That's okay. I was still being a twat, undeserving of great love."

"Huh?"

"Never mind. Holden..." I turn so I can see his face, all of it. My heart floods again at how much I love him. "Thank you...for understanding. A lot of people would tell me I'm crazy to give half my money away, but I love that you get it. You get me."

He kisses me softly on the lips and tips his forehead against mine. "I get you. And I want you. And I love you."

"And I fucking love you."

He laughs. "No! I'm ruining you."

"Maybe. Or maybe you're making me better."

He kisses me once more. "You are deserving of great love, Mare."

I smile at that. "As are you."

Holden

Two Months Later

"We didn't need to fly on a private plane," Molly chides for the tenth time since we boarded the sweet jet provided by the Arsenal owner to ferry us home after our weeklong visit to England. But I know she loved it. Especially the bedroom in the back.

"Only the best for you, Mare." I take her hand and lead her down the stairs, away from the plane. She glances behind as though she's forgotten something.

"The luggage?"

"It'll be in my living room after we get back from the event with the team."

"Wow. Service. A girl could get used to it." She reaches for my hand, and I wonder if I'll ever get used to the bounty that is *her* in my life every day. The barest touch of her fingers curling around mine warms me from the inside out and grips my heart so hard it hurts.

Ah, but it's a good hurt I'll never get enough of, as long as she's with me.

I still get up and look at myself in the mirror each morning and shake my head in disbelief that I've gotten this lucky in one lifetime—the woman of my dreams and the job that feeds the rest of my soul. And in case there's any question about which comes first, I only have to look at her sleeping—blond hair splayed over the pillow, sweet lips waiting to greet me when she wakes up— and I'm a thousand percent certain she's it.

Our trip to England was perfect—some meet and greet time with the team and gladhanding of the coaches and team owner when I signed my one-year contract to play for Arsenal, which emerged as a silent suitor once I met with the other teams.

"You can't pass this up," Molly had insisted. "At least, let's consider it." As soon as I understood that she really was willing to move with me, I booked the trip.

We had a whirlwind week that left time for a little sightseeing and touring of a few flats where we could potentially live in Kensington.

Molly fell in love with every one we visited, so I don't think we'll have much trouble deciding on a place. And I discovered that her affinity for Mediterranean food is only superseded by her love for Indian food, which is plentiful all up and down Kensington High Street.

After my one-year term is up, I'll return as starting keeper for the Strikers, and both the high school and the public library have extended return job offers to Molly after the sabbatical she decided to take so we could have the year in London together.

Her one requirement was that the Arsenal management help her secure at least one job so she can continue funding the scholarship for Troy next year. "Done," the owner said. "In fact, I'll match your salary so we can offer the same opportunity to a student here in London." I thought her face would crack open with the spread of her smile.

Like I said, I have to shake my head in disbelief every damn day.

Which brings me to this moment, when I stop walking in the middle of the giant empty tarmac, pulling Molly into my arms.

Her hands go to my chest, where I've discovered she really enjoys running her palms across my pecs, though she's yet to address another text message to them specifically.

"What's up?" She tips her head up and without even thinking, I lower my lips to tease hers, momentarily lost to the taste of her.

Then I remember why I stopped and abruptly pull away. She casts a skeptical side-eye.

"Holden? You okay?"

It's a legitimate question since I've never turned down a kiss from her. "No." I shove my hands in my pockets. "But I will be."

Taking a step back, Molly studies me, and I'm aware that I have my eyes cast down at the ground. If I meet her gaze, she'll know exactly what I'm planning, and I want to surprise her.

"O-kay…" She waits me out while I gather my thoughts, but I'm apparently too slow because she blurts, "If you don't want me to go to England—"

I cut her off with a deep, hard kiss before she can finish uttering the stupidest sentence in the world. My hands cup her jaw before pushing into her hair. Maybe I don't have to say anything at all. My tongue thrusts against hers, willing her to understand how much I want her to be a part of me. I want her with every atom that comprises me.

When I lean away, still cupping her face in one hand, I see the flush I love across her cheeks. Her eyes look dazed. Her hand grips my forearm, and I know she needs it for balance.

Just like I need her all the time.

"No." My voice is a quiet rasp. I'm grateful no planes are taking off because the airfield is quiet and we're alone. "Don't try to guess what you think I intend to say. Just let me fucking surprise you for once."

Her throat works as she swallows, her eyes never leaving mine.

Shoving one hand back in my pocket, I fish around for what I've been carrying around for a week, looking for the perfect spot to propose. We've been on bridges at sunset, atop ornate towers with views. We've eaten Michelin-starred meals and slept between sheets with a billion thread count.

None of those places seemed right.

"This spot. Remember this spot." I break eye contact to take in our random surroundings and she glances around.

"Okay."

"This spot is where I tell you what I knew that day you chased me down outside the library. Even if I didn't want to admit it to myself, in my heart, I knew you were a force to be reckoned with, and I don't mean that just because you're as fucking stubborn as I am." My throat is so dry I can barely swallow, but I choke down the last bit of nerves. "You're it for me, Mare. You're the one. And I don't know how I got so goddamn lucky that you figured out a way to love me through all my grumpy-ass personality defects, but I'm smart enough to hold on with everything I've got."

She presses her lips together, and I see the moisture in the corners of her eyes, but I'm not done. Stroking her cheek, I tell her the rest. "Wherever I go, whatever path life takes me on, I want to go there with you. I want all your todays and all your forevers if you'll marry me, Mare, because I love you more than anything."

Jesus, fuck. That was harder than defending against Chisholm.
And so much more worth it.

My inhale sounds ragged as I finally suck in a breath. Yanking my hand from my pocket, I pop open the ring box and we both stare down at the two-carat solitaire which sparkles like a midnight star.

Nodding and blinking back what are now generous tears, Molly presses her lips together. She kisses me before she gives me her answer, but when she does, it's just a whisper near my ear. "Yes, soccer star. A thousand times yes."

EPILOGUE

*H*olden
A Month After That

ALL TOLD, the Strikers pulled out a decent season. Some early losses and shaky-looking formations evolved into more solid footing, enough that most of the players now have faith that Charlie knows what he's doing.

Work needs to be done and he'll shuffle around some players, which means the team will likely look a little different when I come back after my year in England. "Change is good," Charlie is fond of saying, and knowing I have job security makes it easier to believe him.

And on a night like tonight, when we're celebrating a big win and mingling with management, spirits are high all around.

So when Tim Cheltenham jogs over to where Molly and I stand near the tables in the back of the stadium's team clubhouse, I put my hand out, expecting him to shove a beer in it.

He doesn't.

I glance at him, and he looks like he's seen a ghost. Or maybe he's the ghost because he's turned a pasty white as all the blood drains from his face. "Fuck, man. You okay?" I ask. He looks like he might be sick.

Stepping slightly behind me, he exhales a deep breath. "Bloody hell, no."

"You need a trashcan?"

"No, I'm not drunk. Not yet, at least. But that'll be the goal now."

Still unclear on the problem, I look around the bar for a sign of trouble but see nothing. It's a crew of teammates, partners, some press, a handful of jersey chasers—in other words, it looks like every other post-game hangout after a win. "What's wrong?"

He opens his mouth, then closes it again. Then it drops open and stays that way, but he says nothing.

"Tim, you look like a dying fish," Molly says, elbowing him in the ribs. He barely reacts, still staring off at an unknown apparition in the opposite corner.

"It's just…Charlie's new hire. The one who's going to handle the stats from here out—first off, I assumed someone named Jordan Elliott was a bloke, but…she's not. Second, she's here." He gestures with his head before sucking down nearly an entire bottle of craft beer.

We subtly turn and notice a striking woman with red hair across the room. Molly looks at me questioningly, but I don't know any more than she does.

The team is on an upswing, with more wins than losses over the past couple months, and we all credit Charlie Walgrove and his algorithms with part of the success. But as team owner, he can't spend all his time analyzing data, so he's been scouting to fill a fulltime position.

"Right, Charlie mentioned he was bringing someone in to analyze the numbers," I recall. "Charlie said she's a genius. Guess he'd know."

Tim looks positively green. "Yeah…" He shakes his head. "She was brainy way back when, from the scant details I remember."

"So, you know her?" Molly laughs knowingly and sips from a tall glass of cranberry juice. I drape my arm over her shoulder and settle in for what promises to be a stellar story.

"Yeah." Tim scrubs his hands over his face so hard I think he might be losing skin. "From when I was an exchange student here for a year, lived with her family. And we didn't exactly part on good terms."

"Oh, I'm gonna need way more details than that." I'm not used to seeing Tim unnerved by anything, let alone a woman. But this one has him practically crawling under the table to hide.

I look at Molly and she's pressing her lips together, forcing back a grin. Tim follows my gaze to her and crosses his arms over his chest. "What? Why are you looking at each other like that?"

Molly shrugs. "Just that this new arrangement ought to be interesting. And I'm a little sad we'll be gone next year and I'll miss the drama."

Tim chugs the rest of his beer and slams the bottle down, muttering as he walks away. "Aw, bloody hell. I'm off to talk to Charlie about a trade."

Pulling Molly in tight against me, I whisper in her ear, just to make sure she always knows, "I wouldn't trade you for anything."

She smiles and tips her head against my chest. "Good thing, because there's nothing anyone could offer that would convince me to go. Not ever."

"Where you go, I go."

She holds out her hand and glances at her ring before I envelop it in mine. "Forever."

THE END

~

TIM AND JORDAN'S story is available now—He's a Player; a second chance fake dating sports romance. Read on for a Sneak Peek.

WANT a peek into Molly and Holden's future? Join my mailing list by typing https://BookHip.com/CBPFKRT into your browser to read an exclusive BONUS EPILOGUE. Mailing list subscribers only receive the good stuff—new release info, exclusive sales, and a monthly free romance from one of my author friends.

onus Epilogue

Molly

Five Years Later

"Hey, who's hungry?" I yell through the screened back door of our house in Mill Valley. I expect to hear three voices, but the only response comes from a frog that's taken up residence in an undisclosed spot under the redwood deck.

"I wasn't talking to you," I tell the frog. "Though it's nice that someone answers."

As soon as I step outside, it's apparent why I'm being ignored. The yelps and laughter and Holden's booming voice echo from behind a row of hedges that separate the back patio from the rest of the yard.

We moved into the new place—a two-story craftsman tucked in between the hills with views of the bay—a couple years ago. It's near the house Holden used to own in Tiburon, but the yard is bigger.

We needed bigger.

Big enough for a sports court that's currently in use by Holden and our twin sons, Liam and Oliver. Yes, the year in England left its mark on me, and I came up with a long list of names for our eventual offspring long before our wedding day.

"Hello, anyone out there?" I yell again, knowing perfectly well where they are—a scant ten yards from the door—and what they're doing. Playing soccer, of course.

The twins, now three years old, didn't have much choice in the matter. Holden told me early on that he didn't want to force the sport he loved on his future kids, but as soon as our boys were old enough to walk, I put a ball at their feet, and Holden's dreams of our kids branching out were dead.

"You can still sign them up for your ice dancing lessons or whatever," I told him. "But come on. They're probably genetically gifted at soccer, so you can't deny them."

"I wasn't thinking ice dancing, but maybe, I dunno…baseball? Tennis? Debate team?"

I cracked up at the thought of our toddlers on a debate team, but given the stubborn personalities of both of their parents, I had no doubt they could hold their own when it came to defending opinions.

"Let's put a pin in the debate team until middle school, yes? But as to the rest, sure. They can all of it," I told him at the time. But secretly, I knew I'd give them a gentle them toward soccer if I had a say in the matter.

I knew it seemed odd that I was the one with the soccer dreams. Holden maintained that it might feel like too much pressure on our kids to follow in his footsteps. "I chose to make this my life, but they should have the right to choose for themselves. If they inherit some degree of athleticism from me, great. But that can translate into any sport. It doesn't have to be soccer," he reasoned. More than once.

I agreed with him about wanting our kids to find their own

passions in life, and I absolutely planned to sign them up for every kid activity that fit into their schedules. But one day when I was leaving a farmer's market, I came upon a stall selling multi-colored soccer balls, and I couldn't resist bringing one home.

Okay, I brought home two.

At Holden's raised eyebrow when I presented my finds, I grimaced and apologized. "He smiled and said, "You know I can't resist those doe eyes of yours. I guess our boys are learning to play the Beautiful Game."

I can't really explain it, but somewhere along the way, my soccer fandom kicked into high gear. Then, once I saw Liam and Oliver's joy at kicking around their new balls, I started fantasizing about the next generation of soccer players that would keep me sitting on the side of one soccer pitch or another for many, many years.

This year, for the first time, the twins are eligible for a tot youth soccer league, and Holden has signed on as coach. It will be familiar territory for him since he's been a Keeper coach for the Strikers for the past two years since he retired from the sport.

"Hey! Guys! Dinner!" I yell once again before giving in and walking to the junior-sized pitch that turns brown every winter because we planted a drought-tolerant strain of grass.

As I round the tall hedge I find my trio of guys in their usual positions, Holden bouncing on his toes, arms outstretched, blocking the pop-up goal on one side of the yard. The boys are conferencing at the other end, no doubt devising a winning strategy for getting the ball past their favorite keeper.

No wonder they're ignoring me. All three are so entirely in their element, it's a wonder they ever stop for food.

I can't stop the grin from spreading across my face at the life I never thought I'd have. My fear of kids all but evaporated the minute I gave birth to the twins, and since then, I've been besotted.

I'm ridiculous. I saw them all an hour ago, and even in that bit of time, I've missed them. These boys have carved out a space so deep in my heart that I can't imagine ever going back to the life I had when I swore I'd never let anyone past my emotional guard gates. It feels like a long time ago.

And my love for Holden has only multiplied from there.

My rule is that I only call for them three times if I know they can hear me. The first time doesn't count, when I called from the house. They get one more chance before I turn around, and they're forced to eat a cold dinner whenever they decide they're done playing.

So far, that's never happened. Smart boys, all three of them.

"Okay, this is it. Last call. Dinner's ready, and it's hot," I yell to them. I know they can hear me. Liam continues dribbling the ball toward where Holden stands ready, but Oliver stops in his tracks, changes directions, and runs right for me.

Liam shoots left, and Holden dives right, making a big show on the ground of how frustrated he is that a goal got by him. Delighted, Liam runs over and extends his hand to high-five his dad before turning toward the house with his brother. Holden stands up, dusts off the stray bits of grass, and strolls toward us, juggling the soccer ball on his foot.

"Better workout that I used to get with the team, no kidding there," he says, exhaling a dramatic breath and putting an arm around me. Tipping my head onto his shoulder, I let him lead me lazily toward the house while the twins rush ahead to wash their hands.

I'm glad we have this moment to ourselves. Not wanting to disrupt the usual afternoon ritual, I kept myself focused on cooking pasta and garlic bread and tossing a salad with home-made vinaigrette dressing. But now, I feel ready to burst with my news.

"So...I grabbed a few extra things when I was at the store earlier."

Holden's eyebrows bounce. "Hopefully, one of them was chocolate ice cream."

"Ha. Yes, I did get that. I also picked up a pregnancy test." I wait for my words to land. He shoots me a side-eye to gauge what's coming next.

I nod. "It's early, but I had a feeling, so…"

He stops walking and turn to face me, putting both hands on my forearms. "Wait, really?" His eyes look larger than I've ever seen, but his smile slowly spreads into a giant grin as I nod some more.

We'd been talking about having more kids, working on having more kids, but after a while, we both counted ourselves lucky to have two healthy boys and stopped focusing on it. If it happened, it happened.

But now I'm one hundred percent focused on the fact that it seems to be happening, and I have zero chill. "Yes, really!"

Kissing my nose, my forehead, and finally, my lips, he doesn't hesitate to show me how delighted he is. He can still kiss me breathless without even trying, and if our kids weren't right inside waiting for dinner, I have no doubt we'd be back behind the hedge, using the big grass field as I've always intended.

Um, yes, okay, fine—I may have had an ulterior motive in choosing a house with a big grassy filled with secluded, shady corners and romantic little knolls. I'm not all soccer, all the time. Don't be silly.

"Do you think it's a girl?" Holden's gray eyes sparkle with delight at the possibility.

I laugh. "It's too early to know, obviously, but…maybe. Hopefully?" He knows I have a long list of English girls' names—Penelope, Philippa, Elizabeth—so this could be fun.

"This is amazing news, Mare. I love it."

"I know. Me too."

"And I love you."

"I know that too." Leaning down to kiss me, Holden almost

convinces me to turn back for the grassy knolls and let the kids fend for themselves. Almost.

We head inside the house, Holden's arm wrapped around me, and find the twins already sitting at the table, hungry and not-so-patiently waiting.

"What're we having?" Liam sat on his knees on one of the kitchen chairs, which give him a view of the kitchen.

"Pasta and garlic bread," I tell him.

"And salad," Holden chimes in, looking right at Liam for his expected groan. Instead, Liam's eyes focus suspiciously on the dish macaroni with breadcrumbs and cheese melted over the top.

"Are there vegetables in it?" He makes a sour face and looks at Oliver, who doesn't share his picky palate. But Oliver's a good sport, so he makes an equally disgusted face.

"No vegetables," I assure him.

There are definitely vegetables. They're ground up in the sauce, and I defy him to taste them. It's the only way I can get anything green past his finicky taste buds.

Once all the food is on the table, Holden and I start serving everything to the kids, including salad, before they can object. When we finally sit, he picks up my hand from where it rests on the table, and if I know him, he won't let it go during the entire meal. As if to emphasize that, he brings it to his lips and kisses my knuckles.

"Why are you so kissy?" Liam asks, his mouth full of macaroni. Oliver, who's quietly studying us, as is his way, merely blinks his large brown eyes. He knows something's up, but while his brother could spend two solid hours guessing and never tire, Oliver is far too pragmatic to mess around.

"No reason," I say. Not going to tell them about a potential sibling until I'm much farther along. Nine months will feel like nine years to them.

"Just tell us. Are we getting a dog?" He wiggles off the seat of his chair and pads around the table to me in his striped soccer socks and no shoes. I have no idea what happened to his shoes between the yard and the dinner table, but I have a feeling they're on the floor somewhere between the two. This kid has a habit of disrobing as he goes. Looking at him in his shorts and t-shirt next to his brother, still wearing a fleece sweatshirt, a beanie, and shoes, I can't help but smile at how much I love them both.

"Ah, someday. We'll get a dog someday, I promise. But not today. Today, I'm just happy because I love you. All of you," I tell him.

Oliver grins and stabs a bite of macaroni with his fork in one fist. "Because we're the best, right?"

It's something I've been telling them for as long as I can remember. "You've got that right. This family, you're the best I could ever ask for."

Then I meet Holden's eyes, and he nods.

It's true. There's nothing better.

HE'S A PLAYER

Jordan

Click, clack.

My shoes sound like a metronome on the parquet floors. A noisy wristwatch counting down the seconds. Counting down my fate.

No, not fate. I don't believe in fate. Or karma. Or destiny. I don't think life operates according to some karmic sense of justice. Karma doesn't have it out for one person or another based on a past slight or insult. And a good deed doesn't earn extra points in life's big swear jar.

Please.

Calling on fate always feels like putting the blame someplace else when it's more likely that life is a big random happenstance. Because a large stellar explosion yielded anxious little life forms looking for explanations.

People cross paths randomly, not because it's meant to be. And if it happens twice, it's just more dumb luck or similar taste in movies or food.

That's it.

I'm a scientist, after all. Sports doctor, but a scientist nonetheless. That means there's no reason to get ruffled over inconvenient events or people. Things just happen. Or don't happen.

Science is the backbone of all things. Want to know whether it's okay to play tennis with a torn labrum? Look at the science.

Want to know whether whole milk or skim milk leads to stronger bones? Science.

Everything that happens has a cause, every cause has an effect, every effect has an explanation. Living with such an impassive, unemotional outlook has served me well. Everything is just one tiny data point in a constellation that will make perfect sense later.

Even if that data point turns out to be my unrequited crush—the guy who led me to make impulsive decisions in the past. If he's the first person I see in a giant room full of people, it's just a big, big coincidence. Tim Cheltenham won't fluster me. My heart won't race in his presence. Even if it's racing now.

For all I know, as the resident newbie, I'm heading into a den of debauchery, hazing, and torture from the team's stupidly handsome defender. My fault for taking a job on his home turf.

Click, clack.

But it's a dream job, and I want to succeed. I don't start work for a month, but my new boss wants me to meet the players in an informal atmosphere. Hence the invitation to a casual post-game gathering at the stadium. "Easy crowd. And I don't like crowds, so trust me on this," the Strikers' owner, Charlie Walgrove, said when he hired me. The awkward genius billionaire famously avoids the spotlight, so if he finds this sort of event manageable, it works for me.

"Sounds good. I don't love crowds either." Not that my previous job at a sports medicine clinic dropped me into a lot of crowds filled with professional athletes.

A nervous butterfly jazz band marches through my chest at

the thought of tall, muscle-bound jocks who view me as the enemy. Yeah. About that…

Charlie just fired the prior team physician for mishandling the health of his athletes. It wasn't as bad as doping, but the good doctor was apparently keeping injured players pumped up on prescription pain meds to keep them in the game, even if it led to worse injuries and other wear and tear.

He kept them bandaged and iced just enough to numb them up, but Charlie, king of data and stats, noticed that some players weren't recovering from games and workouts the way they should. Their speed was slowing. The time it took for them to launch from ready to a full run was a split-second off, which made all the difference when it came to fighting for a ball. And winning games.

The head coach was in on it as well, so Charlie cleaned house and brought in a new coach and a new medical team, with me leading them. I assured him my ethics would never allow for abusing the health and safety of players.

"I don't doubt you at all, Doctor Page," he'd said. His confidence boosted my own. How intimidating can a bunch of jocks be? They'll be like more talented versions of the amateur athletes who came into my old clinic with sprains, tears, and broken bones. Only instead of getting back to spring skiing, they'll be heading back to million dollar contracts to play pro soccer.

I've been preparing for this job with all my heart and soul for more than ten years. Not only is it a chance to work with top athletes, but I'll get a front row seat at my favorite sport. A shot like this comes around once in a career.

Yes, Alexander Hamilton, I know what to do.

Following the signs inside the San Francisco Strikers soccer stadium, I walk past the luxury boxes toward the fancy members-only clubhouse, where a cacophony of voices and music blasts from a hundred yards away.

Click.

Clack.

Not like Charlie gave me much wiggle room when he invited me to the event tonight. "Come meet a few folks and get your bearings before you start instilling fear in the players."

I laughed and nodded because at five feet, three inches, and with what people refer to as "doe eyes," I rarely instill fear in anyone.

I'm busy mulling that over when I trip over something invisible and almost face plant on the floor. Steadying myself, I glance around to be sure no one saw my near-fall from grace.

Damn these two-inch heels. They're not even high, but I want the added stature as long as I can avoid my usual clumsiness.

Slowing my pace, I want to be sure I can walk the last few yards without taking a bite out of the hardwood floor. My stomach churns with a flutter of nerves the closer I get to the stained oak doors that flank the clubhouse entrance. I stop and lean against the wall, fortifying my nerves.

I've always made it my goal to blend into a group. To disappear. My mother would have a lot to say about this. "It's why you're still single. You're a bystander. No one notices how pretty you are when you're hiding behind someone taller."

A whole other issue, my mother. Her goal is to see me married, pregnant, and feathering a nest. My goal is to make a difference in the world by working hard. I'm good at that. I'm *bad* at dating, evidenced by making terrible, impulsive decisions around men.

Starting when I was sixteen. Starting with Tim Cheltenham.

Glancing down at my gray pencil skirt, pink silk blouse, and sensible heels, I look like I dressed for a day at a law office, not a night on the town.

Ugh.

I pull my russet hair out of its clip, so it falls over my shoulders. Bonus points for the loose waves from having it twisted into a bun all day. And I wipe off the pale pink lipstick with the back of my hand and rifle through my purse for a brighter, darker shade. Extracting a tube of red, I feel my party cred notch up a tad.

Then I flick the button just beneath my throat on my blouse, giving me a hint of cleavage that wouldn't pass muster during a workday. Not exactly nightclub-worthy, but less uptight. It will do.

When I reach the door, I don't have time to process my unexpected panic when I see that the couple dozen people I anticipated are easily a hundred. Panic is panic, and mine has just ratcheted my heart rate over a thousand.

A hundred people drinking, talking, laughing. Having fun. They're in groups, smiling and socializing. Some wearing dress shirts and ties, others in casual T-shirts and jeans.

No one wears a pencil skirt and sensible pumps.

"Oh, Jordan. Greetings." Charlie extends his hand. "Welcome to the team. And the post-game madness, as it were. Always nice to have a win." Charlie's easy manner belies the truth—he wants more than just a win. The man didn't build his billion-dollar virtual reality company with modest goals. He wants the Strikers to be the best, and he's put faith in me and his new coach. No pressure.

None.

I try to ignore the sudden stifling warmth in the room. A rivulet of sweat dribbles between my shoulder blades.

"Congrats on the win. I'm thrilled to be here." I compensate for my knocking knees with the biggest smile in my arsenal. Confident. Savvy.

Before I can come up with more empty pleasantries, Charlie is buttonholed by a tall, broad man with slicked-back hair and a navy suit. Probably an agent, manager, financial partner. Doesn't matter. Charlie smiles apologetically as he's whisked away to a nearby table.

With my safety net person gone, I make my way toward the

bar, passing through groups of men and women standing at tall cocktail tables. More groups sit around four-tops and in black leather banquettes. It's standing room only around the four-sided bar in the middle of the room, but I slip between people without being noticed.

The sealed concrete floor and high industrial ceiling make the acoustics extra loud. The only items to absorb sound in the room are some throw pillows with the blue and black Strikers logo on them, and this place would need four thousand of them to blunt the noise.

"What'll you have, miss?" A bartender who looks young enough to be carded grins at me beneath round wire glasses and spiky brown hair. Leaning my forearm on the heavy oak bar, I survey the liquor on well-lit glass shelves.

"Margarita, rocks, no salt, thanks." I watch him pour a jigger of expensive tequila into a shaker with triple sec and lime juice before giving it a shake. He drizzles it over ice and adds another healthy pour of tequila. He winks as he hands it to me.

I'm buzzed after one sip of his strong cocktail and cringe as it burns my throat. Relaxing a bit, I scan the faces in the crowd. Mostly men—trainers and coaches, office staff, and players who look a little different from their roster photos now that they're showered and dressed in street clothes. One pretty brunette in leather pants and tall heels throws her head back and laughs. Another wears a short blue dress, dirty blond hair trailing down her back. They huddle together, easy in the crowd, comfortable with themselves.

"Hello." The voice is accented. Gruff. Deep.

Even amid the din, I recognize the voice as huskier than Charlie's. My stomach drops to my feet, and I fight back a surge of adrenaline mixed with nausea.

I turn, and I'm met by broad shoulders under a tight black Henley with the Strikers logo on the front. Even in heels, I have to look up to see Tim Cheltenham's face.

It's gorgeous. Undeniably gorgeous—angular jaw, olive-colored eyes under criminally long lashes, lips that inspire fantasies among virgins. And everyone else.

Except right now, those beautiful eyes are squinting in confusion, and his luscious lips are pressed into a line. The only thing harder than this man's muscles is the intensity of his stare, and his muscles could tear holes in his shirt.

My eyes go rogue, taking a slow tour of his frame, starting with his ripped, low-slung jeans and those sculpted soccer player thighs, hugged tight by the denim fabric, which is probably having its own orgasm from the contact.

Lucky-duck jeans.

His shirt is tight enough that I can clearly see his six-pack abs, right below carved pecs that have me swallowing hard, so I don't open my mouth and take a bite out of his bicep. It would be embarrassing but so worth it.

"Tim." That's all I can muster.

Bringing my glass to my lips, I feel a tremor in my hand, which I hope he doesn't notice. Fifteen years since I've seen him in person. Same damn reaction.

I take a long sip. Then another.

Thank you, bartender. I'm drunk now.

Just looking at him brings back age-old hurt coupled with memories I've pushed down hard and tried to forget. Tried and failed.

Tim had burrowed in deep, affected me in ways I couldn't fight and couldn't fathom. I stopped thinking about him eventually out of pure self-preservation, but I never forgot about him.

Besides, it's pretty hard to forget when his name and face are plastered all over the sports news, which I started looking at when I applied for jobs as a medical director. And for years before that, right about the time I met Tim. Coincidentally.

"What are you doing here?" His eyes flicker under the dark blond hair that falls across his forehead before he pushes it back with a large hand. His gaze bears down on me, and he jiggles the sudsy remains of a beer in a pint glass.

You've earned this. Own it. Just breathe in and out, in and out.

I choke halfway through my inhale. I sputter my exhale. I don't own a damn thing.

"I work here. Or at least I will in a month." I feel a tic in my cheek.

He stares at me like my words make no sense. Like I make no sense. "Doctor Jordan Page."

"Yes?"

He shakes his head. "You went by Danny. Back then."

"Nickname. Jor-dan. Dan-ny. No one calls me that anymore, except my mom on occasion, and even she mostly doesn't because I've asked her not to. Of course, I think that makes her want to do it more. Or maybe old habits die hard." I'm oversharing. Or under-explaining? Or rambling because he makes me nervous—that hasn't changed at all.

But he still seems flummoxed. "Doctor Jordan Page. Fuck me for thinking it was a bloke," he mutters, raking a hand through his hair. My eyes track the motion, fixated on how much better he looks in person than in recent photos. Pure masculine virility radiates from him.

And yet…

"Because you assume all doctors are men?" My sexism radar flares to life, my bottom lip jutting out with my retort.

"No, I—"

"Good. You shouldn't."

"You're the team doctor?"

"Director of Sports Medicine. Yes. I'm—"

"Part of Charlie's new brigade. Coming to fix what isn't broken. Right. I know all about it. Don't think much of the plan." His accent makes him sound so much more polite than his sharky smirk suggests.

My confidence shrivels like a sunburned grape. I feel my attempted smile pull down into a glower.

Is that what all the players think?

I tell myself I don't care what he thinks, that I'm a professional. But I do care. And I *have* worked hard to get this job. I *should* own it. I'm tethered to my resolve by a fraying thread.

As I try to kickstart the syrup in my brain to find a witty retort, I'm jostled from behind by someone big—big enough to send me off-balance in my stupid two-inch shoes.

I lurch forward toward Tim, who puts his hands on my shoulders to steady me, but not before his entire beer spills down the front of my blouse.

His eyes go to the spill, which makes my shirt virtually sheer. And now it's sticking to my bra, which has demi-cups made of thin baby blue lace—a stupid gift from my mother, who hoped I'd wear it on a date. Instead, I wear it on laundry day when all my plain cotton bras are in the wash.

After a mortifying second or six, Tim wrenches his eyes upward and releases his grip on me. I close my eyes to blot out the image of him. Of everyone.

Tonight was supposed to be the beginning of my future, the culmination of everything I've worked to achieve. It was supposed to be proof to my mother and anyone else that I don't need a boyfriend to be happy. I was supposed to drink and celebrate and meet the players who'd be grateful to have me on their team.

But apparently not. They're not all grateful, starting with this one.

I must have stepped on a puppy in a past life.

Because karma's acting like a little bitch.